THE WOLF AND THE WATER

DELUGE: BOOK 1

JOSIE JAFFREY

For my parents, who have been waiting five years for me to write something that doesn't have vampires in it.

By Josie Jaffrey

The Deluge Series

The Wolf and The Water

The Solis Invicti Series

A Bargain in Silver
The Price of Silver
Bound in Silver
The Silver Bullet

The Sovereign Trilogy

The Gilded King
The Silver Queen
The Blood Prince

The Seekers Series

Killian's Dead (short story prequel)
May Day

Short Stories

Living Underground
Cara Mia (available free to Josie's subscribers)
Bella Donna (available free to Josie's subscribers)

The Valley of Kepos
with tribe animals
The Secret Sea
Wall
Sancta
Cliffs
Cliffs
Kepos
Quarry
Bridge
Temple
Waterfall
Sacred pool
The Eastern Sea

The Dekocracy of Kepos

with abridged family trees

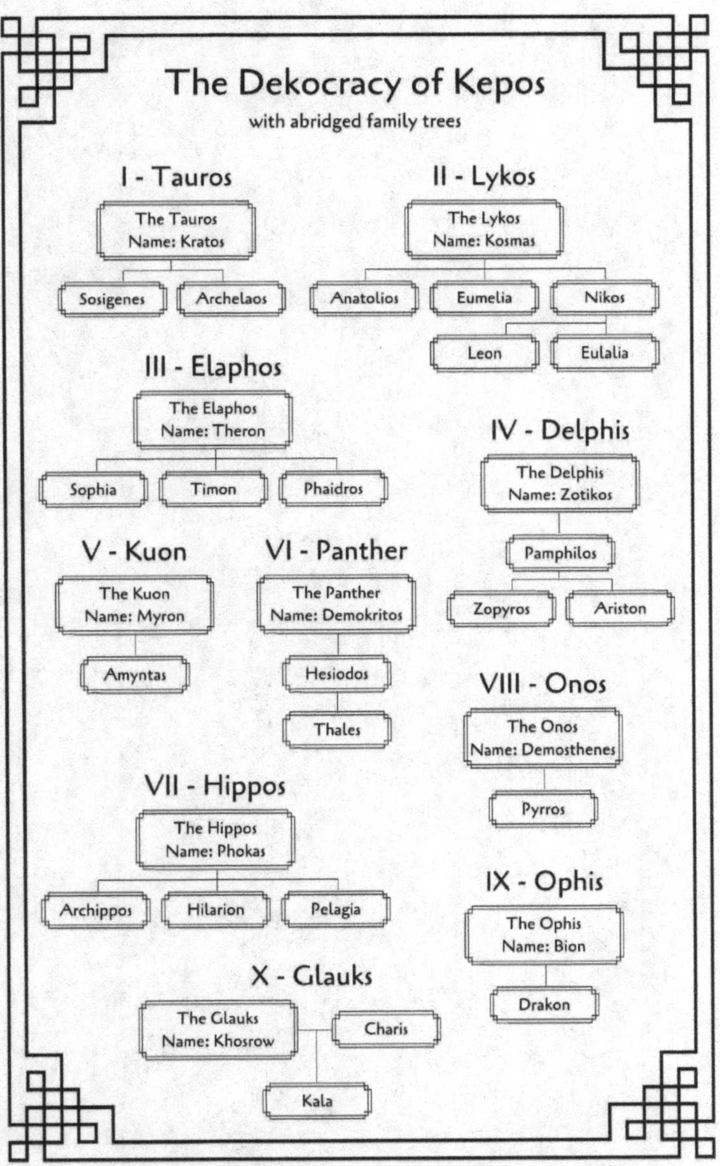

Prologue

They found her by the water. Not the river, not the lake, but the Water. It kissed her toes, icing the dark skin with foam.

'How long has she been here, do you think?' The man's tone was hushed, muffled further by the damp in the morning air.

His companion made no reply.

Dawn stretched rosy fingers towards them, colouring the waves in sheets of light. The two men stood on the dam's wide rim and looked down at the hidden ocean. The city was far beneath them in the valley at their backs, and the cliffs towered above on either side.

The girl was naked, exposed on the coastal rocks below.

'Can we just… leave her? I mean, no one will ever know. We could just walk away, and the tide would take her.' The man twisted the rough material of his cloak between his fingers, crumpling a fistful before releasing it again. His gaze slid towards his companion.

Crumple, release.

'You look to the immediate problem, as always,' his companion said. The light of the new day glinted off his robes. 'You fail to see the danger. I thought I had taught you better than this.'

The girl was waving her hands above her head, shoving away the remainder of her swaddling clothes with her chubby arms.

The first man watched her, trying to puzzle out how the baby could possibly pose a threat.

'What danger?' he asked, giving up.

'Someone put this child here,' his companion replied. 'They know about the Water.'

I

ταῦρος | Tauros | Bull

The god divided the garden into ten parts, one for each of his sons,
and gave to the first-born the central portion, which was the largest and best.
He named him Atlas and made him king over the others,
that he might use his strength to protect the kingdom.

- Kleitos, On the Formation of Kepos

The wall was even older than the city itself. It straddled the narrow gap between the peaks at the end of the valley, marble blocks climbing halfway to the clifftops. Both heights were sacred, cliffs and wall. Both were warded by the acolytes. Both were forbidden to the citizens of Kepos.

While the wall bounded the valley to the west, and the cliffs bounded it to north and south, the sea marked its eastern edge. But there was a second sea, a secret sea, a rising sea, that crashed against the outside of the wall.

This was not common knowledge, and it was certainly not known to the common people. It was not even known to Kala, heir to the tribe of Glauks, as she approached her majority. The wall was forbidden to her. Also forbidden was the pool in which she had chosen to swim.

Her toes clenched in the water, forcing the tickles of bubbles from between them. The cold ached in her ankles as she dropped them into the pool, but she ignored it and let her legs follow, dangling them over the rock until the water reached her knees.

She shouldn't be here. That might have explained the place's attraction, but it had much to recommend it besides the thrill of transgression. The pool caught the waterfall from the cliffs above, the drop immense. By the time it reached her, the cascade was wreathed in mist and spray. On its way down it passed the temple, perched precariously on an outcrop of the cliff, picked out in gold by the sun. She squinted up at it and noted with satisfaction that there was not a soul in sight.

This pool was sacred, and she was sullying it with her toes. She wriggled them with abandon.

The water was so deep that all she could see through the turbulence of the current was blue, blue and black. She imagined that some creature might break through the darkness in a burst of glorious colour, snatching her heels to drag her down to a hidden world in the freezing depths. The thought held no fear, but shivered lightly through her chest, almost as though she wished for it.

She breathed.

She watched the fine hairs rise in goose pimples over the skin of her stomach.

She felt the pressure of her racing heartbeat in the back of her throat.

The moment stretched.

In a single move, she lifted her body from the ledge and knifed feet-first into the water, toes pointed down, fingers stretched above her head. The cold settled on her skin and sank into her thin fat. She spread her limbs, her eyes opened wide into the grey blue, and held herself in place under the surface. But for the distant thud of the waterfall, it was utterly silent.

With a kick of her legs, she flew weightlessly through the water. She danced, graceful as a sycamore seed, whirling around and up until her head reached the air. One gasp, then down again. She forced herself deeper still, until finally her feet hit the bottom of the pool. It was rocky, strewn with stones that slid as her toes touched them.

Arms pushing the water upwards, pushing her feet into the ground, she walked. A perfect line: one foot in front of the other. Toes, arch, heel, step. Repeat. Repeat.

Her lungs flattened, forcing air between her lips in frantic bubbles. Reluctantly, she pushed off hard with her good leg and kicked, long hair trailing heavily behind her, until she broke the surface.

It was late. The sun was painting a rainbow up the sky, red to indigo from horizon to stars. The air smelled warm and rich, the high heat of the day sliding away to let the land exhale its scents.

She shouldn't be here. Her parents would start to worry soon.

It was ten times harder to haul herself out of the water than it had been to drop into it. She struggled, rolling up and over the stone ledge like an inept seal. The shale scraped against her bare thighs as she dragged herself to her feet, supporting herself against the tree where she had stashed her dress and cane.

The air was heavy. She was heavy.

How she wished she could live under water.

It took Kala almost an hour to walk home.

Night was falling when she finally passed from dirt tracks to the cobbled streets of Kepos. Her home was in the centre of the city, amongst the affluent clutch of Dekocrat houses at the very peak of the citadel. The streets were wider here, the roads paved, the wooden houses giving way to stone. It was quieter too. While the lower reaches of the city bustled with people even at night, the heights were so peaceful you could hear the breeze. Kala could almost imagine she heard the souls of the dead singing from behind the distant wall.

Dust coated her sandalled feet, stuck to the moisture she'd brought with her from the pool. With her mucky shoes, dirty dress and dripping braid, she might have been mistaken for a slave if it hadn't been for the cane. There was no disguising herself when the rap of the wood on stone attracted attention to her every wobbling step, so she disguised the mess instead, pulling her cloak over her head and close around her waist. However defective she might be considered by her father's peers, it wasn't proper for the daughter of a Dekocrat to be grubby in public.

She could have stopped at the baths, but tonight she wanted to get home. It wasn't that she would be in trouble for her lateness, or that she had any premonition of tragedy, it was simply that her muscles ached from the swim and from the walk. She had pushed it too far, and now her left leg was so heavy that she stumbled over her steps. She tried to control it, to harness the grace of walking underwater, but she was too weak.

Even if she had been paying attention to her surroundings, she would have seen nothing out of the ordinary when she reached the house of Glauks. There was no sound from within, and the door slave answered her knock with his customary leisure. The pale-haired boy wouldn't meet her eye, but that wasn't unusual either. He owed her deference because of her status, but she knew there were those who thought her deformity was infectious, that they might 'catch' the curse the gods had visited upon her. Nevertheless, she chose to believe the boy's behaviour was a mark of respect rather than revulsion.

So, with the house apparently functioning as normal, it was not until she found her mother washing a bloody rag in the courtyard that she realised something was wrong. Charis's movements were brutal and efficient: rubbing the cloth against the stone of the central pool, rinsing it in the pink water, wringing it in her hands, unfurling it. Slap, splash, slap.

She didn't look at Kala.

'Mother?'

'This soap is worthless.' She took a handful of the ashy substance from a pot at her side and rubbed it into the fabric, coating the material to temper the red.

'What's happened? Is everyone all right?'

'I don't know why Daos lets the tenants get away with this. Maybe it's time we changed his duties, something less strenuous perhaps.'

'Mother, let the maid do that.'

'Oh, don't even get me started on her.' Her movements were frantic now, rubbing away at the fibres so violently that her hands had turned white.

'Mother.'

But she was distant, her eyes fixed mindlessly on her chore.

Charis was widely considered to be a beautiful woman. Her hair was paler than was common in Kepos, a soft brown highlighted with strands of gold and copper. Her skin was light, her face round with dimpled cheeks, made for grinning, but the smile she offered Kala now was small and rueful.

'No one will ever marry you, will they?'

'What?'

Kala knew it was true. Of course she knew. They all knew.

When the disease had crippled Kala, most of the Dekocracy were appalled that Kala's father wouldn't disown her. It had been a wise decision in the end, because she was now his only child. Charis and Kala, together with her father Khosrow, were the only aristocrats who remained in the tribe of Glauks.

But Kala wouldn't do as an heir. Her parents would need to have another child, or perhaps adopt from one of the other tribes. They wouldn't surrender Kala to the acolytes, at least not until then, but they'd never marry her off either. She was now as she would always be: redundant.

'I'll just have to take another husband, I suppose,' her mother was saying. A tear dropped from her cheek.

The pieces fell into place, then: the blood, the tears, and the absence of her father.

Kala ran.

* * *

He was in the library, a scroll unfurling from his fist and blood trailing from his mouth. A meal sat half-finished on the desk in front of him. There were a few salad leaves on his tunic, dripping dressing into the material. His old dog was still asleep by the desk, his head pillowed on Khosrow's foot.

Kala stopped just inside the door. Her face felt full of liquid. It pooled in her nostrils and in her eyes, blurring her vision. A noise escaped from the tightness of her throat; a soft sound, a short sound, out of all proportion with the emotion it expressed.

Her father.

She pushed back the tears and forced herself to focus. There would be things to do, lots to do, and her mother needed her. There was the land to manage, the tribe, her mother's remarriage, the house to prepare. The funeral, of course. She'd need to wash the body.

Her father's body.

The thought was too big. She forced herself to focus smaller. She'd need to clear the food away, tidy the library, put away the scrolls in their correct places so that everything was proper.

She still didn't move.

The scroll he held was Kleitos's history of the city, the book with which he had taught her to read. She wasn't supposed to know how, but he had encouraged it anyway. They read together every night, a quiet hour before bed that they shared together. That they *had* shared together.

'She tried to pull it out.'

Kala hadn't seen the maid. She was at the table on the other side of the room, laying out sheets of cloth. Cloth for wrapping the body, Kala realised. For her father's body.

'I'm sorry?'

'The food,' the maid said. 'From his throat.'

Kala's voice cracked as she spoke. 'You were here?'

'At the end. I was in the courtyard. I heard the…' She looked down, pressing her lips together as though the memory were awkward. It was only then that Kala noticed the bruising on her father's jawline, the scratches around his mouth, now cleaned of blood.

The maid raised her eyes again.

'The Master, the Glauks, your father, Miss. He was choking, you see. His dinner. Your mother, she tried, but by the time she managed it...'

The maid avoided the words, but Kala's mind couldn't stop repeating them: He was dead.

'I'm sorry, Miss.'

She excused herself, leaving Kala alone in the library.

Almost alone. She wanted to approach the body, to approach her father, but she couldn't. It was as though there were a barrier between them. His soul was still there. She knew it wouldn't leave him until they released it to the afterlife, to the place behind the wall. So why did he seem so empty? His body looked heavy. Blank. Like a thing, not a person.

'Linos.'

She whispered, trying to attract the dog's attention without disturbing her father, as though he were only asleep. She clicked her fingers together gently.

'Come on, Linos.'

The dog still didn't move. Anxious now, Kala lowered herself clumsily to the floor and crept closer on her knees. Linos's flaxen fur was cool when she stroked it back from his head, his body quiet. He'd gone to the Shadows with his master, following at his heel just as he always had.

She couldn't hold back the tears.

Crying was a brief indulgence, but it wasn't long before she forced herself to wipe her eyes. She gathered the salad from the floor, from her father's chest, and returned it to the plate. Then she saw the leaves protruding from Linos's lips, the same as those on her father's tunic. She didn't recognise their shape. They resembled parsley, with small sprigs of bright green foliage, but the curve of them was slightly wrong.

'Agathe?' she called.

The maid returned. 'Miss?'

'These leaves, this herb, what is it? Is it from the garden?'

'No, Miss. The Archon sent it over this morning, for your father's trouble.'

He had suffered from insomnia. It was why they always read together in the evenings.

And gods, the Archon.

Kala had already waited too long to report her father's death. The high priest, the Archon, would expect to hear first. Then the Tauros, the head of the Dekocracy's most powerful tribe, then each of the other eight in turn. The house would fill up with strangers, mourners, suitors. The competition for her mother's hand would begin, the title of Glauks to the victor. From the moment she reported it, her father would be not just dead, but erased. The wedding would take place within the week, as though he were capable of being replaced.

But the city wouldn't wait.

'Have messengers been sent?' she said.

'Not yet, Miss. Your mother, well—'

'Yes, thank you. I'll deal with it.'

Her mother was in no state to do anything. Kala could hear her in the courtyard still, sitting by the pool with the bloody rag.

Splash, slap, splash.

Once Agathe had escorted Charis to her room, Kala enlisted the maid and two of the other slaves to prepare the bier: a stretcher of planks bound together with rope, with handles along each side. It would carry her father to the tower for the cremation.

Kala tried not to think about the flames. The smell of the fat.

Whilst they worked in the courtyard she returned to the library, closing the door behind her. Following her first instinct, she folded a piece of papyrus around one of the herb leaves and rolled it up inside the Kleitos scroll, which she prised from her father's grip. Only when the leaf was safely secured did she open the door of the library again to find Agathe hovering outside.

'They'll be expecting the Mistress to send word.'

'I know.'

The Archon wouldn't respond to a summons from Kala. Her mother was a daughter of the city, but Kala was doubly sullied: once by her father's foreign birth and once by disease. She knew her worth to the Dekocracy: nil.

'Fetch a couple of the boys,' she said. 'The twins are probably the fastest. I'll write for her.'

If it hadn't been for her father, she wouldn't have known how. Another mercy she owed to him.

She drew a chair up on the other side of his desk and studied his face for a moment before bending to her task. His eyes were closed, but she knew their colour was as deep as her own. His skin was darker, but there was enough of that colour in hers for others to recognise the kinship. She'd enjoyed that when she was younger, being so identifiably his. It would condemn her now, she supposed, that obvious echo of her mother's first husband. She wondered whether the new Glauks would kill her for it, or if she'd be considered so inconsequential as to pose no threat. She was hardly a challenge to any new heir, broken as she was. She would have no children of her own, no husband to father them.

She wrote in her mother's name, making it appear as though they could afford a scribe. The runners took the letters. The messages returned: they would come in the morning. It was too late tonight.

Kala tried to relax, breathing deeply, and found herself overwhelmed by the heavy scent of the library, a scent that almost resembled her father's. Oil and paper, but soured. Too rich. Too sharp.

She couldn't put it off any longer. The slaves had already gathered in the doorway, waiting for permission to enter. She wished she didn't need their help.

At her nod, they lifted his body. Linos's chin tipped upwards, still resting on her father's foot, following its progress for a moment before cracking down onto the floor, bone to stone. The movement swirled the faecal odour of her father's body into the air. Stripping his clothes, Agathe used them to wipe away the filth from his legs, from the chair, from the floor.

'Burn them,' Kala said. 'The food too.'

'Not the chair, surely?' Agathe asked.

Kala hesitated. Her father had carved it himself, decorating it with owls and bulls, fish and horses, all the animals of the Dekocracy. The wood was darker on the arm rests where his hands had rubbed at the heads of the panther and wolf that coursed along them. She could never replace it.

'No. Wash it carefully, then oil it. Scrub the floor. Leave him to me, please.'

The men laid her father on top of the sheets Agathe had prepared. The table nestled against shelves of scrolls that lined the wall from ceiling to floor. It filled Kala's vision: her father and the wood, the paper, the words. Then the things that didn't belong: bowl, rags, oil, the water.

A hand rested on her arm, the rough touch gentling her heart. Kala knew Melissa by her scent before she spoke, even through the cooking aromas she had brought with her from the fire. She was older than Kala by just a few years, but she was shorter by a couple of inches. She had thick, dark hair that curled uncontrollably, barely restrained by a tie at the nape of her neck. It was a constant annoyance to Melissa, but Kala loved it. Kala loved her.

They had shared their upbringing together. They usually shared everything. But this was a burden Kala had to carry alone.

'Herbs before oil,' Melissa whispered.

'I remember.'

It had been barely a year since Kala had laid out the last body. He had been small enough for her to lift alone, his hair as light as their mother's and his skin as dark as their father's. There had been less of him to wash. His frame had seemed hollowed out when she'd spread the oil, skin sliding over bone beneath her fingers.

Her father was different. He was muscle and flesh, heavy but slack. He had no more strength to protect her.

She was on her own.

There was some comfort to be found when Kala finally reached her moonlit bed: Melissa was already in it.

'Gods,' Kala groaned as she tucked in beside her.

Melissa wrapped her in her arms.

'Are you all right?'

'As all right as I can be.'

'What are you going to do?' she whispered.

'What has to be done.'

'No,' Melissa said, 'I mean about the Archon. Agathe mentioned the herb.'

Kala stilled. 'It was definitely him?'

'I saw the messenger myself. I recognised him. If the leaves are what killed your father...'

'But why?' Kala breathed. 'Why would he want my father dead?'

'I don't know, Kallista. Maybe he didn't. Maybe it was just an accident. I don't know.'

Melissa pulled her close.

Kala cried then. She'd held herself together through the hours spent cleansing and anointing her father's body, but now she couldn't hold back the tears.

They cried together, for the man who had refused to surrender his crippled daughter to the hierophants; who had brought Melissa into Kala's life as her companion when no one else would let their children close to her; who had kept their secret when he walked in on the girls together. He had loved them both, despite all the ways in which Kepos believed Kala had failed him.

And for that, the Archon had killed him.

'He'll come tomorrow,' Melissa said.

'I know.'

'What will you do?'

'What can I do? I'll play the dutiful daughter. Then I'll do what I must to get to the truth.'

Melissa pulled back, concern on her face. She was about to protest when a ringing clang echoed through the silent house, coming from the direction of Charis's room. Kala dragged herself out of bed, bidding Melissa to stay put. She threw a robe around her shoulders then stumbled across the courtyard with her cane.

Her mother's room was quiet by the time she arrived outside. She knocked on the door and called, but there was no reply.

'Mother?'

She hesitated. She would never normally enter without an invitation. Her father's room – the next room along, joined to her mother's by a connecting door – had always been open to Kala. But not her mother's.

'Are you all right?' Kala called through the wood.

When there was still no reply, she opened the door a crack and peeked inside. Her mother was sitting in the centre of the rug. Beside her, a bronze bowl lay on its side, spilling dirty water across the stones. The liquid sought out the gaps between them, forging an angular path towards the door.

'Are you all right, Mother?' she asked again, lowering herself awkwardly to the floor to mop up the water with a discarded linen.

'Where is he?' Charis asked.

Kala stopped her work and looked at her mother's face: her wet lashes, her pink cheeks, her beautiful hair in disarray. It looked as though she had been clawing at it. She was worrying at her fingernails, scraping dirt from underneath them. Dirt and blood, the souvenirs of her attempts to save the Glauks. Her husband. Kala's father.

All in vain.

'He's in the library,' Kala said. 'The bier has been prepared. He has been prepared.'

Charis looked up at her daughter for the first time since she'd entered the room.

'How can you speak of it?' she whispered. 'How can you talk about it like that, as though the whole world hasn't changed?'

Kala pressed her lips together. This is where she and her mother differed: Kala had responsibilities, and she would see them through. Charis had the privilege of ignoring her own, but Kala's dutifulness was her only virtue. She clung to it.

'It needed to be done,' she said eventually.

'I watched him die. He died in my arms. I saw…' Charis broke down, the tears taking her voice.

Kala sat on the rug, putting one tentative hand on her mother's shoulder. She had come here hoping for comfort, but had no idea how to offer it in return. He father would have known. He had always been their intermediary, the thread that bound them together.

'Come on,' Kala said, urging her mother towards the bed. 'You need to sleep. For tomorrow.'

'Tomorrow?'

'I've sent word to the Archon.'

Charis stiffened and moved away. For a moment, Kala thought her mother might also suspect the Archon's involvement in Khosrow's death, but her next words made it clear that their concerns were not the same.

'Then it will start tomorrow,' Charis said coldly. 'How could you? How *could* you?'

'What else was I supposed to do?' Kala asked. 'Hide his death? Let his body rot? Would you have me conceal it?'

'You could have given me a day.' Charis slumped onto the bed. 'A day to prepare, to mourn, before…'

Before the courting started. Before the gifts and suitors and deluge of petitioners. Before the fight for Glauks began.

'There'll be time to mourn him later,' Kala said briskly, suppressing the urge to cry.

'You know that isn't how it works.'

Kala wanted to argue, but there was no arguing against the truth. She was right. There would be no time to mourn, for either of them. They were now nothing more than commodities in a household that would only survive by the grace of her mother's remarriage.

Charis would have to pick another husband, and she'd have to pick soon.

'Tomorrow, Mother.'

Charis curled up on the bed, facing away from her daughter.

'Do you hear me?' Kala said. 'The Archon will be coming with the Dekocrats. You have to be there. Do you promise me?'

'I know my duty,' Charis said.

'And you'll do it?'

Charis showed Kala her back. It was the only answer she would give.

Melissa woke Kala with the dawn. The Glauks tenants were already crowding in the streets outside. Kala was under no illusions that they were here to pay their respects to her father; they just wanted to make a show of their fealty to impress the new Glauks, whoever that might be. By the end of the day, they would know.

Today, the Archon would come.

The bier was arranged in the courtyard, the cloth wrapped up to her father's chin so only his head was visible. His dark curls glistened, oil deepening the colour to rich black. Linos would be cremated with him; the dog's body rested at his master's feet.

Kala wanted to break at the sight, but she couldn't, not until her mother arrived to greet the Dekocrats. Not until

Kala had made sure that she would play her part. But Charis still hadn't emerged from her rooms when a breathless Melissa found Kala in the courtyard.

'The Lykos is here.'

The leader of the second tribe. They'd come out of order. Kala had expected them to arrive in reverse order, with the Ophis coming first, the leader of the lowest of the tribes but her own. The Lykos should have been amongst the last to arrive.

'Why?' she asked. Melissa had no answer, and there was no time to speculate before the door slave was leading him into the courtyard.

It was her mother's duty to greet them. Her mother wasn't here. There was no alternative.

Kala dropped her cane into the shadow of the pool, straightened her back against her exhaustion and prepared to receive the entire Dekocracy on her own. As long as she didn't have to walk more than a couple of steps, she could save face until her mother arrived.

The Lykos was old enough to need a cane of his own. He curved around it, as though it had carved him into shape rather than the other way around.

'You would be the daughter?' he said.

'Yes, Lykos. The house of Glauks is honoured to receive you.' Belatedly, she spotted his companions. 'And your family, of course.'

His wife, she guessed, in dyed cloth and orichalcum jewellery, and two men in their thirties. His sons, probably. She didn't recognise them, but that wasn't saying much. She could recognise all of the Dekocrats, as could everyone else in the city, but her parents hadn't generally introduced her to their acquaintances. No one wanted to meet her.

'Your mother?' the Lykos asked.

'Indisposed, but arriving shortly.'

He looked over his shoulder to one of the men, the younger of the two. His face should have been attractive, his features strong and well-proportioned, but there was something sharp and greedy in his eyes. It discouraged her gaze from lingering.

'Thought you said the girl was a cripple,' the Lykos said to him.

Heat rushed to Kala's face. When the old man looked at her again, his expression was accusatory, as though he had been promised a spectacle then found himself disappointed. He scanned her for defects.

'My leg,' she said, her voice dangerously calm. 'I have trouble walking.' Deliberately, she bent to retrieve the cane from where it lay at her feet.

'Name?' he said.

'Kala, sir.' Her name meant 'beautiful'.

He laughed: a single, harsh bark. 'Really?'

She felt the blush raging on her cheeks, but she didn't reply.

The Lykos looked at her cane and laughed again, glancing back at his family to include them in the joke, and they obliged by joining in. Now he had his entertainment.

Kala smiled, swallowing down her anger. She hated him. She was well aware of the irony of her name, but most people were not so crude as to laugh at it to her face. It was just another reminder that, in Kepos, her twisted limb was all she would ever be.

'Hrm,' the Lykos murmured as his laughter settled. 'I shall await your mother.'

He gave her a final, dismissive glance before turning sharply into the grandest room in the house. He didn't wait for an invitation. His party slammed the door behind them.

Melissa popped her head around the corner from the entrance hall.

'I need her to be out here, now,' Kala said, her voice low and cracking with suppressed anger.

Melissa raised an eyebrow. 'I'll send Agathe.'

'Tell her the Lykos is waiting.'

'The Ophis and the Onos have both arrived too.'

Kala closed her eyes and exhaled, trying to tamp down her frustration. When she opened her eyes again, Melissa had crossed the courtyard towards her.

'They want their cruelty to make you weak.' She took Kala's hand, squeezing hard. 'Prove them wrong. Let it make you strong instead.'

Kala nodded, blinking back frustrated tears, and lifted her chin towards the front door. She needed to do this, and she was going to do it as herself, with her cane, on her own.

It was late morning when Charis finally joined Kala in the courtyard, with only the Archon himself still awaited.

By that time, Kala had greeted all of the Dekocrats, with mixed success. The leaders of some of the tribes had been dismissive, though none quite so unpleasant as the Lykos. Some of them had even been kind. That may have been down to the Delphis, an ancient man with more grandchildren than the gods themselves, who'd stayed at Kala's side to soften the manners of those who came after him.

Then Charis took centre stage. Her audience poured out from the rooms around the courtyard where they had been waiting. She was dressed for the occasion, as a prize, and they treated her as such. Kala was shunted off to one side, where she found a bench with some relief. The Delphis joined her.

'A good cane you have there, my girl,' he said to her. 'Your father carved it, did he?'

'He did.' Kala smiled vaguely, turning the stick in her hands, the tip pivoting in the soil. The handle was an owl, the owl of Glauks. She traced it with her fingers, remembering how her father's fingers had moved over it as he cut the figure from the wood.

'He enjoyed carving,' she said.

'He was good at it.'

'He was.'

Kala watched the Tauros take her mother's hand, leaning down to press his lips to her cheek before turning to introduce her to the man next to him. He was young, maybe twenty, but nonetheless he was dressed for courting. The suitor from the tribe of Tauros had made himself known. Eight more would follow, one from each of the other tribes.

'I appreciate your company, Delphis,' Kala said, 'but don't you want to join your family?'

He laughed, soft and warm.

'I'm too old for all that, my dear, and I'm too old for that nonsense with the tribe title, too. When you get to the age where you lose track of your children's names, it becomes confusing to have two names yourself. Call me Zotikos, please.'

He looked at her with such kindness that she felt as though she might cry.

'Anyway,' he continued, looking away discreetly, 'I'm sure my son can manage on his own.'

He nodded towards the line awaiting her mother's pleasure, towards a young man wearing a tunic dyed the same blue colour as Zotikos's own. He had the old man's friendly eyes, creased with lines, though he couldn't be much older than thirty. He was smiling at a younger man by his side.

'One of your grandsons?' Kala asked.

'Oh, I expect so. They all seem to be, these days.'

The sun had reached an angle high enough to burn their skin and touch her father's shroud. They would need to leave for the tower soon, before the heat perfumed the air with rot.

'Barbaric really, isn't it?' said Zotikos.

'Death?' she asked.

'No,' he said. 'Well, yes, my dear, of course, but I meant this. This spectacle, this grabbing trade. Distasteful, but there it is. Nothing to be done.'

'I suppose not.'

'Well, I'm sorry for it, nonetheless.'

She blinked back tears. The heat in the air made the heat of her emotion almost unbearable. It itched and seeped, salting her skin. She longed for the water of the sacred pool, the icy chill to shock her heart into stillness. Escape. But there was no escaping this.

'Your given name is Kala, isn't it?' Zotikos asked her.

She shielded her emotions, anticipating more pain.

'That's right,' she said.

'It suits you well, just as your father always said.'

She searched Zotikos's face for any hint of sarcasm, but there was none to be found. Despite the flare of injustice she had felt at the Lykos's earlier ridicule, she had suffered it often enough that she had taken it into herself. She believed in her name's irony and felt its sting, even when it passed unremarked. She believed that her leg was enough to unravel the rest of her into ugliness, and so she wore the name as a constant rebuke, a reminder of her failed potential, of the gift that she might have been to her family. She wanted to unburden herself of that guilt, to explain to Zotikos how the weight of disappointment crippled her more than her physical disability.

Instead, she said, 'You knew him?'

'Very well. He was an accomplished and intelligent man. I shall miss his company and his counsel in these dark times.'

They sat together for a moment in silence until Zotikos's son gestured to him, beckoning him towards Charis.

'The Delphis is called to duty, I fear.' He got to his feet. 'Bide well, Kala.'

She smiled. 'And you, Zotikos. Thank you for helping me pass the time.'

After a brief greeting to Charis, Zotikos was ushered away to make room for the Lykos.

The old man presented the younger of his companions to Kala's mother. The suitor was the sharp-eyed son, the man who had told the Lykos that Kala was a cripple. He was handsome, but the hard line of his jaw gave him an air of cruelty that was barely tempered by the softness of his curls. Her mother greeted him with a familiarity that pinched at the back of Kala's neck.

Charis smiled at him, her lips parting too widely, her hand sliding into his even before he reached for it. He kissed it, his lips pressed into her palm.

Something wasn't right. The order was wrong. The Lykos had waited until all the other leaders had given their respects, leaving his family as the last to greet Charis before the arrival of the Archon, as though this final suitor were the climax. Not one of the other tribes had challenged that contrivance, not even the Tauros, who properly deserved that place of honour. He had taken the first greeting instead, as though it were planned.

Charis's smile played on her lips as she met the suitor's eyes.

Kala looked on with uneasiness rolling in her stomach.

They greeted the Archon together. Not Charis and Kala, as it should have been, but Charis and him, the suitor of Lykos. Kala was forgotten. She wanted to leave, but her father kept her tethered in place.

The Hierophants, high priests of the tribes, processed out behind the Archon within minutes of his arrival. Kala tried to catch the Archon's eye, as though her suspicions would be settled just by looking at him, but in the end she had to look away from the glare of the orichalcum disks sewn into his robes. Blinking, blinded, Kala reeled as the sensation dizzied her into nausea.

She could smell the body, too. It would only get worse.

The Dekocracy surrounded the bier, nine men to carry their tenth, hands pulled low, rope imprinting their skin. She joined the column behind them, behind her mother, behind her mother's suitor. The families of the Dekocrats crowded along behind her. The proximity confused her legs, so they became muddled with her cane. The more she tried to watch them, to control them, the more they failed her.

Just as she started to fall, an arm tucked into her free hand, gently edging her upright.

'May I have the honour of escorting you?' The voice was breaking a little. The boy to whom it belonged was tall and wiry, dressed in the pale blue of Delphis. 'I saw you talking to Grandpa.'

He looked familiar to Kala, but she was sure he wasn't the boy who'd been in line earlier. His features were different: softer, with more sunshine in his hair and more pink in his cheeks.

'Do I know you?' she asked, trying to place him.

He smiled. 'We used to play together in the river. Ariston.'

It had been before her illness, back when she'd still played with her peers. Afterwards, things had changed. But, for a few years, she had been one of them.

'Ariston,' she repeated.

She had only the vaguest memory of a chubby boy with soft hair. She remembered him being kind, but didn't recall any particular occasions on which he had demonstrated that attribute. There was only one incident she could remember, in fact.

'Ariston,' she said again. 'You're the one who–'

'Yes, that's me.' His smile faltered a little, pinching awkwardly at the corners. Kala controlled her expression, trying not to laugh.

'I won't say anything,' she promised.

With her attention elsewhere, her feet seemed to be behaving themselves better.

'I'm sorry about your father,' he said.

'Thank you.'

'I still have the fish he carved for me.'

Her father had been practicing the animals for his chair, she remembered. He'd given them to all the children, wooden masterpieces that nestled comfortably in sticky little palms.

They walked on in silence, past the council house towards the highest point of the citadel. Her stomach was churning by the time they reached the foot of the tower, knowing what would come next.

Once her mother had gone ahead, the Dekocracy carried the stretcher awkwardly up the steps. It tipped slightly. Fearing for Linos's security, Kala let go of Ariston's arm and put a hand on the dog's small, cold body. His fur felt different. It was coarser somehow, the lustre gone with his life.

The odour was stronger up close, almost overwhelming in the narrow stairwell. It was sweltering now, so hot that her thighs slid slick against each other, and her dress was sticking to the sweat collecting along her spine. She wanted to be near her father, but she hated the heat and the odour of death and wished again that she were somewhere else. The wish felt like a betrayal.

The sun was directly overhead when they finally reached the top of the tower. The space was wide and flat, featureless except for the stairwell and a large block of stone mounded with wood and flowers, as though they could overpower the scent of the meat.

The Dekocrats lowered the bier onto the framework of wood, settling it securely in place, then crossed the tower to where the Lykos suitor stood with Kala's mother.

Kala's eyes fixed on their joined hands, fingers wrapped tightly around each other. How could this man claim her mother with such confidence, with such widespread acceptance?

She moved reluctantly to her mother's side. Her unclaimed side.

The acolytes of Diaprepes, the god of Glauks, surrounded the bier. They were led by their Hierophant, Straton. He was a bastard brother of Kala's mother, the only one left, but Kala had never known him as an uncle. Her mother wouldn't say why he'd joined the priesthood – an unusual calling for those with aristocratic blood – but the decision had served him well. He had been an acolyte until recently, but it had been a decade of desperate illness. The elder ranks of Diaprepes's priesthood had emptied as quickly as those of Glauks's aristocrats, so now the Hierophancy was his. Maybe he'd be Archon one day.

He stood at her father's head and intoned prayers to the god as acolytes circled the bier, kneeling low as they held tapers to the kindling. Soaked in oil, the wood caught quickly, forcing them away from the heat.

All except one.

She stood on the other side of the pyre, visible to Kala only in strobing slices between the flames. Like the rest of the acolytes, she was heavily robed despite the temperature. Unlike the rest, her dark skin contrasted starkly with the pale cloth. Unlike the rest, she was a woman.

The fire burned hot. Flesh split and peeled, the blood steaming and hissing in the cracks as it evaporated. The smoke was rich with fat, so pervasive that it stuck in Kala's throat. She tried not to cough, because she knew that once she did she would only breathe the corruption deeper into her lungs.

Eventually the fire settled itself, pouring a steady column up into the blue. The wind took it then, chasing it up and over the wall at the valley's end along with her father's soul, taking him to join his ancestors in the world beyond. She tried to mark the moment when he left, but she couldn't feel it. There was nothing but the smell of the meat cooking.

The acolytes began to sing, a low hum, rising into a melody that cut through the valley. They called on Diaprepes to guide his soul to his place in the Shadows. They called on his ancestors to receive him there. They called on her father to go, and not to linger.

Through it all, Kala could hear only one voice: the voice of the girl, quiet but discernible still by its tone. She sang with a hitch of tears, the notes ponderous and flattened, thudding bleakly through the choir. Where they hymned, she wove a dirge between. It was somehow more solid despite its whispered edge. Soon it drew the rest of the voices around it, twisting them from major to minor, drowning their praise in its lament.

Tears dropped down Kala's face, but Charis didn't cry. She seemed frozen, her eyes glazed, as though she had been scoured out and filled with cold wax. But Kala saw the tension in her shoulders and the sharpness of her movements, and in them she saw something like fear.

The Dekocracy left a few hours later, taking Charis with them. Kala watched them go. The Archon and the Hierophants were next, followed in the evening by the tenants and the acolytes, all except the dark-skinned girl. She hadn't moved, her mouth forming the shapes of words that were no longer audible.

The night breeze pulled brighter flames from the pyre as the two girls faced each other through the remains of Khosrow's body. But for Kala's cane, they were so similar that she might have believed herself reflected in the haze. They each wore cream dresses with a pale cloak trailing from their heads, Kala's donned against the cool of the evening and the acolyte's part of her ceremonial garb. They were each crowned in braids of thick black hair. Their skin was almost of a shade, but Kala's was perhaps slightly paler; the falling dusk and the play of the light made it difficult to discern the exact colour.

This was what Kala's past would have been had her father disowned her: a slave to the priesthood, bound to serve a god whose tribe had discarded her. It might yet be her future, if the new Glauks were so inclined.

Someone in Glauks had abandoned this girl.

'Who are you?' Kala asked.

But the acolyte had stepped back from the flames and was already gone, light footsteps tapping down the stairwell and away.

Kala could concentrate on nothing else as she walked back to the house of Glauks. The colour of her skin, the colour of her hair; the acolyte even had the same shaped eyes as her. They were traits Kala had inherited from her father.

She was maddened by it. Had it not been entirely forbidden, she would have gone to the temple that night to find the answers she needed, but they would never let her up on the plateau. She would have to wait until she saw the acolyte in the city again.

Or she could ask Melissa.

But Melissa was busy when she entered the house. All of the slaves were. The families of the Dekocrats hadn't gone home, not all of them. The suitors had come back to the house, and they were being handsomely accommodated. The contest proper had started sooner than Kala had expected, and she guessed that it would end tonight, one way or another.

They were not quiet. Ten of them filled the dining room, her mother and the nine men.

Laughter and the sharp odour of new wine and lust rolled against the walls. It spilled out into the courtyard when Kala rushed by. She stood in the darkness, just beyond the aurora of light that danced through the doorway. Jasmine bloomed in the courtyard, but she could smell only the smoke from the oil lamps and the fatty spice of the meats Melissa was serving.

The feasting was in full swing. Charis was seated in the middle of the longest bench, two suitors on either side of her. She was laughing, her eyes shining brighter than Kala had ever seen them, and yet they were dark and blank beneath the surface. She was covered with an unpleasant sheen, as though she were a cold creature on which the heat around her condensed, never penetrating her skin.

While Kala watched, her mother leaned towards the man on her right, the suitor from Lykos, and brought her lips to his ear. They were close, so close that the brown curls at his neck moved as she spoke. It was like a caress, as though she were stroking his hair with her mouth. They might have been alone.

He looked down, smiling with satisfaction, then brought his eyes up to meet Kala's.

He saw her.

She saw him.

She saw his hand on her mother's leg, his eyes on Kala's, but his attention on the rest of the room. She saw his absolute control and in that moment she knew him for what he was: contained but limitless, hungry and dangerous, son of the Lykos.

The new Glauks.

II
λύκος | Lykos | Wolf

The god gave music to his second son, Eumelus,
so he might charm the people with his song and win their
adoration.
His portion of the garden was second in size only to that of
the king,
and it was filled with fruit and the singing of birds.

- Kleitos, On the Formation of Kepos

Kala left the house before her mother had risen the next morning, heading down to the river to wash the pyre smoke from her best dress. The slaves would have done it for her, but she wasn't sure the man from Lykos had left last night, and she preferred to absent herself than to have her fears confirmed.

Those fears weren't the only ones playing on her mind.

In the long night she'd had time to reflect on her father's death, and her suspicions had swelled with the dawn. As she walked into the city they spilled over into certainty. Her father had been murdered.

He had been healthy and strong, with no obvious infirmity. He might have choked, maybe, but now that her head was clearer Kala could finally name the inconsistencies that had prompted her to save the strange herb. The desk had been unusually messy. Her father would have found it intolerably disorganised, she was sure. He had also not been accustomed to taking his meals in the library, because he worried for the scrolls, so why had he done so that night? And then there was Linos. He could have died from old age, but perhaps he had died from the same cause as her father: poison.

It all pointed to the herb her father had received from the Archon, and that left Kala powerless. How could she accuse such an important man? And why would he want her father dead?

She wished she had more time. It wouldn't be long before her father was replaced, forgotten. That was all that mattered to Kepos: the traditions of the past, and the future of the tribe.

When she arrived at the river crossing west of the city, she saw that she was not the first. The blue tunics of Delphis littered the banks, the slaves who wielded them eyeing her suspiciously as she approached. She opted to continue on to the sacred pool. There, at least, she would be alone. She walked a little faster, but there was only so much speed her gait would allow on the uneven path.

The temple on the outcropping above was busy at this time of day, so she skirted close to the cliff until she reached the edge of the water, where she stowed her cane. There was a shallow pool behind the waterfall, in a cave churned into the rock. That was where she headed now, carefully stepping along the stone until she could wade into the sanctuary, letting the water take her weight.

It was cool and dark, and the roar of the cascade gave Kala a perverse sense of silence. This was a place in which words and noise meant nothing, because there was nothing to be heard except the crash of the water. Here, the water ruled.

She washed the dress she was carrying, then stepped out of the one she was wearing and did the same. It didn't take long. After that, the morning was her own. The water here was too shallow for her to stand fully underwater, so she contented herself with lying back into its dark arms. But it was cold in the secret shade, so before long she clawed her way back into her wet dress and, carrying the other, waded out into the sunshine.

And stopped.

There was a girl there, at the edge of the pool. From her clothing, Kala guessed that she must be one of the acolytes, but she was too slim and pale-skinned to be the one Kala had hoped to see. She hung back behind the curtain of water and watched until the girl was out of sight, carrying a pot of water up the precarious stairway to the temple. It was the first time Kala had seen anyone here, in the place she thought of as her own. She had the uncomfortable feeling of being intruded upon. She couldn't stay here to dry the dresses, as she had planned.

The soaking fabric sucked at her flesh as she collected her cane and stumbled quickly south, following the river into the woods. Once she was concealed by the trees, she hauled herself up into the low branches of an elm, off the path, and secured herself in the crook of its arms, spreading her good dress beside her to dry. The tree held her comfortably in the morning sunshine and so, for the first time since her father had died, she slept deeply. She slept until the afternoon.

And that is why, by the time Kala next saw her mother, the deal had already been struck.

'Where have you been?' Melissa's tone was urgent and unhappy. She was wringing her hands, a gesture at odds with her usual stoicism.

'I'm sorry. I lost track of time.'

Kala handed the clean dress to her and pushed through into the courtyard.

'Have you heard?' Melissa asked.

'I can guess.'

'Nikos, his name is. Second son of the Lykos.'

'And the wedding?'

'Tomorrow.'

That surprised Kala enough to bring her to a halt. There would be a new Glauks tomorrow. Her mother would be remarried tomorrow. Kala would be replaced within the year, as soon as a child had been produced to carry on the line. An unbroken child. Her mother was not so old, after all.

Would Kala be allowed to stay in Glauks? Would she be thrown to the mercy of the Archon, as an acolyte of Diaprepes? Or was she too much of a threat for Nikos to tolerate her remaining alive?

She could see the same anxiety in Melissa's face.

'All will be well,' Kala said. She offered Melissa a tight smile, then retreated to her one remaining bastion of peace, the one place in which she still felt it was possible for all be well: her father's library.

Only to find that it, too, had been invaded.

A tall, dark-haired young man was walking along the shelves, fingering the scrolls. He held a few in his arms, one of which looked suspiciously like Kleitos's history, the scroll in which she had hidden her sample of the unfamiliar herb. Kala's chest tightened in panic.

'What are you doing in here?' she said.

He raised a single eyebrow. His composure riled her.

'Don't touch those,' she yelled, as though he were a slave whom she could command. He was not; that much was clear from the orichalcum torc circling his bicep. Nonetheless, she snatched the scrolls from his hands and began returning them to their rightful places, muttering irritably as she did so.

'You must be Kala.'

She was busy reassuring herself that the herb was still rolled safely into the Kleitos, and didn't reply.

'I'm Leon.' His voice was tinged with amusement, which served only to aggravate Kala further.

'And what exactly,' she asked, 'are you doing in my father's library?'

He looked away, his expression awkward.

'It's still his,' she insisted, but they both knew that was a lie.

'Of course. I didn't mean to intrude.'

'Then what did you mean to do?'

'Find a peaceful spot,' he said, 'but I see this one is already taken.'

He moved towards the door, but Kala stopped him with a hand on his chest. She hadn't finished with him yet.

'Who are you?' she asked.

'Leon.' His mouth shifted a little, as though he were trying not to smile.

Kala's patience was running out. 'Yes, so you said, but who are you?'

'Ah.' His tone was almost embarrassed. 'Grandson of the Lykos. Son of Nikos.'

'Son of the Glauks,' Kala murmured.

'So it would seem.'

And the new heir. Her mother wouldn't need to produce a child after all.

He looked down at her, his hazel eyes threaded with green. A question played across his eyebrows. She realised that her fingers were still resting on his tunic and pulled her hand away. Still too close for comfort, she moved to her father's desk, idly stroking the bull on the back of his chair. Its head was central, dominant, as befitted the animal of the ruling tribe.

'Is it just you?' she asked.

'I have a sister. About your age. Eulalia, her name is.'

'Where is she?'

'With your mother. She likes, you know, things.' He gestured towards his torc. 'She used to help mother with her hair. She says she likes the combs, the jewellery, the perfumes. I think she just misses her.'

'She chose that for you?' Kala asked, pointing at the torc.

He smiled. 'She likes to dress me up.'

'And your father?'

The transformation in his expression was unexpected. His eyes clouded with shadows, but he didn't reply.

'He's not a good man?' Kala asked.

'He's a powerful man.'

'And?'

'Do you think it's possible to be both?'

She thought about the Dekocrats she had met the day before. Did she think they were good men, with the way they had treated her? Maybe Zotikos. She didn't know any of the current Dekocrats well enough to say, but she had known one.

'My father was,' she said

'You loved him?' Leon asked.

'You don't love yours?'

'Should I?'

'Are you always this obtuse?'

'You sound like my sister.'

She laughed harshly and said, 'Well, I'm not.'

Kala couldn't imagine anything more ludicrous than the thought that she might be considered kin to this reluctant prince. She'd be happier with the slaves. With Melissa.

'You don't want a brother, then?' he asked.

'I had a brother.'

He must have heard the edge in her tone, because he didn't push.

'I loved my mother,' he said. 'Very much.'

Kala examined his face for sincerity. There was something she recognised in the hard vulnerability of his eyes, as though he were daring her to crack the seal of his pain. It was as familiar to her as the carvings under her fingers, the shape of the shield she held over her own loss.

She gripped her cane and ranged along the shelves, looking for a particular scroll. When she found the one she wanted, she pulled it out and handed it to him.

'Love poems?' he asked, his eyebrows eloquently conveying his disbelief.

'There's more than one kind of love, Leon.'

His laugh was so derisive that she snatched the book back.

'Fine,' she said, 'go and find some other way to amuse yourself then, and get out of my library.'

'I thought it was your father's library.'

'Well, it's mine now.'

He laughed again, ruefully this time, and gently took the scroll from her hands. She let it go.

'I wish that were true,' he said.

'Really?' Her tone was sceptical.

'Just as much as you do. I assure you.'

'Is he that bad?'

Her own impressions of Nikos had not been favourable, but she was surprised that his son would share her dislike.

'Worse,' he said. 'You'd better come with me.'

Leon led Kala to a dining room at the back of the house. Nikos had installed himself there, surrounded by scurrying slaves and scrolls, as he took account of the household he would be acquiring. His head was bent over a wax tablet on which he was taking notes, the stylus dwarfed by the size of his fist.

'Father?' Leon said to him.

He looked up after a pause of some moments, clearly irritated by the interruption.

'May I present Kala, daughter of Glauks?'

Nikos's sharp gaze roamed between the two adolescents for a second before settling back on his son.

'Your sister is in the gardens.'

'Yes, I'm aware–'

'Well, then.'

That was apparently the end of the matter. Kala's own father had talked to her as he worked, asking for her advice and encouraging her to participate in the management of their property. Tomorrow, it would be Nikos's property, and it didn't appear that he would be extending the same courtesy to his son.

Leon didn't look surprised. As he ushered Kala from the room, he raised his eyebrows at her as though to say, 'I told you so'.

They passed through the house, navigating shaded colonnades to the walled garden behind. Leon had no trouble finding his way, which Kala found irksome. She was denied the superiority inherent in guiding him, in claiming greater knowledge of their surroundings. It was as though she were no longer permitted any advantage in the house, as though Glauks had already been ceded to the newcomers.

They found his sister alone, sitting on a bench near the entrance to the garden. Charis was absent, once again.

Kala had expected Eulalia to simper at her, and was surprised to find an intelligent gaze underneath her sculptured curls. The girl rose to her feet to greet them.

'Kala?'

She nodded in response.

'I'm sorry for the circumstances,' Eulalia continued. 'I hope we might be friends.'

Kala nodded again, rather addled by her forthright manner.

'I think we're the same age,' Eulalia said. 'You were born in the nineteenth year of Ophis?'

Kala started to nod once more, but stopped herself. She didn't want the girl to think her a mute or, worse, an idiot.

'Yes, that's right,' she said. 'I'm sixteen. And Leon is older?' She turned to him for confirmation, only to find that he had wandered off into the alley of cypress trees that led past the pond.

'Don't mind him. He mopes.'

'Excuse me?'

'Oh, you know. He's bored because Father never lets him do anything, so he gets frustrated and goes off with his friends, drinks too much wine and breaks things.'

'The obvious solution.' Kala would never understand boys.

Eulalia sighed. 'The problem is, the more he does it, the less father trusts him. And Leon won't listen to me, of course.'

They watched as he reached the far wall at the end of the garden. He lingered there, testing and plucking figs from a tree that was pegged out against the sun.

'He's not really as wild as they say,' Eulalia said.

Kala had heard nothing about Leon before she had met him, but she refrained from saying so, worried that her ignorance might offend.

'Still,' Eulalia continued, 'it always works in his favour at the Proaulia. For some reason, the daughters of Kepos seem to find the wild ones exciting. Personally, I find them tiresome.'

Kala might have been inclined to agree, had she any frame of reference. As it was, she tended to keep to herself and to her household. The fact that she was about to participate for the first time in the Proaulia – the city's annual marriage festival – was a source of anxiety. She knew she'd be left without suitors, so what was the point?

'And you?' she asked Eulalia.

The girl smiled. 'Oh, I make sure that I'm only wild in private.'

Kala was shocked enough to laugh. 'I meant, what are you going to do? Are you going to the Proaulia this year?'

Leon was making his way back towards them now, a handful of purple figs clasped loosely at his side.

'Oh yes,' she replied. 'My first year.'

'And your last, I expect,' Leon said as he joined them. 'You'll be snapped up, Lali.'

She smiled at him with more pleasure than Kala had expected. There was a slight pinking of her cheeks, the most demure of blushes.

'We'll see,' she said.

Kala found herself reflecting Eulalia's smile, despite her grief. It was magnetic. She had a transparency to her emotions that made Kala feel as though she had known her for years.

'You like someone, then?' Kala said.

But Eulalia wouldn't be drawn on it. Instead, she diverted the conversation.

'You're going this year, aren't you?'

'Yes,' Kala replied.

Of course she was going. She was of age this year, so there was really no choice. If her mother had intended to marry a childless man then maybe Kala might have found a suitor. Someone might have been willing to overlook her deformity for the opportunity to become the heir to Glauks. Now, with Leon shortly to be in line before her, that would never happen. She tried to care about that, to feel its loss, but with all that had happened over the past few days it seemed beneath her concern.

'And you, Leon?' she asked, as eager to deflect attention as Eulalia had been moments before. 'You'll be going too?'

'Pff,' Eulalia huffed. 'He's gone for the past two years and approached no one. I'm not sure why he even bothers.'

'I'll be there,' he said.

Eulalia leaned forwards and whispered loudly to Kala. 'Everyone's saying he prefers men, that he's delaying because he can't stand the thought of sex with a woman.'

Kala's cheeks burned, but the siblings seemed unperturbed, as though this were the usual tone of their bickering.

Leon laughed, full-throated but bitter. 'Oh, yes,' he said. 'Father would love that. At least I'd be out of the way then. But no, I'm afraid the rumours aren't true.'

'How do you know?' Eulalia said, prodding his arm as she relieved him of one of the figs. 'It's not as though you have any experience with girls.'

'Oh really? And how do you know that?'

'A sister knows.' She winked at Kala and they shared a smile. It felt like family, that intimacy, that acceptance, and Kala wanted it keenly.

Eulalia bit into the fig, but before she could move it away from her mouth, Leon had covered her hand with his own and pushed, rubbing the fruit across her face. She yelled her outrage, grabbing the remaining figs and hurling them at him as he fled across the garden, gasping with laughter.

To her credit, it only took Eulalia a minute or so to catch up and push him into the pond.

* * *

There was still no sign of Kala's mother when the three of them trooped back through the house, and Nikos remained engrossed in the accounts. Leon hovered at the door to his room for a few seconds, as though hoping for some acknowledgement, but it never came. That was probably for the best, since Leon was soaked through and tinged green with pond scum. The only acknowledgement he could have expected in that state was one of censure.

'Please don't tell my father,' Eulalia whispered to Kala as they made their way back along the colonnade, Leon trailing soggily behind them.

'That you two had a food fight?' Kala laughed. 'Don't worry, I won't.'

'No, not that. That there's someone I, you know…'

'Like?'

'Yes.'

'Why not?' Kala asked, but Eulalia just begged her silence and refused to say more.

When they reached the courtyard Kala called for Melissa, who soon had Eulalia cleaned up and Leon in a dry set of clothes. The time it took Leon to change was long enough for Kala to come to a resolution.

'I want to go to the wall,' she said to Melissa.

She was catching at ghosts in this house, and her father was being dissipated by every new intrusion. She needed to go to the edge of the Shadows so she could feel his proximity, or at least know that she felt nothing.

'I'll come with you,' Leon offered.

'No.'

'Yes,' Melissa said. 'I don't want you going there alone.'

Kala knew she meant well, but the implication that Kala couldn't look after herself made her skin burn. She didn't want a tag-along, and in particular she didn't want *him* tagging along.

'I don't need an escort,' she said, lifting her cane pointedly. She already had a weapon to hand.

'I know,' Melissa said, 'but you're going to take one anyway.'

Kala started to protest again, but Melissa stopped her words with one of her looks. It was the tenderness of her touch that finally won Kala over, rough fingertips stroking the back of her hand, and so she allowed Leon to follow her out of the house and into the city.

They walked westwards, out beyond the citadel, pushing through the fragrant bustle of the street markets in a snaking path that made their progress slow. Spit-roasted meats filled the air with a rich scent that flared her appetite, then made her queasy as she realised what it reminded her of: the body on the bier.

'Have you eaten?' Leon asked her.

She shook her head at him, unwilling to open her mouth, to taste the smell of the flesh burning.

'Do you…'

She shook her head again, pushing past him to lead them away from the meat. He followed reluctantly, but once they were out of the cloying atmosphere of fat and smoke, she stopped at a kitchen selling baked goods. He looked on as she acquired fruit pies and breads filled with vegetables and cheese. The woman at the stall eyed Leon with open mistrust, but she smiled at Kala warmly, her wide face wrinkling into comfortable creases as she wrapped the food in a length of rough cloth, slipping a couple of honey cakes into the bundle.

'For your father,' she said.

Kala smiled painfully, mumbling her gratitude as she slipped back into the crowd. Although she was hampered by her leg and her new burden, Leon still struggled to follow. She knew how to move with the people, weaving amongst them, but he just seemed to slam up against the flow.

'One of yours?' he asked as he finally made his way to her side.

'Excuse me?'

'That woman. Was she one of the Glauks tenants?'

'Why? Are you keeping count for your father?'

His expression simmered for a moment. 'It's not always about him,' he said.

But Kala didn't want to talk to him about Glauks or their tenants. It was the world she had inhabited with her father, and she didn't want to share it.

They walked in silence until they reached the meadows west of the city. There Kala stopped, finally putting her bundle down into the long grass, and sat to rest her legs. Leon didn't join her, but instead stood off to one side, looking out towards the wall.

There was a clear view from their vantage point. From here, they could just make out the shadowed shape of the staircase that jinked across its face. The wall was many stones deep, a series of walls in fact, one stuck to the face of another. The front layer was the shortest, its stepped diagonal top forming the first part of the staircase up from the ground. The wall directly behind it was a little taller, the lowest point of its top taking over where the first wall had left off. The series continued, each wall taller than the one in front of it, their tops angling in alternating diagonals to create a continuous staircase zig-zagging to the very peak, where the wall was at its thinnest.

No one except the priesthood was permitted to set foot on those steps. No one else knew how thin that upper reach of the wall was, but it was always growing. The wall was fed every year without fail. Every year, the priests built it up with blocks decorated by the people of Kepos for the harvest festival, by putting a single new stone on each step of the staircase. It took ten years to complete that process from the bottom of the staircase to the very top, and last year had been the ninth of the latest layer. Kala could pick out last year's stones by the brightness of their colours, near the top of the wall. The colours faded as her eye trailed downwards from one staircase to the next, triangular slices of marble that bled from bold to pastel to washed-out hue, bleached by years in the sun. It was like a map of passing time.

As she traced its patterns, she untied the cloth package and pulled out one of the vegetable-stuffed breads, still warm from the oven.

'Hungry?' she asked Leon.

He didn't answer, but he did at least sit down on the other side of the cloth and take a bread for himself. While they ate, Kala thought about Eulalia, about the secret she had asked Kala to keep. She decided to break the silence.

'Your sister,' she said, 'the boy she likes, is he not someone suitable?'

'He's nice enough.'

'No, I mean—'

'I know what you mean. And he's good enough.' As he spoke, Leon looked off towards the wall again. He was holding back.

'But?' she persisted.

'Good enough isn't always good enough, and father has other plans. So long as he doesn't find out that she likes Ariston, we might be able to make it happen. Otherwise…'

'Ariston? She likes Ariston? Delphis Ariston?'

That brought Leon's attention firmly back to Kala.

'You know him?' he asked.

'I saw him yesterday. Does he know?'

'Oh yes,' Leon chuckled. 'He knows. He's pretty smitten himself.'

'And your father?'

'He has someone else in mind for her.'

'So why doesn't she talk to him about it? Tell him she'd rather be with Ariston? I mean, it'd be a pretty good match for her.'

Leon gave her an odd look, as though he were surprised she had to ask the question.

'Knowing what someone wants gives you power over them,' he said, 'and he has enough of that already.' Anger lit something dangerous in his eyes.

When Kala spoke next she did so tentatively. 'What did he do?'

Leon picked up a fruit pie and fiddled with the pastry, breaking off the edges that had been singed in the oven.

'Did you know that our parents were lovers?' he asked.

'What? You mean my mother and your father?'

He nodded.

This was news to Kala. She thought about Nikos's hand on her mother's thigh, her hand in his at the funeral, and the unspoken accord of the Dekocracy to his claim. Her stomach churned.

'Since when?' she asked.

'Since they were teenagers. You didn't know?'

Kala just looked at him.

'You didn't know,' he said.

No wonder her mother's remarriage had been presented as a done deal. No wonder it had gone unchallenged. Everyone had known about it, everyone except her. Had her father known? Had he found out? Was that why he had been killed? Had Nikos done it? The questions were piling up so quickly that she could barely parse her thoughts.

'Did they... I mean,' she said, 'when my father was alive, all this time, or... how long?'

'I don't think so. It happened when they were our age. Then my father married my mother instead, because the Lykos demanded it.'

'Who told you?' Kala asked. She didn't trust him, and she didn't want to believe it was true.

But his source wasn't the idle gossip she had hoped for.

'My mother told me,' he said, 'a few days before she died.' He looked haunted, his expression hollowed out into one she recognised from their meeting in the library earlier that day.

She was about to ask for more details, to steer him back to the story and away from his mother's death, but before she could do so he was on his feet, striding away into the meadow. He started to gather wildflowers into a bunch.

After a moment, Kala bundled up the food and joined him.

* * *

It was late in the afternoon by the time they reached the sacred precinct. The land sloped down to the base of the wall, so Kala had been able to swing her way there on her cane. But she had slowed by the end of the journey, and her leg was now aching so much that it burned. Leon had adjusted his pace with no comment, for which Kala was grateful and resentful in equal measure.

There was farmland and grass all the way up to the holy space itself, the sancta: a wide arc in the shadow of the wall filled with offerings, statuary and dedication stones. There was a section for each of the tribes there. A monument to Kala's father would appear soon enough, discreetly, to honour him without dishonouring his successor. The dead Glauks would have no ceremony other than the one he had already received.

Leon made his way towards the centre of the wall, where the Lykos sanctum stood between those of Tauros and Delphis. Glauks was to the far side, as befitted its low status. That was where Kala headed, her bundle of cakes and flowers slung across her shoulders.

Straton was tending the offerings that day and gave her a nod of recognition from his place at the stone altar. It was unusual for a Hierophant to mind his sanctum himself, but Kala was not surprised to see him here today, the day after the funeral of his Dekocrat. However, he seemed surprised to see her. His face was calm, but his fingers were nervous, gathering the cloth of his robes into his fist, then letting it go again. Crumple, release.

'Gennadios brought his finest bull yesterday,' he said to Kala when she joined him. 'I performed the sacrifice to Diaprepes in your father's name just before the dawn.'

She hadn't expected Gennadios to be so generous, but the tenant farmer always had been close to her father. He could expect very different treatment under the new Glauks.

'Thank you,' she said.

'You have offerings of your own?'

She shrugged the bundle from her back and unwrapped it so that Straton could lift out the honey cakes and flowers. He placed them carefully on the altar, the cakes resting on the bed of foliage to keep them from the filth that coated the stone. Straton would deliver them to the hands of the needy who came to pray at the altar that day, together with cuts of roasted meat from the slaughtered bull.

That task done, Kala went to visit the dedication to her brother, a tall stele cut with words of praise he'd barely been old enough to earn. What he had been was cheerful, cheeky and full of energy in a way that had exhausted and delighted everyone he met. There was no way to capture that spirit in cold, carved stone. There was nothing of him here, just as there was nothing of her father in the sanctum. She stood a moment longer then drifted away with a nod to Straton, moving past the altar and towards the wall.

Such vegetation as could grow in its shadow was lush, the ground moist and bouncy under Kala's feet. Her cane was practically useless here; the point just sank into the marshy ground. She balanced her paces carefully on tired limbs, following a track through the greenery to where the steps started, the first one higher than Kala's head. Two acolytes stood there, both men, neither of whom were familiar to her. They bobbed their heads at her approach.

'Good afternoon, Miss.'

'Hello,' she said. 'What tribe are you?'

'Both Panther, Miss. We cede to the Hippos acolytes at sundown.'

They matched their shifts with the segments of the day, then. Each day was divided into ten sections, each dedicated to a different god, to a different tribe. The Glauks acolytes would take the last shift of the day, the hours just before dawn. That was the time sacred to Diaprepes. If she wanted to have a chance of seeing the mystery girl, she would have to come back in the dark.

'The first step is taller than I remember it being,' she said, thinking how difficult it would be for the priests to haul the new stones up at this year's festival. And this year, they would have to carry them all the way to the top.

'Too tall,' the same acolyte said. 'Next year we'll have to dig the foundation for a new wall, to bring the first stair back to the ground.'

He didn't seem enthused by the prospect. Judging by the height of that first step, a new layer was several decades overdue. The Archon had been procrastinating.

She smiled at them and trailed a little way along the wall, her fingers tracing the colourful lines that decorated the stones. Each of them was painted separately, one stone every year from every family of every tribe in Kepos, so the pattern of each stone was different from the next. It was gloriously noisy, although the colours mellowed the farther she walked from the stairs. The marble was cool to the touch and slightly damp from the occasional trickles of water that meandered down its face from above.

She closed her eyes and breathed, tasting the smell of the Shadows. It reminded her of the sea at the other end of the valley. Her father had sometimes taken her to see the little boats there, to see where Kepos found its fish. The smell of the wall was like that, salty and fresh, but with a dankness to it that lingered in her nostrils, like wet soil and mould. It was a dead place, this close to the souls of her ancestors. She pressed her palm into the wall, pushing with her fingers as though she could reach them through the marble.

She felt nothing. Her father wasn't here. There was nothing here but damp and ashes.

'Kala.'

She turned to see Ariston standing by the altar that was now behind her, and realised that she must have walked as far as the Delphis sanctum.

'Ariston,' she said. 'How are you?'

They walked towards each other and met in the middle of the ferns.

'How are *you*?' he asked.

'Well enough, thank you. Your grandfather?'

'He's well, as always. I sometimes think he's indestructible, the amount he runs about.'

'Spry.'

He laughed. 'Yes. Very,' he said, but then his expression dropped into concern.

'Look, Kala, we were talking about this business last night, me and Grandpa. You know, the wedding, Lali's father, you.'

'Oh?'

'Yes,' he said. 'And I know that with your father, and your home, well, it's difficult. But look, we just want you to know you have other options. There are lots of us in Delphis, I know, but there's space for more, and Grandpa is always pleased by more grandchildren, so if you wanted to leave home then, well, there are options. That's all.'

Kala was staggered. Was Zotikos really offering to adopt her into Delphis?

'Are you saying what I think you're saying?'

Ariston laughed. 'Well, we could be siblings. I mean, you already know the most embarrassing story from my childhood, and I bet I remember some things about you that you'd rather I didn't.'

She laughed, her eyes pricking with dangerous tears at the generosity of his offer. What was it about the kindness of these Delphis men that always made her cry?

'Thank you,' she said, and pulled him into a hug. 'It means a lot.'

'So you'll think about it?'

'I will, I promise.'

He squeezed her tight then let her go, smiling bashfully. Kala smiled back, and hoped she wouldn't need their charity.

Ariston looked off to the side and Kala followed his gaze to see Leon approaching. He was standing tall, but Kala didn't miss the shine of moisture in his eyes. He had been to see his mother's monument.

'Ariston,' he said as he joined them. There was no warmth in his tone.

'Leon.'

They were glaring at each other. Kala looked between the two of them, trying to work out the source of their animosity. Leon was trying to arrange for his sister to marry this man, so why would they be at odds with one another?

'Your sister is well?' Ariston asked.

'Yes, she is, no thanks to you.'

Kala expected retaliation, but Ariston's aggression quickly crumbled into despair.

'I didn't know,' he said. 'If I'd known, then I would never have said anything. You know I wouldn't, Leon. You know it.'

Leon sighed.

'I know.' He clasped the back of Ariston's neck and they pressed their foreheads together. It was an expression of such intimate pain that it made Kala feel like an eavesdropper.

'I'm sorry,' Ariston whispered.

'It's not your fault, my friend. We both know whose fault it is.'

'Can I make it right?'

'We can try. Tomorrow. I'll find you.'

They clasped each other's forearms and then pulled apart, sealing some unspoken resolution.

'Stay safe,' Ariston said to Kala, with a sincerity that raised a flare of anxiety. Was she in danger? And then he left them both, wending his way back through the ferns to the Delphis sanctum.

'What's going on?' Kala asked when the other boy was out of earshot.

'He did something stupid.'

'What?'

Leon walked away towards the Lykos sanctum, Kala trailing behind him with her laboured stride.

'Leon,' she said, but he just kept walking. 'Leon!'

He stopped this time.

'I have an overwhelming desire to push you into a pond,' she said when she caught up with him. 'You can't just walk off every time I ask a question you don't want to answer.'

He raised an eyebrow at her. 'I rather think I can.'

It was the wrong thing to say. Her temper flared. She stuck her cane out to the side, catching it between his feet, and down he went, face-first into the marshy ground.

'Very mature,' he said, spitting mud.

'Says the boy who starts food fights.'

He wiped his face on the sleeve of his tunic. 'Living with you and Lali isn't going to end well for me, is it?'

'Probably not.'

His grimace was so ill-disguised that she couldn't help but laugh.

'Come on,' she said, extending a hand to help him up. 'It looks like you need another costume change.'

Eulalia had already left for Lykos by the time they got back. Leon begged another clean tunic and ran over to the baths so he could clean up before his father saw him. It didn't save him from Nikos's anger; when the men finally left together Leon's lip was split and bleeding. Kala couldn't guess what might have incited the incident, but Leon's posture was not one of defeat. He offered her a bloody smile on his way out of the door, the redness settling between his teeth, and she could see nothing in his expression but glee.

Once again, Nikos ignored her, reserving his sharp glances for his son. And once again, Charis was locked away in her room.

Kala stopped by the library to collect the Kleitos scroll. It would be safer in her own rooms, where none of the new household would wander. She made her way there now to stash the history of Kepos at the bottom of her clothes chest, feeling exhausted. Her hand had been rubbed into blisters under the cane. The skin was tough enough that it would heal quickly, but she would have to use a different walking stick for the wedding the next day. She would miss the comfort of her owl, but perhaps it was inappropriate for her mother's remarriage anyway.

She should have gone to the baths with Leon to soak away the stiffness in her limbs, but the thought of leaving the house again had been more than she could bear. Besides, she hated communal bathing. She much preferred the solitude of her pool, but it was hardly practical at night. Instead, she asked Melissa to bring warm water and a cloth. The slave set it down on the table in Kala's bedroom and helped her to the chair beside it.

'You've tired yourself out,' Melissa said.

'I know.'

Gentle fingers reached up to Kala's hair and teased out the pins that kept her braids in place. The plaits unravelled down her back and into Melissa's quick hands, which pulled each strand loose and free.

'I saw Ariston again today,' Kala said softly.

'The Delphis boy you used to play with? The one who–'

'Yes,' she chuckled. 'That one.'

'And?'

'He made me an offer. To move to Delphis, if I want.'

Melissa's hands stilled.

'What's wrong?' Kala asked.

'At the Proaulia?'

'Lissa–'

But she rushed on, saying, 'I know you'll marry soon. You need to. I know I won't have you to myself much longer.'

'No, it's nothing like that,' Kala said, turning to take Melissa's hand in her own. 'This isn't about Ariston. The offer came from his grandfather.'

'What? You don't mean adoption, surely?'

'That's what he said.'

The slave was silent for a moment. 'And why would he offer that?'

'Why indeed.'

It was a question Kala had asked herself on the trek home. What did Zotikos know that made him willing to take in a liability like Kala? The man had been kind, but his offer went far beyond courtesy. Was it out of some duty to her father? Did he want something from her? Or did he know something about Nikos that would prompt him to offer her sanctuary? It was not a comforting thought.

'And what did you think of your new family?' Melissa asked.

'I think Eulalia might be a friend, but Nikos…'

Melissa ran her hands across Kala's scalp, massaging away the tightness the braids had left behind.

'Yes,' she said. 'Nikos.'

It seemed that no more words were needed.

'I think Leon feels the same way,' Kala said.

'About his own father?'

'From what I could tell. Did you know that Mother and Nikos were lovers?'

Melissa's fingers stopped moving. She dropped her hands from Kala's head and put the bowl of water on the floor, wetting the cloth as she did so.

'Yes,' she said eventually, her eyes downcast. She lifted Kala's feet into the bowl. 'I knew.'

Kala leaned forwards with a jerk, tipping the bowl to one side so it splashed water onto the floor.

'Why didn't you tell me? How long have you known?'

'I've always known,' she said quietly, then she looked up at Kala and sighed, resigning herself to the disclosure. 'I was a just a baby when it happened, but I grew up hearing the story. Your mother was your age at the time.'

'So it really was that long ago?' Kala said.

Melissa raised her eyebrows, marking the interruption.

'I'm sorry,' Kala said. 'Go on. I'm listening.'

'It was about eighteen years ago, give or take. Just after your grandfather took my parents in. Apparently, your mother had been seeing this boy. Nikos. They were in love and they wanted to be married. But then, well, she started to show and the Lykos hit the roof. He wouldn't own the child, wouldn't bear the marriage, and made his son marry a daughter of Tauros instead. My parents thought that was the end for your mother, that she'd be sent to the temple to spend her days serving the god.'

Melissa lifted each of Kala's feet out of the bowl and dried them in her lap with a fresh cloth.

'What are you saying?' Kala asked. 'That I have a brother or sister out there?'

'The baby was stillborn.' Melissa got to her feet and tipped the muddy water out of the window into the garden. 'That's what they said, anyway. No one knew about the pregnancy. They still don't, except for a few people in this house. I always wondered about it. I suppose the little thing could have been adopted. Or exposed.'

Her last words were whispered, so quiet that Kala could only decipher them because they were what she had expected to hear. Kala knew where Melissa's mind had gone, because her own followed it there.

Perfect little fingers, too many but perfect nonetheless, clutching at the air.

'Lissa...'

Kala reached up and caught her around the waist as she passed. The two women looked into each other's eyes as they remembered the pain they shared: the little baby girl they had found together a year ago, and the tragedy that had brought them to her. They didn't talk about those days, which had been dark enough to rival these.

Melissa cleared her throat, and the moment was broken.

'Anyway,' she said, examining Kala's blistered palm, 'your father showed up later that year.'

'But why didn't I know this?' Kala said. 'Why didn't you tell me?'

'Not my secret to tell.'

And yet Kala would have expected to hear it from her, of all people. Not from Nikos's son.

'I'll fetch the medicine chest,' Melissa said, leaving the room.

Kala sat alone with her thoughts. It seemed cruel that Nikos would keep his daughter from marrying the partner of her choice when Nikos had been prevented from doing exactly that by his own father. Still, it was no mystery why the Lykos would suddenly approve of the marriage now. The title of Glauks would make it worth Nikos's while, and with their history, no one would challenge his claim to Charis's hand.

Whichever way Kala looked at it, it sounded like motive. Which begged the question: how close was Nikos to the Archon?

By the time Melissa returned with a poultice for her hand, Kala had pulled the herb out of its hiding place in the Kleitos scroll.

'You kept it?' Melissa said.

Kala placed the leaf and its wrapping onto Melissa's palm.

'Don't touch it,' Kala said. 'Just in case.'

Melissa stared at it for a moment, turning it this way and that in the light of the oil lamp.

'Do you know what it is?' Kala asked.

Melissa stuck out her bottom lip, apparently stumped. 'I'm not sure. My cousin Eirene would know. I can ask her.'

'I don't want to drag you into this.' Kala took the leaf, wrapping it back into the scroll. 'Maybe I'll go and see Eirene myself, though. She lives out by the quarry, right?'

Melissa nodded as she bound the poultice onto Kala's palm, securing it tightly with strips of cloth that wrapped between her fingers.

'There was an acolyte at the cremation yesterday,' Kala said. 'A female acolyte.'

'A female Diaprepes acolyte? A Glauks acolyte?'

'Yes. My age. Maybe a bit older.'

'And you think that she might be the child? Your mother's first?'

Kala thought about her dark skin, dark hair and dark eyes. They were her father's features, not her mother's.

'No,' she said. 'Or at least, I don't see how she could be. She looked just like me, and you said that my father didn't arrive until after the baby was born.'

'That's what I heard.'

'So, who is she?' Kala asked.

But if Melissa had any theories to offer then she kept them to herself. The most likely answer was what Kala feared: her father had another child, another girl, whom he had abandoned to the priests. She just couldn't shape a version of her father who would do that to any child, much less his own. Not a version she recognised, at least.

'You need to sleep,' Melissa said, helping Kala out of her dress and into the tunic she wore to bed, gentle fingers stroking her skin. 'The wedding starts before sunrise.'

'Will you stay tonight?'

Melissa cupped Kala's cheek in her palm.

'What are you getting yourself into?' she whispered.

'I don't know.'

'I don't like it.'

'I don't have a choice.'

Melissa kissed Kala's forehead, her cheek, and finally her mouth, lingering on the last. Kala pulled her close and caught Melissa's lips with her own, unwilling to let her go. Not tonight. The bed was big enough for the two of them to fit comfortably, one curled around the other.

'Will you take me with you if you go to Delphis?' Melissa whispered against her mouth.

Kala pulled away slightly so that she could meet the other woman's eyes. 'I would never leave you behind.'

Melissa smiled at that, but there was more concern than joy in it. 'And will you go?'

'I don't know. I don't trust Nikos.'

'You shouldn't.'

'He doesn't seem to know I exist. He certainly didn't want to meet me when Leon tried to introduce us.'

Melissa exhaled and some of the tension passed out of her frame, her arms relaxing around Kala's body.

'Good,' she said.

And it was true: Nikos hadn't even looked at her. He hadn't shown any interest in her at all, but something about his disregard had felt artificial, as though he were deliberately turning his attention away.

Kala was reminded of a conversation she had shared with Gennadios when she was a young child. She had asked the name of one of his cows, and the man had said the cow had no name, because he was a boy cow, bred for meat. She had asked her father about it afterwards, and he had explained gently how much harder it was to kill a creature when you had named it, when you had recognised it as a living thing.

The memory kept her awake that night while Melissa's breath warmed the skin of her neck. For the first time Kala could remember, her proximity was not enough to bring any comfort.

III
ἔλᾰφος | Elaphos | Deer

The god surrounded the garden with water,
bracketing the edges of paradise.
He gave the shores to Ampheres, his third son,
and charged him with guarding the frontier.

- Kleitos, On the Formation of Kepos

It had been years since Straton had found the child by the Water. It had served him well to keep her origin secret, but now she was grown, that secrecy was being threatened. The pressure ate at the edges of his patience. The last thing he needed right now was a wedding, an uncontrollable congregation of the child's tribe. It could all unravel today, and then he would be finished.

But still, with every risk came opportunity. As the Glauks Hierophant he would officiate the ceremony, close to the Dekocrats and their influence. He craved their power. Today was a chance to insinuate himself into the families, to find the information he needed, and control the information he needed to suppress.

He arrived at the sanctum before dawn to perform the sacrifice that would start the festivities. The only light was provided by a single torch set into the ground, but they wouldn't need more. It would be a small crowd. The rite required close family only, which was just as well given the early hour.

The two houses arrived separately in horse-drawn carts, Lykos first and Glauks shortly afterwards. The Lykos was the first to the altar, his family matching their steps behind his, and Kala was the last. There had been no one in the

Glauks cart except her, her mother and the slave who drove the horses, and her mother didn't wait for her.

They'd spoken little on the journey. Kala had waited for her mother to say something, anything, to break the silence that had fallen between them since the night of her father's death. They'd made it halfway across the meadows when she'd decided that she'd waited long enough.

'Why him?'

'Hmm?' Charis said, dragging herself out of her reverie.

'Why Nikos?' Kala asked.

Charis was silent for a few long moments, playing with the fringe of her shawl, before she replied.

'I know him.'

'So I've heard.'

Charis looked away.

'We were children,' she said. 'Too young. But I know who he is. Better that than one of the others. And he's willing to leave Lykos. Isn't that enough?'

'Enough?' Kala looked at her mother incredulously. 'You're handing him the title of Glauks and you think *you* should be grateful to *him*?'

'If I don't give it to him,' Charis said, her gaze drifting away, 'then he'll take it for himself anyway. It's what they do.'

'What who do?'

But Charis didn't reply, wouldn't even look at Kala after that.

She was vacant. Her eyes fixed on nothing. Kala was beginning to worry that she might have lost her mind. It seemed that there were only glimmers of it left, flashing brightly for a few moments, but unable to sustain the spark for long.

Kala took her hand in an attempt to reach her, but her mother just stared ahead, saying she was fine even though everything in her bearing told Kala she was moments from fracturing apart.

It was too late anyway.

Charis would marry Nikos, and there was no going back. Perhaps it was easier for her to dive in headfirst than it was to brave the water one cold inch at a time.

The Hierophant intoned the opening prayers in the small area of light by the Glauks altar.

Eulalia and Leon were standing behind their father, and neither of them looked happy. Nikos seemed eager enough, his face chiseled handsome and bright-eyed by the torchlight, but the Lykos was clearly delighted. He must have been staggered at his good fortune, that the girl with whom his son had scandalised Kepos had turned out, years later, to have the key to Glauks in her gift.

The unsteady light played on his hunched figure so that he seemed now to be twisting not just around but also through his cane. His half-rotten grin, together with the reflection of the flame playing on his eyeballs, gave him the appearance of a feral rodent.

Two acolytes approached the altar holding a lamb on a tether. They had been standing outside the sanctum, and their sudden appearance in the glow of the torchlight startled Kala. She was under-slept and jumpy. Every rustle of the ferns and every glimpse of changing shades in the darkness made her clench her fist more tightly around the unfamiliar handle of her replacement cane. She wore a glove to protect her blisters from further damage, at Melissa's insistence, but its only effect was to make her palm slide along the polished surface. The more her hand slid, the tighter she gripped to make it secure, until the tendons in her fist ached with the tension.

In one quick movement, the acolytes scooped the lamb onto the altar and Straton dragged a flint knife across its throat, directing the spray away from the small congregation. In the poor light the blood was black, like hot tar coating the stone, running down its sides and into the earth. He released even more as he slit the animal's belly open to examine the entrails. The smell of raw flesh filled the air, but for the moment the odour was fresh rather than heavy. Kala was glad that she could see nothing but monochrome shapes. The festive reds and blues and browns of death would have felt like an assault. Grey and charcoal were better suited to the day.

Straton declared the result of his augury to be positive and, wiping his bloodied fingers across the cheeks of the bride and groom, he passed the knife to Kala. She had to join him in the small circle of light to take it from him. There was no avoiding the colours here.

He was soaked in red up to his elbows from where he had plunged his hands into the carcass, and the spray flecked the skin of his face and neck. His hands dripped with it so liberally that the blade nearly slipped from her hand. She had to pull it back against her body to catch it, trapping the hilt between her hand and her stomach, and so she was bloodied too.

She walked carefully towards her mother and stood at her back. She knew her role, but it felt like a hollow gesture in the circumstances. Together with the sacrifice of the lamb, the cutting of the bride's hair was intended to symbolise her virginity up to this point, but Charis was clearly no virgin. That was why this task was Kala's; the aristocracy had convinced themselves some time ago that the ritual remained valid if the woman's child performed it.

Kala thought it was ridiculous, particularly as she now knew that her mother had not even been virginal for her first marriage. Had her father known? Had he seen this ritual for the farce it was, as Kala did now?

Nonetheless, she was required to participate. She stood behind her mother and balanced her cane against her leg so that she would have both hands free. The hair shone in the flickering light, blonde strands picked out by the flames as they rippled down to her mother's waist. Kala could see the beauty in it.

She gathered it carefully in her gloved hand then pulled it gently until it was taut. The knife slid easily enough through the filaments, leaving Kala with a handful of gold and her mother with hair that was a foot shorter than before. The blood from the knife's hilt had transferred onto the new ends, so that it appeared as though Charis had dipped them into a cup of wine.

So Kala's role ended. The Hierophant threw the hair onto a pyre that the acolytes had built on the altar, then followed it with the body of the lamb. Between that and the bull Gennadios had brought the previous day, the poor of Glauks would be feasting well this week.

By silent consensus they left before the meat started roasting, much to Kala's relief. She glanced back as they walked to the carts, hoping to catch a glimpse of her acolyte twin at the base of the staircase, but the morning was still too dark for her to see past the flames on the altar.

That quickly, with no protest at all, her mother was remarried and her father forgotten. The couple left as they came: separately, the bride silent in the shadow of the wall.

Kala was not invited to join her mother in her preparations for the nuptial feast. It was the custom for the bride to bathe in her rooms beforehand and she would normally be attended by the women of the family. However, Charis had asked only for Agathe, so Kala went to the public baths to make her own preparations. There was no way she could avoid them today.

The baths were on the southern edge of the city, next to the gymnasium. Their location made them convenient for athletes returning from their exercise, but the gymnasium had been built around the baths, and not the other way around. The baths had been placed on that spot because of the hot springs that bubbled to the surface there, dedicated to Euaemon, god of Delphis. They obviated the need for heating: conduits brought fresh, hot water from the springs, and overflows channelled the used water away to the river.

The building was simple: a rectangular space filled with steam rising steadily from baths of varying sizes. They were separated by tiled walkways that continued around the inside walls, where columns supported the wooden roof.

Kala squinted through the steam. It was still early, but there were a few elderly gentlemen at one end of the room, a woman on her own in one of the central pools, and in the largest pool, a group of slaves were washing themselves clean before the day. The smallest of the pools, however, was both unoccupied and distant enough from the other bathers that she might escape their notice.

She made her way to the bath as quietly as possible, pressing the tip of her cane gently against the tiles. She could barely see through the hot fog, but no one appeared to be paying her any attention.

Deep breath.

Cane down, dress off, step to edge, slide in.

Exhale.

She sat for a second, relieved to have made it into the cover of the cloudy water. The heat burned on her cold skin, pervading her battered limbs and soothing away the aches of the past few days. She closed her eyes as it settled in her chest and brought her back to herself, centring her resolve.

She had to find out how her father had been killed, and by whom. To do that, she needed to speak to Eirene about the herb. That would tell her where to start looking.

But first, she had to get through the wedding feast.

There was a splash nearby and she opened her eyes to see that Leon was already waist-deep in her pool. He'd clearly come from the gymnasium because his skin was slick with sweat, which did interesting things to the musculature of his chest.

'Really?' she said irritably. 'You couldn't find another pool?'

'Good morning to you too, sister.'

'I told you not to call me that. I am not your sister.' The fact had never been clearer to her.

'Well, then,' he said, 'Kala. How are you today?'

Her gaze trailed across his swollen lip. 'I think I should be asking you that.'

'Oh, this is nothing. You should have seen what he did when I broke his favourite drinking cup.'

'And what did you do this time?' she asked.

He lay back against the tiled wall. 'One of the slaves saw me at the sanctum and decided it was his duty to report back to my father.'

'About Ariston?'

'No, thank Eumelus. He didn't hang around for that.'

'Then what?'

His eyes emptied out into an expression Kala recognised.

'Your mother,' she said. 'You visited her stele.'

'It was "inappropriate", apparently, in light of today's event. The truth is, he'd rather I didn't think of her at all. He never does.'

'He didn't love her?'

Leon laughed. 'You think this is about love? You think it has anything to do with love?'

'The wedding, you mean?'

'Not just that. I mean the Proaulia, the tribes... I just don't think love's something we get to have. We marry for a purpose, for the tribe, not because of love. It's what we sacrifice for the status we have, for the power.'

She thought about her own parents. When Kala had been small, there had been so much warmth in their home. Her mother hadn't always been this way, this cold, she was sure. Even if Kala's father hadn't been her first choice, she was sure her parents had loved each other. She was sure.

'It doesn't have to be that way,' she said.

'Not for Lali, I hope. Not you either. But for me, for our parents, it's not about choice.'

'They chose each other once.'

'Maybe, but that was a long time ago, when they thought it was just a fling. Lykos doesn't marry Glauks, Kala. You know that.'

She was a little affronted on behalf of her tribe. 'They do today.'

'Yes, but you know why, and it still has nothing to do with love.'

She wiped her hands over her face, pushing away the drops of moisture that had collected on her skin. She didn't want to accept it, but she knew it was true. She wanted to believe that Nikos still felt something for her mother, because if he didn't then they were both in danger. She had never seen her mother so vulnerable, so breakable. And if Charis was unable or unwilling to speak on her behalf, Kala might well find herself in need of the asylum Zotikos offered. It was a decision she would have to make quickly, before Nikos made up his own mind, but it would mean leaving her mother behind.

Kala needed to speak with her, today.

'Did you know about their baby?' she asked.

His lips pressed together. 'It's not a good idea to go asking about that.'

'Why not?'

He sighed. 'Do you never listen? You're always digging, always turning over stones, as though you're entitled to know everyone's secrets. But some people are prepared to do anything to protect theirs. I'm asking you: please stay away from my father's.'

'Are you threatening me?'

'Kala, *I* don't even know his secrets. But I know him. Don't go looking for trouble.'

Her gaze dropped down to his lip. The moisture of the baths had reopened the wound and it was red with fresh blood. 'I think you need to learn to heed your own advice.'

'Ah, but then life would be so dull.'

He grinned and stretched his arms out along the edge of the pool to either side. The gesture was so self-satisfied, and Kala was so irritated, that she couldn't resist disturbing him.

She flicked at the surface of the bath, sending spray into his face. He reciprocated by splashing an armful of water at her, so much that she was left rubbing her eyes and spluttering.

So she retaliated, and he retaliated, and soon they were laughing in each other's faces as they competed to make the biggest waves, and Leon's hands were around her wrists as he tried to stop her from splashing him. Her skin was touching his under the water, her legs sliding against his, rough and hard and nothing like Melissa's.

She had started this, she knew, but its trajectory shocked her. She abruptly let the tension go from her muscles, so she no longer struggled against him.

He let her slip away.

'Kala,' he said softly.

She smiled at him, because nothing was really wrong. But everything had changed.

The evening's feast would take place in the garden of Glauks. That way, there was enough space to accommodate a number of the tenants along with the families of the Dekocracy. They would sit at different benches, of course, but they were still invited to share in the spoils of the celebration.

Kala trailed through to the courtyard alone. A stream of acolytes was pouring through the house with buckets full of sacred water for the couple's bridal bath. There, right at the back of the line, was the face Kala had been searching for. She started to move towards the acolyte, but the girl made a tiny shake with her head and tipped her chin towards a figure at the other end of the courtyard: Straton.

'Is that the last of it?' he asked one of the older acolytes.

'Yes, Hierophant.'

Straton followed them down the corridor, but not before he had noted Kala's interest in the acolyte girl. She kicked herself for not hiding her stare. She already suspected the Archon, and if she couldn't trust him then how could she trust Straton, even if he was her mother's brother?

The slaves were busy setting out benches and preparing food for the feast so, with nothing else to do but fret, Kala went to help. If she had been a proper aristocrat then her behaviour would have been considered scandalous, but most of the slaves were happy enough to have her assistance, even if she wasn't much help with the heavy lifting.

It was while she and Melissa were finishing the flower garlands in the courtyard that one of the twins came rushing up and slipped a shred of parchment into her hand. The little boy hesitated just long enough to say, 'You told me to give you this, Miss,' before rushing off again.

She unfurled the paper quickly, spreading it between her fingers. The writing was not well-formed, but angular and smudged, as though it had been scratched with charcoal in a hurry. Nonetheless, and despite a number of errors, it was legible.

'Kala?' Melissa said.

'He didn't mean me,' she whispered. 'He meant the girl who looks like me. The acolyte. The one I've been looking for.'

'She's here?'

'Yes, and she'll be at the wall tonight. She wants me to meet her there, before dawn, during Glauks watch.'

She folded the parchment carefully and slipped it into the pouch that hung at her waist. She was finally getting somewhere. Tonight, maybe she'd start getting the answers she was looking for.

'I'm coming with you,' Melissa said.

'Lissa—'

'I'm not letting you go alone, not at that time of the day, not to meet someone you don't know, and not that far from the city. I'll slip away with one of the horses and meet you by the gate at the end of Ophis watch.'

There was no point in arguing, and in truth Kala would be grateful for the company. She took Melissa's hand in her own.

'Thank you.'

Kala started to lean in towards her, but then Leon arrived with Eulalia, bringing their belongings to their new home. Seeing him recalled to her the sensation of his skin on hers, the flush of his cheeks as he laughed through the steam, and the little kick in the bottom of her stomach that had scared her away from his touch. She dropped her gaze to the tiles at her feet, ashamed to relive the memory whilst she sat next to Melissa.

'He seems kind,' Melissa whispered. 'Not like his father. I know what they say, but I hear from those that know better.'

Kala didn't know how to react to that. 'I don't know what they say.'

'Just as well, then. He'll make someone a good husband. An understanding husband, one who sees what matters.'

'Lucky her, then.'

Kala was not at all comfortable with Melissa's new marriage obsession. She knew the Proaulia was fast approaching, but she wasn't yet ready to let go of what they had. Melissa's eagerness hurt.

She squeezed Kala's hand gently then stood, taking the garlands with her. She had seen what Kala hadn't: Leon was crossing the courtyard towards them. Melissa nodded at him as she passed then left them alone.

'Good evening,' he said.

She looked at the colour of the sky and realised that it was, indeed, evening. Sunset was close, and the other guests would be arriving soon. She stood to greet him, using her cane to push herself upright.

'Hello,' she said.

'You look nice today. I mean, your hair, you look…'

She laughed, wondering how much he had been drinking with Ariston.

But Leon wasn't amused, and she belatedly realised that he wasn't drunk at all. An awkward silence threatened.

'So,' she said, 'did you enjoy the ceremony this morning? I thought the acolytes sang well. How is Eulalia? I thought I saw her arrive with you.'

Leon seemed to have recovered his composure while she babbled, but there was a steady resolve in his eyes that presaged further awkwardness.

'Yes,' he said, 'they did sing well, Lali has gone to her rooms, and Kala, you are beautiful tonight, as always. Can I take you through to the gardens?'

She smiled at him. 'There's really no need for this.'

'What do you mean?'

'Leon, we're only weeks away from the Proaulia. Every eligible maiden of dekocratic blood will be arriving shortly, ready for you to escort the one of your choice to the feast. You don't need to worry about me.'

'What if you're the one I choose?'

'Come on, be serious.'

'What if I am?'

'Then your father will do more than split your lip.'

A smile played around the edges of his mouth, but the look in his eyes was one of surrender. He knew his duty; they had spoken of it only that morning. He couldn't escape it by hiding with her, using her cane as an excuse to sit out the dancing.

'Later then?' he whispered.

He was now standing so close that their hands touched. He caught one of her fingers between his own and stroked up its inner edge. His body heat warmed her and she wanted to lean into it, to let him chase away the chill of the dusk, but instead she unwound her fingers from his and stepped back.

'Yes,' she said, 'later, so you can tell me about Ariston.'

He took a step back himself, but was saved from any explanation by the arrival of Eulalia.

She had clearly made an effort for the occasion. She was draped in a rich, peach-coloured dress that fell from her waist in a multitude of dense folds. Her hair was pinned with orichalcum and gems into a pile of curls that trailed elegantly down towards her neck, and jewels twinkled at her throat.

'You've changed,' Leon said to her. He and Kala remained in their clothes from the ceremony, which were not quite so dramatic.

'Well, why not? Don't you think it's nice?'

'You look beautiful,' Kala said.

'So do you, dear Kala. Let's leave my ill-mannered brother to pout in private, shall we?'

With that, she took Kala by the arm and didn't speak again until they were out in the gardens, wandering the paths. The night was closing in, but with a few bonfires and lanterns strewn around the garden, it was easy enough to see. Slaves bustled around putting the finishing touches to the decorations and tending to the feast. The meats had been on their spits all day out in the garden, and there was no escaping the smell of their charring. Kala's mouth watered at it even while it turned her stomach. She hadn't eaten yet today.

'Are you all right?' Eulalia asked her.

'Of course. Why wouldn't I be?'

The look Eulalia gave her was worryingly direct. 'Kala, please. Do you think it's possible for that boy to keep a secret from me?'

'What? You mean his meeting with Ariston?'

'No,' she said, her expression darkening. 'But don't think I'm not going to have words with him about that too.'

'What happened?'

She flapped her hand dismissively. 'Oh, a ridiculous fight. Father had intended that I should marry Timon, the son of the Elaphos, and that Leon should marry Timon's sister, Sophia. But I met Ariston and, well, that was that. Then last week, Ariston told Timon that he was going to ask for my hand at the Proaulia, without knowing that Timon had been told that I was promised to him.'

'Oh dear.'

'There was a fight, and Timon got the worst of it.'

No wonder Leon had been angry. Elaphos was the third of the tribes, and they'd see it as a breach of protocol for a suitor from Delphis, the fourth tribe, to be preferred to one of theirs. More than that, they'd see it as an insult.

'Anyway, it was a problem,' Eulalia said. 'But what my dense brother doesn't seem to realise is that it's all academic now, because we're not Lykos anymore, we're Glauks. There's no way Elaphos will abide by their agreement. Delphis is far better than I could expect in the circumstances, so surely even Father can't object now.'

She was right. Glauks was at the bottom of the heap, and Delphis would be a good match. Kala hadn't appreciated how far the siblings' own marriage opportunities might have been disadvantaged by their father's choice to wed her mother.

'Have you spoken to your father?' Kala asked.

'Not yet.'

The other guests began to arrive then, laughing as they gathered around the fires and benches, where slaves had set up barrels of water and wine. The Dekocrats settled themselves into the best seats whilst their families fetched refreshments for them. In the middle of it all was Zotikos, in the thick of the crowd, laughing with the Glauks tenants as he served his family himself.

It could be her family too, if she wanted.

Then they arrived, the bride and groom, fresh from their bath. Nikos prowled the tables for a while, smiling wolfishly as he formed alliances with the press of skin, but his smile had disappeared by the time he joined Charis and the rest of Glauks. Kala sat by them that night, her current family, and all she could hear was the silence of Nikos.

The women didn't stay long. Some of the men left with them after a couple of hours, but more stayed behind to drink the barrels dry. Kala's bedroom was too close to the uproar of the garden for her to think of sleep, and so she found her way to the courtyard instead. The torches had been extinguished, but the moon was bright. There was enough light to lead her to the bench she sought, but not enough for her to notice that she wasn't alone.

'It's you.' The voice was almost a whisper, so quiet that Kala didn't immediately recognise it. She found its owner lounging against the back wall of the courtyard, a cup of wine in her hand.

'And it's you,' Kala said. Her mother was hiding in the dark. 'How are you?'

The reply was an unsteady nod.

'Are you sure?'

Charis drained the wooden cup and let it roll from her hand to the earth at her bare feet.

There was a border around the edge of the courtyard. Ivy and jasmine grew in great profusion along the wall, so thickly piled that their tendrils enveloped Charis, making her appear like a dryad emerging from a creeper-covered tree. With her moonlit skin and hair, she herself was not entirely of this world.

'So,' she said, 'what did you think of the wedding?'

'Is it what you wanted?'

Charis shrugged, her eyes out of focus, but made no other reply.

'Will you love him?'

'I don't know,' she said, her words slurred. 'I'm not sure I'm capable of that anymore.'

Kala almost laughed. She wasn't even capable of loving her daughter. Where had she been, these past few days? Charis was her mother, the person who should have held her close while they dealt with their private loss together, but she had been gone. She wasn't even here now, not really.

Kala leaned back against the wall and traced the constellations above them, remembering the charts her father had shown her with a gleam in his eye. She used to feel that excitement too, but not anymore. There was nothing vibrant about her or Charis now, as though his soul had sucked theirs out with it.

'It hurts to think that you could ever love someone else,' Kala whispered.

A tear dropped onto Charis's cheek and shone there for a second before tracking down to her chin.

'Sometimes,' she said, pressing her fingertips into the flesh beneath her sternum, 'I think that if I could just push my fingertips through the centre of my chest, I could pull my rib cage open like wings and let it all fly out of me. It keeps me awake, so sharp, gnawing at my insides.' Her fingertips found purchase under her ribs, pulling at their edges through the material.

When had she lost so much weight?

'Mother,' Kala said, 'please.' She pulled her mother's hands away from their bruising, twisting, prodding, and cocooned them in her own. 'What are you doing?'

'There's never a choice,' she whispered.

Kala tried to coax Charis to her rooms, but she couldn't move her from the wall. Her body felt like a cage, rows of hard lines that trapped her in, skin sliding over bone in a way that reminded her of another body.

When had she become so sick, and how had Kala not noticed?

She called for Agathe and soon her mother was bustled off to her chambers, wrapped in blankets against the cold. Kala was left alone with her guilt. She had let her mother fracture under the weight of her father's loss, under Nikos's suit, because she had been too busy doing what she thought needed to be done. She may have needed her mother, but her mother had needed her, too. Now they were both beyond need, and it seemed as though Charis might never find her way back.

The men were still drinking when Kala slipped through the garden to meet Melissa at the gate. Leon was amongst them, but she avoided him and the other men by making herself invisible. She drew her cloak over her head and skirted the edges of the walled garden, muffling the end of her cane in the dirt. They were all so deep in their cups that the effort was probably wasted.

The horse Melissa had brought was an old bay mare called Hypatia. She was grumpy and stubborn, but she had always been Kala's favourite because she was so solid and surefooted. For a night like this, with two of them to carry, she was the perfect choice. Melissa helped Kala into the saddle then climbed up behind, wrapping her arms around Kala to grasp the horse's mane, and then they were riding into the night.

The journey was short on horseback, shorter than expected, so Glauks watch had not yet begun when they arrived at the sancta. They were far enough away from the wall that they weren't illuminated by the torches that lit the base of the stairs, and the moist earth muffled Hypatia's hooves. Melissa slipped down Hypatia's side and tied her reins to a Glauks monument before helping Kala to the ground, then they huddled in the shadow of the altar and waited. The chill seeped through into Kala's marrow. She wore her cloak, but the morning dew was forming around them and soaking through her dress.

'Here they come,' Melissa whispered.

Kala watched the torch trailing through the Onos sanctum on its way to the wall. She could see only one figure in the moving circle of light. It wasn't her twin.

'Where is she?'

Melissa put her hand on Kala's shoulder and pointed at the wall. Halfway to the top, climbing slowly upwards, there was a light.

'No,' Kala whispered. 'It can't be.'

They kept pace with the acolyte carrying the torch across the sanctum, creeping from monument to monument before stopping at the edge of the altar. At the foot of the stairs, the newcomer was handing his torch to the two Ophis acolytes who guarded it. They exchanged some words that were too quiet for Kala to hear, then walked back to the city the way the Glauks acolyte had come. He was left at the foot of the staircase alone.

'What now?' Melissa asked.

The acolytes warded the wall to placate the souls of their ancestors in the Shadows beyond. The watch of each tribe was time in which the acolytes should renew those prayers, so why did they seem instead to be guarding the staircase? Why was a figure ascending it now, when the only time it should be climbed was during the harvest festival, when the new stones would be laid?

'There's something wrong here,' Kala said softly.

Melissa seemed even more perturbed. 'It's not the first time I've seen this,' she whispered.

'Seen what?'

'A light on the wall. Not just me either, but some of the others too. You've heard of the dark shades?'

'What?'

Melissa clicked her tongue in irritation. 'You know, the lost souls, the ones who can't rest. They say that's why the acolytes really ward the wall, to keep them where they belong. But then, every once in a while, when there's something calling them back here strong enough, a dead man might break through the wards and find himself on that stair. Then the acolytes have to go up after him, shining their torches to chase the shades back behind the wall.'

'And you believe that? You believe that the dead return to us?'

'You think there aren't things out there bad enough to pull a man back from the Shadows?'

'Well,' Kala said, 'shades or not, we're not going to learn anything by hiding here.'

But she had to admit that the wall was not an inviting destination in the dark. With the colours bleached from its surface, the swirling patterns that decorated each block took on a more sinister aspect. The grayscale shapes seemed to form the edges of figures and creatures so numerous that she felt as though a whole city of shades was watching her.

With her cane sticking in the marsh and catching on every fern, it was not a dignified approach. The acolyte heard them long before he could have seen them.

'Who's that then?' he called into the dark.

'Kala,' she replied, 'daughter of Glauks.'

He smiled with relief. 'Been expecting you. My Theodora, she's gone on ahead and says to meet her there.'

'Meet her where?' she asked as they joined him in the light.

'Well, up there.' He pointed to the staircase.

'What?'

'At the top. She put it in her note: meet on the wall.' He suddenly looked uncertain. 'Didn't she?'

Kala remembered the scratchy handwriting. She could have misread it, but that didn't matter much now. What mattered was that her answers were at the top of the wall, and she was down here. With her walking stick.

'Can't she talk to me here?'

The young man shook his head. 'You need to see this for yourself, she said.'

'See what?'

'You'll see, she said.' He looked jumpy and awkward, which didn't fill Kala with confidence.

She contemplated the task; calculating the distance, planning her movements, assessing her strength. She had climbed the tower, but it was not so many steps and they were not so high. She had walked a greater distance over and over on her way to the waterfall and back, but that was on relatively flat ground. The wall had hundreds of steps, and even if she could haul herself up them, she might not be able to get back down again before dawn.

Melissa interrupted her thoughts.

'There must be another way,' she said to the acolyte. She gestured at Kala's cane, trying to express what she wasn't prepared to say: climbing the wall might be beyond Kala's ability.

But her doubt had pricked Kala's pride.

'How do I get up to the first step?' she asked.

'Kala,' Melissa said, 'this is ridiculous. You can speak to her another day, in another place. What if you fall?'

'The stones are wide and flat, and Nikos could kill me tomorrow anyway. What do I have to lose?'

'Kala–'

'I'm sorry, but I need information and I think she has it. You don't have to come with me.'

Melissa looked up at the marble blocks rising into darkness. She shuddered and then set her jaw.

'Come on then,' she said. 'I've always wondered what the land of the Shadows looks like.'

The acolyte dragged a ladder from amongst the ferns at the base of the wall and set it against the bottom step. Melissa went first so she could help Kala from ladder to stone, but it wasn't an easy climb. Kala began to think she might have let her pride get the best of her.

'I'll be here when you get back,' the acolyte said as he handed Kala her cane. 'You can't risk a torch, not with two of you, but keep one hand against the wall and you'll be fine. The moon's bright enough.' He hesitated for a moment, as though he were going to add something more, then said, 'Diaprepes guide your steps.'

'Thank you,' Melissa said.

Kala was too busy gathering her nerve to respond. She reached out to the wall and felt its surface. It was slimy under her fingertips, damp and cold. She remembered the water trickling down the marble and wondered how slippery the steps might be. Why had she agreed to this?

It was too narrow for the two of them to walk abreast, so Melissa led the way. The steps were each about a foot tall, so their knees had to bend at right angles to accommodate the height. It was not a movement that Kala's twisted leg could make, so she had to lead with the other. It would have to do double the work to compensate for the deficient one, but it was used to that. That didn't mean it wasn't going to burn, though.

She followed the acolyte's advice and kept her free hand up against the wall. They hadn't climbed long before the empty air at her side felt as though it was beckoning her out into the space. Her cane and her weak limb walked that outer edge, and the darkness seemed to pull at them. If her leg buckled now, the momentum would send her straight into that void, so she leaned into the wall and propped her weight against her arm. She just had to get to the top of this section, then they'd turn and her weak side would be next to the stone.

The turn came sooner than she expected. Melissa had stopped, her hand on the cliff face in front of them as she tested the stones beneath her feet.

'It's a bigger step,' she said.

Kala crowded in behind her and looked for herself. The staircase they had been walking finished abruptly at the cliff face. The top of the wall beside them formed the second staircase, but its first step was up to her waist. They were going to have to clamber onto it.

It wasn't dignified, and Kala felt as though she might roll off into the darkness at any moment, but she managed to scramble up eventually. Melissa followed.

After a few steps, it became clear that travelling in this direction was going to be even more precarious. Kala's weaker side was now against the wall, which meant that her cane was as well. Instead of her free hand supporting her against the stone, it now trailed uselessly in the air. She had to drag her shoulder along the wall to keep her balance, whilst manoeuvring her cane on the same side. Between that and her tiring muscles, their pace started to slow.

It was then that they began to hear the noise. It was something between a whistle and a scream, a handful of different pitches scrambled into each other, and it raced down Kala's spine like ice water. At first it was quiet, so quiet that she could believe she might have imagined it, but it increased with their altitude, along with the dead smell of ash and salt.

After two more turns, Melissa's steps faltered behind her.

'Lissa?' The darkness sucked Kala's voice away into a whisper.

'I'm fine, I just missed my footing.' The response sounded distant and weak, but a second later Melissa's hand was on her waist. Kala startled at the touch until she turned and saw her friend.

'I didn't realise you were so close.'

They might have been the only people in the world. They could no longer see the torches at the base of the wall. The only light came from the moon and the distant city, where pale pools of colour marked torches and lamps burning through the night. Only the richest houses would waste the fuel.

'Can you go on?' Melissa asked.

Kala's legs were tight and hot with pain. 'I'm fine,' she said, because she had no choice.

After a few more turns the screaming whistles became punctuated with crashes that shook the stones beneath their feet. The higher they climbed, the more layers of the wall they left behind, and the thinner the barrier between them and the Shadows became. The stone felt colder under Kala's fingers, wetter and almost sticky with a residue that smelled like salt and decay. It caked the shoulder of her cloak so the material set in stiff waves when it was exposed to the air. The skin beneath it itched and froze.

When they were just three staircases from the top, Kala's knees and hips started to lock. The stars were still bright above them, with no sign of light on the horizon. She had no idea how long they had been climbing, or how long it was until dawn. She wanted to turn and sit on the marble, stretching her legs down the steps in front of her, but they couldn't afford the time, so she clamped her teeth together and, on unsteady limbs, pushed herself on.

'What do you think it will look like?' Melissa asked. She had to speak loudly now to be heard above the thundering screams that surrounded them.

'It sounds like a captive storm behind the wall,' Kala said. 'Like wind and rain and splitting clouds.' And yet the sky above them was clear, the air completely still. There was no breeze, no tendrils of aether catching at her cloak and dress. She was glad of that, but the images the tumult raised in her mind made her reluctant to reach the top of the wall.

'Is it safe?' said Melissa.

'The acolytes come this way all the time,' Kala said with a confidence she didn't feel. 'Anyway, if Diaprepes disapproved of our journey, he would have turned us back.'

'Maybe he's trying to do that right now, and we're just not wise enough to heed it.'

'One of his acolytes invited me here.'

And Kala hadn't stopped to wonder why. She'd been so desperate to know who the girl was, to find her and speak to her, that she hadn't questioned why the acolyte would want to show her the Shadows. It had to have something to do with her father. Given her appearance, the girl herself had to have something to do with her father. But what?

She was an acolyte, so perhaps she'd been close enough to the Archon to hear something about the herb. Maybe she knew who had killed her father. But then why bring her here? The only possible reason was so they could talk to his shade.

That thought pushed part of her onwards and the other part back. She longed to see him again, but the prospect of seeing him as a shadow image of himself pushed a pinch of pain through her chest. It was too late to give up now, though. They had reached the bottom of the last staircase. The air was thick with moisture and the rotten smell of the Shadows. Melissa hung back, but Kala kept climbing until she could finally see the top of the wall.

She stopped, confused. A wide expanse of marble stretched out in front of her, perhaps fifteen blocks thick, to create a flat platform. Beyond that was just a plain of darkness that merged into the sky, the moonlight picking out occasional pale sparkles across its surface. It seemed to mirror the firmament above: black crowded with clusters of light.

She climbed the last few steps onto the marble platform. The top layers of stone were unpainted, so the blocks beneath her feet glowed in the moonlight all the way to the far edge. The crashing whistles drew her on, but somehow they were less sinister here than they had seemed as she scaled the staircase. The tone was clearer, and without the barrier of the wall to muffle the sound, it started to sound familiar.

The wall's opposite side disappeared down into a cresting darkness about twenty feet below the platform. The cliffs cambered down to meet the gloom, sloping close in a way that they didn't in the valley. Rocks gathered in behind the wall, stacking up against it and disappearing beneath the fluid cloak of black that covered everything from wall to cliff all the way to the horizon. The blackness was all-consuming. It bubbled like ink boiling up the stone.

For a moment, it seemed like nothing less than had been promised by the priesthood: a dense fog of dark ghosts, breaking against the wall, clamouring to push back through to the land of the living. This was the land of Shadows from her childhood stories. This was where the shades lived who stalked the wall in Melissa's tales, breaths of ashy smoke that had managed to pull themselves from the grasping hands of their fellows. Kala could almost distinguish fists and fingers reaching out of the mire and up against the wall beneath her feet, clutching and hungry.

Without meaning to, she took a step backwards.

And then she saw it. She saw the buildings clustered on the shore, the dock pushing out into the darkness with its boats tied fast, and finally she understood.

IV

δελφίς | Delphis | Dolphin

To his fourth son, the god gave the waves themselves.
He filled them with plants and fishes of all manner to stretch
the nets of his people.
This son he named Euaemon, which means 'prosperous',
for the gifts of his domain were so great they might conquer
the garden itself.

- Kleitos, On the Formation of Kepos

They found her by the water.

It was a steep scramble down from the wall to the rocks where the acolyte sat. Kala didn't even try to stay on her feet, opting instead to slide down the slope on her backside. Her clothes were already ruined by the crust from the wall, which she now realised must be saltwater residue, so a little dirt wouldn't hurt. Melissa followed with more grace.

The truth didn't seem to have shocked her. She was used to being controlled by stories, Kala supposed, and used to having reality rewritten to suit the needs of those who had power over her. But Kala had never felt so deceived.

The ocean stretched away as far as she could see, waves churning white into the lacquer black of the water. This wasn't the eastern sea, small and contained by the cliffs. This sea was immense, filling a landscape bigger than Kala's entire world. She would never be able to look up at the wall again without feeling the weight of the water it restrained.

'You're Theodora?' she asked the acolyte.

'Yes, and you're Kala. And this is?'

'Melissa,' Kala replied. 'My…'

But she found she had no words to describe her. Melissa was her rock, her lover, and her best friend in the world. There was no name for that.

'Maid,' Melissa interrupted. 'I'm her maid.'

Theodora nodded. 'I imagine you have questions.'

Kala looked along the rocky shore, at the warehouses and boats and all the other trappings of trade. Their edges were discernible in the moonlight, but not their colours. They could have been gleaming and new, or broken by disrepair. There was no telling how long they had been here.

'Who knows about this?' she asked.

'The Archon, the Hierophants, the few acolytes trusted with laying the topmost stones. Your father. You, now. You wouldn't have believed me if I hadn't shown it to you, and it's important that you understand.'

But Kala didn't understand at all.

'Who are you?' she asked the acolyte. 'What were you to my father?'

'I'm his sister.'

Kala looked at Melissa, but she just shrugged. Apparently, this was news to her too.

'You're my aunt?' She was barely older than Kala.

'I was as surprised as you are, but when I saw you for the first time I realised he had been telling the truth. And now he's gone.'

'My father,' Kala said.

She nodded. 'Neophytos and I were in the forest, and he ran into us. He started shouting at me, telling me to go home, but then he stopped and just... looked at me. Called me Soraya. It was my name, he said. My real name.'

'But not the one you use now,' Kala said.

She looked out at the black waves. 'This is where the Archon found me, on these rocks. He called me Theodora: a gift from the gods.' She rolled her eyes.

'You disagree?'

'I know I didn't come from the gods. I came from up there.' She pointed at the cliffs. 'And so did your father.'

***

The Empire's Heart was the wealthiest city in what people called the Plain. People other than the citizens of Kepos, that is. To them, it was the heavens, the top of the cliffs towering above them to the north, the realm of the gods. Had they met its gold-draped princes, they might only have been confirmed in that belief.

The palace was a many-tiered glory of gardens and stone, the emerald of the Plain. Limestone promontories loomed at its back and half-circled its sides like embracing arms. The only access was via the north gate, along a wide avenue that stretched through irrigated parks and fields until it reached the prettiest of the merchant streets. There the geometry of the palace devolved into alleys of twisting brick buildings, propping each other up as they baked in the sun.

Those alleys were no longer Khosrow's home.

He had been just ten years old when the king first saw his mother. She was beautiful, undoubtedly, but the king would never have noticed her if she hadn't punched one of his guards. The man had more than deserved it, and the relentless momentum of her right hook had landed her in the ruler's lap with a broken hand.

They were married within a single moon. Khosrow had twin half-brothers born within the year, another brother two years later and, finally, Soraya. As she arrived, their mother's spirit left, bleeding out onto the flagstones of the birthing room. The liquid pooled between the cracks, slipping jerkily along the channels in the floor to the corridor beyond, where Khosrow waited. It stained the soles of his boots.

It would have been unbearable, had it not been for Soraya. She was a gift indeed, a baby who seemed blessed in her temperament. The four brothers wanted nothing more than to be near her, to hold her, and to bring her colourful gifts to make her smile. But more than anyone, she adored her eldest brother, Khosrow.

Unlike the little princes, he had no royal blood and so there was rarely room for him at court. No one missed his presence, so he was free to spend his time as he wished, and he wished to spend it with his sister. If she groused, he would let her pull at his lips until she smiled. If she was sick, he would tend her through the night. If she couldn't sleep, he would take her from the wet nurse and hold her to his chest, humming to her softly until she stilled. She consumed him.

Then, in the nineteenth year of Kuon by the Kepian calendar, merchants arrived in the harbour to the west. Merchants in general were not strangers to the Empire's Heart, a city that gathered much of its wealth through trade, but these particular ships had not been seen before. They sat high in the water, sharp and fast, and their passengers were interested in only the lightest, most precious wares.

In the end, Khosrow's treasure was all they took.

He woke to find the palace in disarray. There were bodies in the nursery, the wet nurse and two slaves dead, but no Soraya. Blood congealed slowly on the floor, trickling into the grout in a sickeningly familiar fashion. There were stains again, but this time on the knees of Khosrow's trousers, in the cracks of his hands and pushed into his hair with his tears. The king, so distant over the past moons as he mourned his wife, shouted orders that Khosrow couldn't hear. They wouldn't find her, he knew.

The little princess was gone.

The harbour master had seen the ships heading south along the coast, so Khosrow followed them on foot. There was nothing else he could do. It took him less than an hour to scale the promontory above the palace, clambering up the goat path that rose from the harbour. By the time he reached the top there was nothing to see. There was no trace of the ships on the horizon and, soon after, there was not even daylight to see by. Still he walked on, tripping across the wind-scoured grassland. He didn't sleep that night.

By morning he had reached the end of the land, where cliffs dropped hundreds of feet down into the water. It was the most vertiginous view he had ever seen, at least until he followed the headland round to the wall and saw the city beyond, where the ledge pitched sheer into the depths of the valley.

That was his first glimpse of Kepos.

But there was no way down, and no way to cross the valley, so he walked east, past the city, past the temple, through the river that fed the waterfall, until he was overlooking what he would later come to know as the eastern sea.

Then he found the rope. A protruding boulder secured it to the cliff, so it dangled freely all the way to the waves beneath. It was in constant motion, swinging with the pull of the current, but apparently secure. He crawled along the stone on his belly to reach the rope, but it was too heavy to pull up. There were knots at regular intervals along it, about a man's height apart, as though it were designed for climbing.

There was no way to tell whether it would take his weight, but there was no other way across the valley. It was broadening as the sea spread it wide, making the crossing longer with every step he moved away from the city, and he couldn't make out an end. He had to risk it. Strapping his satchel around his shoulders, he inched out onto the rock and grabbed the rope, hands fisting above the first knot.

He breathed.

He tested the grip of his fingers on the blackened fibre.

He felt the pressure of his racing heartbeat in the dry back of his throat.

The moment stretched.

In a single move, he lifted his body from the ledge and out into the air, bracing himself for the jolt as the rope took his weight.

It held.

He climbed down, alternately crouching and stretching as he made his way down the rope. First his hands slid down to meet the knot at his feet, then he slid his feet down to meet the knot below. He was thirty feet down before he noticed the first bone, a shard of vertebra lodged in a twist of rope. From that point onwards he found evidence in every knot: a scrap of fabric, a fingernail, a slew of sun-dried meat. The fibre of the knots that held them was lighter than the rest, tar leeched away by the fluids of decomposition.

A hangman's rope.

The bodies that had been displayed along its length were gone, but they had done their damage to its fibre.

Khosrow was close to the water when it snapped, but not close enough. He fell awkwardly, the rope twisting around him as he dropped, but that wasn't the main danger. He had been so intent on reaching the sea that he hadn't noticed the way it crashed against the cliff face. As he shrugged off the coils of rope, the tide rolled him into the stone, cracking his head against it, and shadows took his sight.

He woke with his face pressed into salty wood. He burst into motion, feeling again the clutch of water around his body. But it was rain this time, not sea, moistening the planks to loose his bristled cheek from their surface. The fishermen didn't speak to him, only occasionally glancing his way from the corners of their eyes until their small boat made it back to the shore.

Then they sent for the Archon.

The man was the tallest Khosrow had ever met. The plates of metal sewn into his tunic were blinding and his guttural language was a strange assault. He was an immense edifice of shiny, incomprehensible anger. Khosrow's senses spun with dehydration and he found himself horizontal once more, this time with his cheek pressed to the earth.

When he woke again he was in the city, in the shadow of the wall he had seen from the clifftops. The priests saw to it that a few Glauks tenants helped him gain his health, the basic language, and an understanding that there was no leaving the valley. He tested that tenet as soon as he was able, but found no way to scale the cliffs. When he tried to climb the wall he was pushed away by the acolytes, and even if he had managed to slip past them, how would he get from the top of the wall to the grassland above? The eastern sea posed the same problem; even if the flimsy Kepian boats had been able to take him as far as the broken rope, he wouldn't have been able to reach it, and there was no other route. He'd seen the terrain from above, and he knew he was trapped.

By the time he learned what the Kepians thought lay on the other side of the wall, and on the tops of the cliffs, he knew enough to keep his peace. He told no one the truth, holding his secret loss close to his heart.

He had failed. He had lost Soraya, and trapped himself in a hole in the ground from which there was no escape. With no other option, he settled with the Glauks tenants and paid his way with woodworking, the trade he had inherited from his father. Then he met Charis and her father agreed to their marriage, mostly because she was never expected to inherit. After that, Kepos didn't seem like such a bad place to be marooned after all. But he never forgot Soraya, and the pirates who had stolen her from him.

The stars had faded as Theodora told Kala the story. Now dawn was threatening, and Kala needed to leave, but her questions wouldn't wait.

'You think pirates left you here?' she asked. 'And you think the Archon is trading with them?'

'That's what your father believed.'

'But why?' asked Melissa.

'The valley's safe,' the acolyte said, 'and rich. We have orichalcum, gems, the finest marble, and more food than we need. He can trade that for what we don't have: power. The Dekocrats may think they run the city, but the Archon is the one who bargains to keep the raiders out.'

'By holding you ransom.'

Theodora nodded. 'As far as the outside world is concerned, the Archon is the king of Kepos. They call it the Secret City.'

'And my father knew this?' Kala asked.

'Not until he came here. He found his way up the wall a few months ago and saw this place for himself. He worked out that the priesthood were trading with the pirates.'

'The Archon sent a herb to my father the day he died,' Kala said. 'I think it could have been poison.'

All three of them were silent for a moment.

Kala had failed to discern the real shape of her world. The Dekocrats were children playing in a sandbox while the grown-ups organised their world around them. They had no power beyond this wall.

'The Archon was one of the reasons he wanted to leave,' said Theodora. 'He was going to take us back home, us and your mother. We were just waiting for the harvest festival.'

'Why then?'

'Because all of the acolytes will be hauling blocks around, so the temple will be empty. That's our way out. We have a pulley lift up there that we use to reach eggs and plants on the cliff face. We would have had to climb the last stretch, but he had a plan for that. And now he's dead.'

Theodora was on the verge of tears, but whatever this girl had meant to Kala's father, she herself had barely known him. These were tears of frustration and fear rather than loss. She wasn't mourning Khosrow. She was mourning the escape that his death had denied her.

The acolyte fingered her pendant nervously. It was a green stone in a silver setting, dangling from a leather thong around her neck. She saw Kala's attention on it and held it out towards her.

'They found it on me as a baby. Your father said it was a protective amulet given to all the children of the Plain, though this one is a more precious stone than usual, since I'm a princess.'

There was a hint of injured pride in her tone. Kala didn't like that and wouldn't indulge it, but it did explain the acolyte's desperation to leave the valley: she thought she was owed a better life.

Kala changed the subject, finally asking the question she came here to have answered. 'Did the Archon kill him?'

'I don't know, but if he found out about our plan...' Theodora blinked and looked at her strangely. 'No one leaves Kepos.'

That was the edict. To everyone else it need not be spoken, but her father had seen beyond this valley. He had seen the world outside.

'Will you still go?' Kala asked.

'I have no choice,' said Theodora. 'I don't think either of us is safe here now.' She pulled her hair away from her face then looked at Kala. 'We have a home out there. Won't you come with me?'

She was scared to go on her own. It was plain in her eyes: the pleading, desperate hope that she might not have to do this alone. She was a year or two older than Kala – Melissa's age – and yet, with her closeted life in the temple, Theodora was still a little girl.

But Kala had never considered that leaving this place was a real possibility. That was the point, of course: the people of Kepos didn't understand that there was anywhere else to go. They were hemmed in by the cliffs, the wall and the sea. For as far as they could sail in their little fishing boats, there were only more cliffs and more sea. The occasional foreigner washed up on their shores, as her father had, bringing stories of faraway lands and peoples. She had dreamed of them: sultans, adventurers, pirates, nomads and treasure hunters, exoticisms from the bedtime tales her father had whispered as she fell into sleep. But she was the only one. To the rest of Kepos, the sea held only dangerous creatures and more dangerous people. In Kepos, 'foreign' was a dirty word.

Kala had never seen the Plain. It didn't seem real.

'The Delphis offered to adopt me,' she said to Theodora. 'He would keep me safe.'

'Not from the Archon. And anyway, that's not enough. Don't you see the water? Don't you see the gaps between the stones, the way they've tried to shore up the wall?'

It was difficult to make out details in the moonlight, but the blocks here did seem less snugly-nestled than those on the city side. They were slightly askew, as though they had been pushed out of alignment.

'It's breaking,' Theodora continued, 'and the water's rising. This is low tide, but when it's high the water starts pushing up over the edge. They think they can keep everything the same by trapping us in, but it's changing more every day, and it won't be many more moons before it's too late. We're not safe here, Kala. Moving to Delphis isn't enough. We have to leave this valley before the water drowns us all.'

They left Theodora by the Water. The sky was lightening above them, and so far they were only two staircases down from the top.

'Her story was so familiar,' Kala said. 'The places, the names, even the way she described it. I feel like I've heard it all before, when I was very young.'

'It's true then?'

'I think so.'

Kala was finding that it took more concentration to go down the stairs than up. With each step she felt a lurch in her chest, because with each step she felt like she was pitching forwards to teeter on the edge of her balance. Her heart jumped like a rabbit in her chest.

'She was exposed,' Melissa said. 'Abandoned on that shore by the pirates.' Her voice was so thick that she might as well have spoken the subtext: Exposed like the girl we found, the one we tried to save. Six little fingers on each hand.

Kala chose her next words carefully. 'We don't know that.'

'They found her on the rocks.'

'But Theodora was taken for a reason. To ransom, or to sell to the Archon so he could ransom her. Why would they just give her up? If she really did end up on the rocks then it must have been a mistake. She had value.'

There was silence, and Kala realised it had been the wrong thing to say. There was no way that the other baby, the baby they had found, had been exposed by mistake. She had been left there deliberately, at the top of the cremation tower where her cries would go unheeded. If Melissa hadn't lost her own baby that morning, if they hadn't gone together to that place of flesh and smoke, then no one would have heard her at all.

Kala turned and reached up for Melissa's hand.

'I didn't mean to imply that our little girl didn't have value too,' she said.

'She didn't, not to whoever left her there.'

'But she did to us, Lissa.'

For just three days, Kala had fulfilled a purpose instead of just being redundant. But it had been as short-lived as their little girl and ended just as abruptly.

'You'd come with me?' Kala asked. 'Up there?'

'Of course. I can't swim.'

Kala kissed the back of her hand and released her, smiling gently against the pain in her heart. They had to keep moving.

'I need to speak to Eirene,' Kala said. 'Can you send one of the boys with a message for her?'

'Still? You've seen what's on the other side of this wall. You've heard what Theodora had to say. Do you really need to know any more?'

Logically, there was only one choice here: they had to go with Theodora. The harvest festival was still a moon away, so they had agreed that they would meet her again in ten days' time to give their answer. But in the meantime, Kala needed to find out who had killed her father. If Nikos had something to do with her father's death then she couldn't wait; she needed to move to Delphis now.

When they finally reached the ground, the torches of the Tauros watch were already moving across the meadows. Kala bade Neophytos a quick farewell, then she and Melissa hid behind the Glauks memorials until the new acolytes had taken up their stations. Even if the men noticed them mounting Hypatia and racing back to the city, Kala was certain they wouldn't have recognised her in the poor dawn light.

The house of Glauks was silent on their return. Melissa took Hypatia back to the stables while Kala slipped into the garden, pulling her cloak up over her head to hide her face. She wondered how much sleep Melissa would manage before Hagne missed her. The older woman was nominally in charge of the household, but she wasn't often in control these days. That much was evident from the state of the garden.

Although the spits had been removed and the tables cleared of food, the benches were still occupied. Snoring men were arrayed variously along them, some lying down and others sitting with their heads pillowed on the tables. The wine casks had been upended to drain the last drops from the barrels. They now rested next to the sleepers in gritty puddles of lees, half-concealing two figures propped up against the garden wall. One was a kitchen slave, a few years older than Kala. The other was a more predictable deviant.

'Leon?'

He didn't move, but the girl startled awake. She stared at Kala, looked down at Leon's head on her shoulder, then shrank away from his embrace.

'Miss,' she whispered as she extricated herself. 'It isn't… I mean, I didn't, it's just… The Glauks asked me to stay for a drink, then the Master–'

'It's all right. Go on, or you'll catch it from Hagne.'

The girl's footsteps were already racing down the colonnade when Leon blinked his eyes open.

'Kala?' His gaze was unfocused, but amiable.

'What are you doing out here? Do you want a black eye to add to your broken lip?'

He squinted up at her. 'Have you come to share some wine with me?'

'No,' she said, helping him to his feet, 'you've drunk it all. I've come to help you to bed.'

His eyebrows shot up, then he started to smile. 'Really?'

'Not like that. I think you've had enough female company for the night.'

'What? Oh, her. Nice girl,' he said. His voice was so slurred that it took some time for Kala to decipher the words. 'Not very smart,' he continued. 'Saved her from Father.'

'I'm sure you did.'

'Reminded me of Lali.' He grinned, then squinted at Kala again. 'Where's Lali? She here?'

'She's sleeping, like you should be. Come on.'

She slung his arm around her shoulders. He reeked of sour wine and wood smoke, and his unsteady weight was almost too much for her. She leaned heavily onto her cane.

'Help me out a bit,' she said. 'There's no one here to save you from your father, and I can't carry you alone.'

'Stay and have a drink.'

'Another time.'

'Promise?'

'If you'll keep your voice down and come quietly to bed, then yes, fine, I promise.'

'Your bed?'

'No.'

'Shame.'

She sighed and steered him into the house along the dark colonnade, wrapping her arm around his waist. His tunic was damp from the puddle of wine in which she had found him. She could feel its sting on her fingertips, seeping into the grazes she'd picked up climbing the wall.

'Why're you all... crunchy?' he asked, rubbing at the hard patch of salt on the shoulder of her cloak.

'Why are you all covered in wine?' She poured indignation into her tone, warning him off.

'D'you want some? There's more somewhere, I'm sure.'

He stumbled, stressing her tired muscles beyond their limit. Her cane skidded away across the tiles as his momentum carried them both into a column, then dragged them to the ground against the wall. That seemed to sober him a little, which was just as well since Kala was winded from the fall. She was also pinned beneath him. He sat crumpled between her legs in the stretch of her dress, his side pressed against her chest and his head resting on hers.

'I'm so sorry,' he said, leaning back to look at her. 'Is anything broken?'

He ran his hands along her arms, moving the joints of her elbows, her wrists, her shoulders. He felt her scalp for bumps then cupped her face in his hands. His fingertips moved on her skin, his thumb across her lips.

In a moment of absolute silence, they looked at each other.

'Kala.'

She pushed him away and got to her feet unsteadily, leaning on the wall for support. 'I'm fine,' she said. 'Nothing broken.'

'Kala.'

She didn't meet his eye. 'Would you pass me my cane, please?'

He crawled across the floor to fetch it, then stayed on his knees as he presented it to her. She reached out to take it, but as her fingertips touched the wood he caught her hand in his own, lacing his fingers with hers.

'Kala, please.'

Her gaze snapped to his. 'What?'

'I'm sorry,' he said.

'It's all right. No harm done.'

'No,' he said, gently squeezing her hand, 'I mean I'm sorry. I'm an idiot when I'm drunk.'

She laughed. 'Only then?'

'All right, more of an idiot. I didn't mean to upset you.'

'Leon, what can I say that will make you go to bed?'

'Let me make it up to you. Let's have dinner together tomorrow. You know, get to know each other.'

'I prefer to eat alone in my rooms.' With Lissa.

'Make an exception. Just once. Please.'

She sighed. 'Fine. Now go to bed.'

He jumped to his feet and grinned. 'Goodnight then, Kala. Until tomorrow.'

She would never have guessed the depth of his inebriation from the way he walked down the colonnade. At least, not until he veered into one of the columns in the corridor that led to his bedroom.

Her own bedroom was on the other side of the house, near the kitchen and the slave quarters. The walk had never felt longer.

The house slept late into the afternoon, so Kala's own lie-in went unnoticed. She saw no one but the door slave as she left for the baths, craving the hot water to soothe her aching body. She could face the crowds today for the relief the springs would bring. Her limp was so pronounced that she took two walking sticks with her, and could still only move at half speed. When Ariston stopped his litter in the street and offered her a ride, she could have cried with relief.

'Did he tell you?' Ariston asked as he helped her into the vehicle. It was carried by four slaves, who moved along the streets as fluidly as water.

'Lali did.'

His face crumpled. 'I had no idea she was promised to Timon. What am I going to do now?'

'Lali said to do nothing.'

Ariston looked like his heart was breaking.

'No,' Kala continued, 'I mean, you don't need to do anything. With the move to Glauks, she thinks Elaphos will want to break the deal anyway. She's going to talk to Nikos.'

His face burst into a smile, but he still looked a little worse for wear.

'Did you overdo the wine last night too?' she asked.

He started nodding, then thought better of it. 'Yes, hence the litter. I take it Leon's still abed?'

'As far as I know.'

'Lucky bastard.'

Ariston was going to the gymnasium, so he dropped Kala at the baths on his way. She thanked the slaves as they helped her to her feet, but declined their offer to help her into the building. She wanted to be as unobtrusive as possible.

The pools were so busy that she had to share with some elderly Glauks tenant ladies, but they recognised her need for solitude and didn't try to involve her in their conversation. They were talking about the upcoming festival, discussing which colours they would grind and how best to seal the paint. Kala let their lyrical voices wash over her as the heat coaxed the pain from her muscles, but it wasn't enough to soothe out the tension in her shoulders. She would be sore for a few days yet.

She returned to the house late in the afternoon, with unsteady legs and wet hair. Melissa met her in her rooms wielding combs and pins and wearing an expression that said she was ready to fight to install them in Kala's hair.

'Must I?' Kala said.

'You're dining with the Master tonight.'

'He told you?'

'Who do you think's doing the cooking?'

Melissa pulled out one of Kala's finer dresses, handed down from her mother. The border was studded with orichalcum and although the colour had faded, the weave was so fine that it was barely visible.

'It's only Leon,' Kala said. 'I don't need all… this.' She flopped onto a cushioned chair and abandoned the two walking sticks, flexing her hands to relieve the pain of the walk.

'He's a good man.'

'So you say, but it's not as if I'm going to marry him.'

'Why not?'

'Why not? Are you joking?'

Melissa spread the dress out on the bed.

'Will you tell him that we're leaving?'

Kala stilled. 'It's what you want, then?'

She looked into Kala's eyes for a moment before responding. 'Kepos holds too many memories. We can't forget the past for as long as we stay here. Leaving is what your father wanted. I think it's what you want, too.'

'Well, then there's no point to this,' she gestured to the dress, 'to any of it.'

'You'll leave them all behind?'

'They won't believe me.'

'They'll die.' Melissa's voice was a whisper.

'We don't know that. We don't know that any of it's true. I'm not even sure I believe it, and I've seen the water.'

In her memory, it took on a sinister aspect. Black fingers clawing at the marble blocks, pulling them down into darkness, digging through the wall to unleash an army of shades on the city. Despite all she had seen, her fear of the valley flooding was still less real than her childhood nightmares of being inundated by the Shadows. She had let them distract her from the danger she should be focusing on, the one that had broken her home.

'Did you send a message to Eirene?' Kala asked.

'She says to come tomorrow. You can collect the blocks for the festival from the quarry, pretend that's your reason for going south.'

'Thank you.'

Melissa smiled tightly and came to stand behind her, gathering Kala's hair into her hands. It was time for her scalp to be tortured with braids again.

'It feels like years have passed in these last few days,' Kala said. 'I start to think I'm done with the grief, but then I get to the evening, and he's not here to read with me.'

Melissa's fingers stroked through her hair, separating sections to comb free of knots, but she didn't reply.

'I haven't been to the library in days. I think I miss him more there.'

But it wasn't just the library, it was books in general. She had buried the Kleitos scroll in her clothes chest, not just because it held the herb she had saved from his last meal, but because she couldn't bear to look at it. The feel of the paper, the smell of it, it was her father. In a city where women didn't read, where scrolls were precious and few, she could avoid books entirely by avoiding the library. It was his place, their place. She wasn't sure whether she wanted to live there forever or burn it to the ground.

'There's a reason I never go into the woods,' Melissa said.

'Hmm?'

'Euphranor.'

Melissa's husband. He had been a Glauks carpenter's slave, and he'd worked in the woods all day, every day, until he'd missed his swing and taken an axe in his thigh. Melissa had been three moons pregnant.

'It's funny,' she continued, 'but I didn't even like him to start with. He was so cocky. Hagne thought I was mad.'

'You loved him though.'

'I did. It was like having a second pair of hands. That sounds like it's nothing, but it's everything. I want that for you, too.'

'I have it. With you.'

Melissa smiled, but there was something broken in it. 'No,' she said softly, 'you don't. I love you, Kala. You know that. But this, what we have? It's not the same. You know that.'

'Do I?' Kala felt as though her heart was breaking.

'You don't have to keep clinging to me,' Melissa said. 'You can let go. You don't need me. You're comfortable with me, and I'm comfortable with you. But we aren't the end for each other.'

Kala knew there was truth in her words, and that if she reached past her own selfishness she'd feel it too, but all she could hear was: *She doesn't want me. She doesn't love me like she loved Euphranor.*

'Are you telling me it's over?' Kala asked. The horror of the question made her tongue go numb, but she had to ask it.

'No,' Melissa said, leaning down to kiss Kala's neck. 'No. But it will be, my love. You'll want a family of your own one day, and children.'

'I won't.'

'But if you do,' Melissa insisted, 'then it won't be with me. It might be with someone like Leon.'

Kala laughed.

'I doubt it,' she said.

Melissa shrugged. 'It won't if you're not open to it. But I'm telling you: you should be. I give you permission, if that's what you need. What we have is comforting, but you need something fierce. You want to fight.'

'You don't know what I need.'

Melissa didn't dignify Kala's petulance with a response. Instead, she returned to combing her hair.

'Is that what you had with Euphranor?' Kala asked after a moment. 'Something fierce?'

'I wouldn't call it that. I know we weren't together long, and gods we were young, but we still loved each other at the end. That's more than most have.'

The afternoon was darkening into evening outside the window, but Kala could still see across the garden to the empty barrels of last night's revelry. Her mother was shut away in her room again, her mind so lost that it was difficult to imagine her ever recovering.

'Did my parents have that?' she asked.

'Your father loved your mother more than anything in the world.'

'And her?'

Melissa thought for a moment before answering. 'I think she grew to love him.'

'Leon thinks the Dekocrat families don't get to have that, that all we have is duty. I can't imagine her learning to love Nikos.'

Melissa's hands slipped down Kala's neck to her shoulders, squeezing them gently. Kala turned to look at her.

'What is it?'

She sighed. 'I think she's always loved him, Kala. She lost your father, and she misses him, but in the end she got Nikos. It was just what she'd always wanted. That can be a terrible thing.'

'You think she feels guilty?'

'Wouldn't you?'

Melissa put the final touches to Kala's hair, pinning the braids around her head so the dark locks that remained loose were gathered onto her crown.

'I think I assumed I knew her,' Kala said. 'I assumed that we were close. She's my mother, after all. But I don't know her at all, do I?'

'Children need to think their parents are better than normal people.'

'I'm not a child, Lissa.'

'I know.'

But it wasn't entirely true. Kala may have been old enough to go to the Proaulia this year, but until she was married she would always be a child in the eyes of the city. She was fully prepared to be a child for the rest of her life. Melissa clearly thought she still was.

'Don't judge her too harshly,' Melissa continued. 'She didn't have much of a choice, about any of it. She's as trapped here as we are.'

That was at the heart of it: Melissa was trapped. She was a slave here. She and Kala were as close as they could be, given the circumstances, but neither of them would choose this life if they had another option. It was a hard truth that Kala didn't want to face, but perhaps things would be different in the Plain. Perhaps they wouldn't choose each other outside the walls of Kepos.

Melissa helped Kala out of her clothes and into the dress, pulling the neck wide to avoid sending her braids into disarray. Charis's cast-off was a little too short, and a little too tight, but it would serve.

'You look just as beautiful in it as she did,' Melissa said as she watched Kala fidget. 'Darker, and different, but beautiful all the same.'

'Broken, though,' Kala said, 'just like her.'

'To some maybe, but not to me.' Melissa pressed her lips to Kala's then whispered, 'Never to me.'

Leon's chambers were bathed in light despite the dusk. In the central room, shelves of lamps illuminated two dining couches that flanked a low table. With the windows shuttered, it created an atmosphere of mischievous intimacy.

'Are you trying to start rumours?' Kala asked as he ushered her inside.

'What?' His expression was all innocence. 'I'm having a quiet dinner with my new sister.'

'I'm not your sister, Leon.'

'Well, that's a relief. Come, sit.'

Her dress stretched tight across her thighs as she relaxed back onto the couch. She wished Melissa hadn't insisted that she wear it.

'Where is your sister tonight?' Kala asked.

'She's dining with Ariston. But if father asks, then she's in bed with a headache.'

'Has she spoken to him?'

'About Ariston? Not yet. Aha,' he said, turning as Melissa entered with a pitcher, 'now for that drink you promised me.'

'You mean that promise you extorted from me?'

Melissa smiled at Kala. She served new wine mixed with water and honey while their eyes held across the table.

'I wanted to apologise for last night,' Leon said.

Kala switched her attention to him. 'For getting drunk, or for fondling the staff?'

'The former, of course. I'm entirely innocent of the latter.'

When Kala looked back, Melissa had slipped away. She returned a moment later with their meal, starting with a dish of figs and chickpeas that she placed on the table between them. She left the rest of the food on the tray, gave Kala an encouraging look, then disappeared. The message was clear: Kala was on her own.

'You're close to your household?' Leon asked. He hadn't missed Melissa's glance.

'To Lissa, yes.'

She sipped the wine. It was sweet and refreshing, with a pleasant bitterness under the flavour of the honey.

'I've never had that,' he said. 'Father changes the slaves every year, moves them around the property. To discourage attachment, I think.'

'That makes no sense. What's the use of a kitchen slave in the fields?'

'He'd say he has even less use for a son weakened by affection.'

'Gods.'

He lifted a pinch of chickpeas to his lips. 'He would call this meal decadent, decry my waste of lamp oil and have you confined to your room against the deranging effects of wine on the female constitution.'

Kala thought of her mother in the courtyard last night, drunk and distant, and wondered whether there might not be some wisdom in that.

'But thankfully,' Leon continued, 'his virtue usually has him in bed at sundown after a solitary meal of barley gruel and water, so his loss is our gain. Your Lissa is a sorceress in the kitchen.'

'She never disappoints. You should try her mutton stew.'

A smug look crossed his face.

'You didn't.' Kala gaped at him. They could rarely afford to slaughter their livestock, so most of the animals they consumed were game. Mutton was an occasional treat.

'There was some meat left over from last night. It seemed a shame to waste it on my father, since he prefers his watery porridge anyway.'

He collected the tray and brought it over to the table, removing the covering cloth with a flourish.

'I think this is your plate,' he said, putting it down in front of her. 'I'm told that you like an obscene amount of garlic on your leaves.'

The sight of the dish set her mouth watering in seconds. It was her favourite: a rich, thick stew that Melissa cooked with root vegetables and spice, and served with piles of wild greens. There was a basket of toasted flatbreads too, so they could scoop the food into their mouths and mop up the juices afterwards. The breads were still so hot they burned her fingers, but she grabbed one nonetheless and leaned forward to sink it into the gravy.

Then she saw something she recognised in amongst the greens: leaves that resembled parsley, but with a shape that was slightly too sharp, and leaves that were slightly too small. There were none on Leon's plate.

Her stomach dropped. She pulled a leaf from the tangle of wilted greens and stood to examine it in the light, then raced to the door to call for Melissa.

'Kala?' Leon hadn't moved from his place on the couch. 'What's wrong?'

When Melissa arrived, Kala dragged her into the room and shut the door behind them.

Leon was on his feet. 'What's going on?

Kala showed the herb to Melissa and her eyes went wide. 'In my greens, Lissa. Just mine.'

'But… it can't be.' She shook her head in bewilderment. 'I prepared them myself.'

'Who else was in the kitchen?'

'Well, everyone. Hagne, Agathe, Daos, the twins, the men in from the fields, a few tenants, the serving girls and maids. You know what it's like in the kitchen at dinner time. Anyone can walk in.'

'But you'd notice the Archon or,' her eyes cut to Leon, 'one of the Dekocrats, or their families.'

'Of course, but if they sent a slave? Probably not.'

Leon put his hand on Kala's shoulder, turning her to face him.

'Will you tell me what's going on? What is this leaf, and what does it have to do with the Archon?'

'I'm sorry, Leon. I have to go. Thanks for dinner.'

She bustled Melissa out of the door and followed after her, leaving Leon in their wake. However much he might hate Nikos, Leon was still his son. Kala couldn't tell him that she thought her father had been murdered, or that she seemed to be the next target. She couldn't tell Leon that she suspected the Archon and his own father might be behind it.

A thought occurred to her. She rushed back to his rooms.

'Don't eat my greens,' she said, then hurried towards her own chambers.

She may not trust him, but that didn't mean she wanted to see him dead. Despite her best efforts, part of her was rather beginning to enjoy his company.

Kala was already pulling pins from her hair when she and Melissa got back to her room. The braids were unravelling over her shoulders, thick strands sliding away from their restraints.

'Well,' she said, 'that didn't exactly go to plan, but at least I can take this dress off now.'

'How can you be so glib?'

Kala turned to see Melissa leaning back against the door, her hand at her chest. She was trembling with rage or, worse, fear.

'Someone tried to poison you,' she continued. 'With my cooking.'

If Kala had died, the Dekocracy would have put Melissa to death. Their society had been built on the back of slavery, and on the trust and fear that perpetuated it. Slaves who betrayed their masters suffered tenfold to serve as lessons to the rest.

'Then they wanted us both out of the way,' Kala said. 'Maybe it wasn't Nikos. I can see him wanting to dispose of me to clean up the Glauks lineage, but he'd have no reason to want you dead.'

'Unless I was just an easy scapegoat.'

'Perhaps, but there's a more obvious explanation: someone knows about our meeting with Theodora.'

'She wouldn't tell anyone about it.'

'No one except Neophytos, I think. Maybe he let slip, or maybe someone saw us.'

'The Tauros acolytes?'

Kala remembered the poor light that morning, and the deep shadows of the sanctum that had hidden their return. 'I don't think so.'

'Then who?'

The truth was that anyone could have seen them. The garden had been full of revellers when they left last night, and the ride to the wall took them across the entire western side of the city. They could have been followed from any point on the journey. A spy who knew the truth about her father and the Water would only have needed to see the two of them scaling the wall, and Theodora descending after they had left, to understand what had happened.

'Look,' Kala said, 'we don't even know that it's poisonous, not until I've spoken to Eirene.'

'Really? You think a passing slave decided that your greens, and only yours, needed a little more flavour? Of course it's poisonous.'

'Not necessarily. Maybe it was intended to make me sick, to drive Leon away from me. Or maybe it's a soporific, like the Archon told my father it was, to make me spend the night with him. Maybe this is about him. Doesn't that make more sense? Who really cares about me, after all?'

As she spoke, Kala dug around in her clothes chest for the Kleitos scroll and picked out the folded paper in which the original herb was pressed. It was dry now, and wilted at the sides, but even in its degenerated state it was easy to compare the two leaves.

'They're not the same,' she said.

The first herb had been lighter in colour, even before it had started to fade. Its leaves were larger and more curved, with a slight fuzziness to the stems. But the new herb was dark green with a waxiness to it that made the leaves shiny, and its stem was blotched with purple.

'Two different poisons?' Melissa asked.

'Maybe.' Kala folded the second leaf into a scrap of cloth and hid it with the first, then sat down heavily on the chest. Melissa joined her.

'Are we going to survive until the harvest festival?' Melissa asked.

'We could always go to Delphis.'

'And how will that help, when we can't even trust the food I cook myself?'

Kala had no comfort to offer. Someone had got to Kala in her own home, just as they had got to her father. Until they could escape from the valley, nowhere would be safe.

V

κύων | Kuon | Dog

The domain of the fifth son was modest,
but to him the god gave a gift greater than wealth.
He taught him the hidden thoughts of man, opening their
mysteries to him,
and the god called him Mneseus, for his mind would hold the
secrets of the world.

- Kleitos, On the Formation of Kepos

Kala left at first light the next day. It took two hours for the cart to get to the quarry, and the journey back would be even longer. Five blocks of marble were more than enough to tax the two-horse team, particularly when added to the muscled weight of the two slaves who accompanied her. She was glad of them, because it was clear when they arrived that they wouldn't get much help loading up the cart.

'What's going on?' she asked a passing slave.

'Rock fall, Miss. A dozen men dead.'

The site was wreathed in clouds of dust that cloaked the quarry in fine powder. It stuck in the back of her throat. Slaves and masons ran towards the rock face, called on by sickening cries that made Kala clutch at her cane. She pulled the horses to a stop and slid from the driving seat, which Daos had indulgently ceded to her.

'Can we help?' she asked.

The slave shook his head. 'Nothing to be done, Miss.' He turned to Daos, pointing towards the stacks of stone ready for collection. 'Can you manage to load up on your own? There's slats and ropes behind.'

He didn't wait for their answer, but rushed away towards the commotion.

'So,' Kala said to Daos, 'can you manage?'

'Easily,' he replied, but he seemed anxious. 'It'll take us some time.'

'In which case, I'll get out of this dust and take Hypatia for a ride, if you don't need me?'

'Leave it to us.'

He unharnessed the horse for her, then helped her up onto the cart, and from there into her seat on Hypatia's back. The other slave had already started building a platform from the ground up to the cart. Kala reckoned she would have at least an hour before they managed to wrestle all five blocks into place.

'I won't go far,' she said, stuffing her cane down the back of her dress, then she sped out of the dust and onto the plains.

'You take care, now,' Daos called after her.

Melissa had told her she couldn't miss the house if she followed the river, so she headed along the towpath. It wasn't long before she reached a small, brick building roofed with timber. It was about big enough to hold two rooms, and nothing more. Bunches of herbs hung from the eaves, and a rack of tomatoes was laid out to bake in the sun on the slope of the roof. A man sat outside the door turning a spit-roasting rabbit over a small fire pit. He didn't look pleased to see Kala.

'Help you?' he said as he got to his feet.

She realised her hair and skin were caked in dust. If Eirene had told him a daughter of the dekocratic families would be visiting, then this was not what he would have expected.

'I'm looking for Eirene,' she said.

A woman stepped out of the house. In colouring and build she was the twin of Melissa, but their facial features differed.

'You'd be Miss Kala?'

She smiled her relief. 'That's right.'

'There's a mounting step round back, if you want to leave your horse there. I'll get some stools and we can sit out in the sunshine.'

By the time Kala returned to the front of the house, Eirene was pouring cups of watered wine. She offered one to Kala and ushered her towards a stool on the riverbank. The man didn't join them, instead returning to his place by the fire.

'So,' Eirene said, 'I hear you have something to show me.'

'Two somethings now, I'm afraid.'

'Oh?'

Kala reached into the pouch at her waist and drew out the two packets: one wrapped in paper and the other in cloth. She spread them open across her lap then offered the first to Eirene, the herb she had found on her father's body. The woman lifted it from the paper wrapping and laid it on her palm, stroking the leaves and stem.

'Cow parsley,' she said. 'It grows all round these parts. See here.' She reached out and grabbed a stem from a tall plant growing next to the river, offering it to Kala. It had wide sprigs of leaves and clusters of tiny white flowers.

'Is it poisonous?' Kala asked as she turned the stem in her hands.

'Not at all. Plenty of folk eat it, but it's also used in poultices and for treating coughs.'

'What about as a sleeping remedy?'

'That too. Some say it has a calming effect, though I've never found it helpful myself.'

So the Archon really had been trying to help with her father's insomnia. He hadn't been poisoned after all. It really had been an accident.

'Now this one,' Eirene continued as she took the second herb, 'this one is poisonous.'

'It is?'

'This is hemlock. It grows in the woods, mostly, and it looks a lot like cow parsley, but don't go confusing the two.

There's many a fool made a nice dish of hemlock greens thinking it was cow parsley. They start out thinking they've drunk too much wine, slurring and dizzy, but then things start to go numb, and pretty soon their breaths are gasping through their chests till they can't get the air in anymore.'

'It's fatal?'

'Always.'

Kala couldn't explain this away. It wasn't about Leon; someone was trying to kill her. Lissa was going to be frantic.

'Where did you find it?' Eirene asked.

Kala hesitated. Spreading rumours wasn't going to help.

'I only ask in case we need to warn people,' the woman continued. 'I worry, with the children playing in the woods. They put anything in their mouths, you know.'

'There's no need for you to be concerned about that,' Kala said, conjuring a lie. 'It's growing wild in the Glauks garden, just one plant, but I'll have it dealt with this afternoon.'

'Well, that's good to hear.' Eirene smiled. 'Anything else I can help you with, Miss, while you're out this way? Do you need any other herbs?'

Kala wrapped up the two leaves and stowed them back in her pouch.

'Not today, thank you. I should be getting back. Can I give you something for your trouble?'

'No, Miss.' Eirene was adamant. 'You look after our Lissa, so we're happy to help.'

'It's rather the other way around.' Kala's throat was tight with guilt. If someone was after her, they were probably after Melissa too, and that was her fault.

She said her goodbyes and trotted back to the quarry, taking the time to enjoy the bright morning. Daos was just hauling the last of the blocks into the cart when she arrived, so it was the other slave who helped her down from Hypatia's back.

'We've got a passenger, Miss,' he said, 'if that's all right?'

There was a young man sitting in the cart, cradling his arm towards his chest. It was splinted and bound, but blood seeped through onto the dusty cloth. A victim of the rock fall, she guessed. Daos saw her looking, finished tying down the last of the marble blocks, then ambled over to join them.

'My brother,' he said. Here was the source of Daos's earlier anxiety. 'He's slave to one of the Glauks masons. Hoped maybe you might find him some employment at the house, get him seen by the healer in the city.'

'Good idea.'

His face flooded with relief. 'Thank you, Miss Kala.'

Such gratitude panicked her, because a position for Daos's brother wasn't in her gift. It was Nikos's decision, and he didn't strike Kala as a generous man.

'You'll still have to ask the Glauks.'

'Of course,' Daos said, but his face fell a little. 'Are you ready to be on our way?'

'If there's nothing more we can do here, then yes.'

Daos harnessed Hypatia next to the other horse and, at a much slower pace, they returned to the city.

Melissa went to meet Theodora the very next day. Now that they knew Kala's father had died accidentally, there was no reason to hang around. Much though Kala wanted to find out why she was being targeted and by whom, Melissa had convinced her that it was more prudent to leave the mystery unsolved and just run. So they set their leaving date – the harvest festival – and now there was nothing to do except wait.

They would be able to take nothing with them except what they could fit in a small pack, so Kala spent much of her time debating how many scrolls she could carry, and which were the most important. When Melissa pointed out that she would also need to leave space for food and water, she resigned herself to taking the Kleitos and just one other. Its identity changed on a daily basis.

Her remaining time was split between sneaking out to the pool under the waterfall, and avoiding Leon and his father. She'd considered moving to Delphis, but it seemed to offer little benefit, especially since they would be leaving the valley soon anyway. If the would-be murderer was resourceful enough to infiltrate the Glauks kitchen, then the Delphis kitchen would be no safer. At least here, Kala knew she had friends.

And one enemy.

It was the noise of smashing crockery that drew Kala to the dining room. She thought perhaps a bird had become stuck inside – it had happened before – and it wasn't until she was right outside the door that she heard the voices.

'I'm talking to the Hierophant tomorrow,' Nikos said, his voice low and rough. A threat.

'No.' Her mother's voice.

Kala pressed herself against the wall outside and slid down to the ground, out of sight.

'You should have done it a decade ago. It's a disgrace.'

'It's no reflection on you. You're my husband, not her father.'

'I'm the *Glauks*. Everything that happens in this tribe reflects on me.'

Kala was weighing up the morality of eavesdropping on a private conversation between a married couple when Nikos said, 'Besides, she's corrupting my children.'

They were talking about her.

'Nikos–'

'Do you have any idea what the other Dekocrats say about her? Bad enough that she's crippled. Bad enough that her father was a foreigner. But the rumours about her and that slave, that *female* slave, are an abomination. And you've done nothing about it.'

'They've been friends since they were children. That's all.'

Kala was surprised to hear her mother standing up for her. Lying for her. Charis was well aware of the true nature of her daughter's relationship with Melissa.

'I'm summoning the Hierophant,' Nikos insisted. 'It's past time that she was handed over to the care of Diaprepes. Let him decide what should become of her. Maybe she'll make a better acolyte than she does a step-daughter.'

'No,' Charis said, with a level of vehemence that surprised Kala. 'Please, Nikos. Please don't send her away.'

'Are you telling me what to do?'

'She's nothing. She's just a crippled girl. She's no one. Forget about her. Please. We have our family. You, me, Eulalia and Leon. Isn't that enough?'

Every word landed like a dagger in Kala's heart. Perhaps they were disingenuous, intended to protect Kala from Nikos's anger, but they hurt nonetheless, because they were true. She was no longer part of her mother's family.

'I'll tell you this much: she'll not go to the Proaulia while I'm Glauks,' Nikos said.

'Of course not,' Charis said, her tone placating, wearing him down.

'And she's to stay away from my children.'

'Of course,' Charis said. 'But better just to forget her. Don't draw attention to her by making her an acolyte. Let her fade into the background. She's good at that. Concentrate on us.' Her voice turned seductive. 'Concentrate on me.'

Kala crawled away as the door to the dining room slammed shut, sealing the couple inside together. She didn't want to witness what came next. But she still heard Nikos's muffled voice as she crept away.

'Don't think you can convince me that easily, woman.'

'Can't I?'

Nikos's laughter chased Kala back to her own room, shivering down her spine.

But Straton never came to the house.

* * *

Despite the tension between the newly-weds, the next couple of weeks passed in relative quietude. Nikos spent his time bullying the tenants and Charis remained 'indisposed' in her own chambers for most of the day. Neither was interested in speaking with Kala. Leon had tried to corner her on several occasions, but she'd made up excuses to slip away every time. The atmosphere between them became chillier with each rebuff, but since she was leaving in a few weeks' time, since his father might be trying to kill her, and since Nikos had made it very clear that he didn't want Kala anywhere near his son, it was probably for the best.

The only member of the family with whom she spent any time at all was Eulalia. One of the five marble blocks from the quarry had been deposited in their courtyard for the house of Glauks to decorate and since Kala was no painter, the task had fallen to Eulalia. Kala had taken to watching her in the afternoons as she coaxed the oily paints into swirls and shadows with her fingertips, punctuating planes of colour with shiny starbursts ground from copper and silvery orichalcum. Layer upon layer, it was becoming a thing of beauty.

'Did you speak to him again?' Kala asked.

'I tried,' Eulalia replied, 'for the hundredth time.'

'And?'

'He says he hasn't heard from the Elaphos, and refuses to discuss it further.'

Eulalia had first approached her father about her marriage two weeks ago, pretending concern that her engagement to Timon might be broken. She had yet to mention Ariston by name.

'So he won't contact the Elaphos himself?'

'Of course not,' Eulalia said. 'If there's any chance that the engagement is still on, he won't endanger it by implying there's a reason it shouldn't be. He'll leave it to the Elaphos to make the decision, which might not be until the Proaulia itself.'

'You think they'd really wait until then?'

Eulalia shrugged, but there was weight in the gesture that was less than carefree. If Timon waited until the last minute to declare the engagement broken, it would leave her unclaimed at the end of the Proaulia. Once snubbed, young women in Kepos were rarely given the chance to attend again. If he was feeling vindictive, the Elaphos could render Eulalia unmarriageable.

There was a commotion in the entrance hall and Nikos came striding into the courtyard, dragging Daos's brother by his broken arm. The young slave had tears streaming down his face.

Daos hurried in behind them. 'Glauks, please. I'm begging you.'

But Nikos was incandescent. His cheeks were shining red and his movements vibrated jerkily with anger. 'The slaves run the house of Glauks, do they? You think you can decide what goes on under my roof, that you can steal my money for whatever purpose you see fit?'

Kala and Eulalia scrambled out of the way as Nikos threw the boy to the floor by the marble block, sending the paint pots spinning across the flagstones and into the grass. They left trails of colour in their wake: purple and green and ochre. Only then did Kala notice what Nikos was holding.

He dragged the boy's arm across the block and swung back with his other hand, bringing the axe down fast and hard. The boy screamed. And screamed. The blade slammed down again and again, crunching into bone. Footsteps thundered along the passageways from every part of the house, but stopped at the edge of the courtyard. The screams went on, until the blade finally hit stone.

The boy curled around the stump of his arm, muffling his cries against his shoulder. Nikos stood and looked at the slaves who had assembled. His face and tunic were covered with blood. It dripped from the axe head, mixing with the colours already spread across the floor in a pattern that would have been pleasing had it not been made of gore.

The marble block ran silver and red.

'I am not your old master,' he said, his voice more powerful for all that it was quiet. 'If you make the mistake of thinking me as weak as him, then I will have my daughter paint a tribute to our god in your blood.' He looked at each of the slaves in turn and then, briefly, at Kala.

Her eyes stung and her skin chilled with sweat.

'Now get back to work,' he shouted.

Daos crept forward to retrieve his brother, but Nikos kicked him away.

'I will take care of the boy.'

He waited for the courtyard to empty out and then, with a last glance at Kala and Eulalia, dragged the boy towards the gardens. He was still carrying the axe.

Kala vomited her breakfast into the flowerbeds. When she turned back towards Eulalia, the girl was looking between her dress, pin-pricked with blood spray, and the amputated limb on the ground.

'He's going to kill him, isn't he?' Kala said.

Their eyes held for a moment before Eulalia turned and ran to her rooms.

That marked the end of her painting that autumn, so Nikos sent the block to be varnished as it was: half masterpiece, half sacrilege. He was apparently unable to tell the difference.

There was a fire that night by the pond, stacked high with dry foliage and logs. It crackled through the darkness, sending the scent of the funeral pyre through Kala's window. She dreamt of her father's soul flying up from the tower, of dark eyes watching hers through the flame, and of shadowed fingers clawing wetly beyond the wall.

Obedience made the house quiet. Nikos began visiting the Glauks tenants the next week to evaluate their yields, but his absence had little effect on the tense mood. Slaves walked silently and quickly down corridors, making themselves invisible at the edges of the family's life. The children no longer laughed, and no one smiled. Melissa even stopped staying late in Kala's chambers, anxious that one of the others might seek to curry favour with Nikos by telling him he could catch her there. The harvest festival couldn't come quickly enough.

One place in the house remained safe for Kala, the one room that Nikos still declined to enter: her father's library. She spent most mornings there, then slipped away to her pool in the afternoons. If she stayed out until after dark, Nikos would already be ensconced in his rooms by the time she returned. So far, she had managed to avoid seeing him at all.

She was engrossed in her morning reading – a particularly interesting scroll regarding the nature of the elements and their effect on the humours of man – when there was a knock. Leon poked his head around the library door.

'Do you mind if I join you?'

Sadly, she hadn't had as much luck avoiding Leon as she had his father.

'Go away,' she said.

'You can't stay in here alone all day.'

'I don't.'

'Oh?'

'No.'

'Then where do you go?'

She refused to be drawn further. If the library was the one place she was safe from Nikos, then the pool under the waterfall was the one place she was safe from everyone else. She wasn't about to surrender that secret.

She leaned back in her father's chair and returned her attention to her scroll.

When she had been small, her father had let her sit on his lap as he read to her. He would tell her stories of the tribes and their sacred animals, and she would stroke each of the carvings in turn as her father's voice coloured them into life.

Now she rolled her palm across the wolf that decorated one of the armrests, the wolf that had invaded her home.

'What are you reading?'

'A scroll. Go away, Leon.'

He sat down on the other side of the desk and leaned towards her.

'What did I do?' he asked.

She glared at him. 'You interrupted my reading.'

'No, I mean, what did I do? Why won't you talk to me?'

'We're talking now. Now go away.' She looked back down at the scroll.

'Just tell me what I've done wrong, and I'll do whatever I can to make it right.'

'There's nothing to make right,' she said, without looking up. 'Goodbye.'

'Will you just stop?' His tone was so despairing that she finally met his eye.

'Was it the dinner?' he asked. 'Do you think I tried to poison you or something? Was that what that leaf was all about? Because I wouldn't do that, Kala. Surely you know me well enough to know that. Or is this about the serving girl at the wedding? Because I told you nothing happened. Whatever it was, can you please just tell me?'

His pleading softened her resolve. 'You haven't done anything wrong,' she said, more gently than she intended. 'I just don't think it's a good idea for us to be friends.'

'Well, if I can't be your brother,' he said, 'and I can't be your friend, then I have to assume you want me to be something else entirely.'

She immediately regretted her sympathetic approach.

'Yes,' she said, 'I want you to be a distant acquaintance.'

'I don't believe you.'

'Then that's your problem, not mine.'

'Is it my father? Is it because of what happened last week?'

Blood swirling with metallic paint.

'It didn't help,' she said.

'I'm not him.'

She rolled up the scroll, resigned to abandoning her reading for the day. 'You may not be him, but you don't make any attempt to avoid his anger. Why would you provoke such a dangerous man? Why would you expect me to do the same? He doesn't want me spending time with you or your sister. He's made that very clear.'

'You're scared of him.'

'Of course I am! Aren't you?'

'I suppose I'm used to the fear. I've never known anything else.' His tone was too matter-of-fact for such a bleak statement. He couldn't hold her gaze. 'If I defy him, then at least Lali doesn't have to.'

They were both trapped here: by the cliffs, by his father.

Kala nearly broke then and told him about the Water, about the wall, and about her plans for the harvest festival, but something held her back. It wasn't that she mistrusted him exactly, it was more that she feared his impulsiveness. He was too reckless. He wouldn't stay out of Nikos's way until they could make their escape. He didn't feel the fear like she did.

'I'm sorry,' she said. 'But I don't know what you want from me.'

'Nothing more than you want to give.'

She laughed bitterly. 'You make it sound so easy.'

'And you deliberately complicate it. Why do you have to fight every little thing?'

'Because this,' she gestured between them, 'whatever you're trying to do here, it's pointless. Why can't you understand that? You treat everything like a game, as though everyone's time is yours to waste, because you don't care enough to take anything seriously.'

'That's not fair.'

'Well, I'm not playing, Leon.' She got to her feet and slid the scroll back onto its shelf before walking to the door. 'Go bother someone else.'

'Kala.'

But she was already gone, swinging the door shut behind her.

She stopped only to grab her cloak before leaving the house, heading towards her pool as fast as her leg would let her. Her blistered hand was well recovered now, the hardened skin providing a welcome barrier against the quick movement of her cane. She passed only a few people on her way across the river. At this hour, those who could afford to rest were driven inside by the sun.

She stowed her cane against the cliff and stopped by the water close to the falls. The vegetation in this spot was lush, the bank crowded with trees and grasses. There was also a profusion of what she now recognised as cow parsley, which made a fine hanger for her dress.

She was sitting naked at the edge of the sacred pool when she heard the sound. It was a soft skittering, as though someone had kicked a pebble over dirt. She spun around, but there was no sign of anyone on the path down from the temple, or on the precipice above. Her eyes swept the sacred grove and there, in the darkest section, she saw a shadow ducking behind a tree.

A shiver swam down her spine. The shadow had definitely been human. If the person to whom it belonged had a right to be here, then why had they hidden?

'I can hear you,' she sang softly.

There was a rustling from the same direction.

'You may as well come out,' she said, grabbing her dress to hold over her naked chest.

'I'm sorry.' The voice was familiar. 'I just–'

'You followed me.'

Leon stepped out from under the trees, his eyes turned away from her. 'I'm sorry. I just wanted to know where you were going.'

'After I made it very clear that I didn't want to tell you.'

'Yes.' She detected a faint blush, but he kept his eyes averted. The posture looked strange on him, a man who was better suited to looking problems in the face with a cocky smile.

She sighed. 'Let's just get this over with, shall we?'

'What?'

'You can look.'

He did, hesitantly. The dress covered her front, but he would be able to see the curve of her naked back, the spread of her thighs against the ledge and, of course, her twisted leg. His eyes focused on the point where her feet met the water, as though he couldn't bear to look at her deformity.

'I'm sorry,' he said again.

'You think you're the first person who's been curious?'

'So you just strip off for anyone, do you?'

She shrugged. 'I'd rather that people get the staring out of the way. I see them in the baths, trying to hide their glances. I'd rather acknowledge my deformity than watch people pretending they don't notice it whilst they look at me out of the corners of their eyes.'

He blinked in confusion, and his eyes moved to her face. 'Your leg?'

Clearly it hadn't been the thing about which he had been curious after all. But this wasn't the first time she'd been naked in front of him; there had been that time in the baths, although the steam there had afforded her some modesty.

She laughed. 'Do you really expect me to be ashamed of my nudity, when you were the one spying?'

He definitely blushed this time.

'Anyway,' she continued, 'haven't you heard? I'm cursed, and the curse is contagious. The only part of me people are ever interested in seeing is my leg, preferably from a distance.'

She balled up her dress and chucked it into the bushes, then slid into the freezing pool. The water wrapped around her body, pulling her under. When she surfaced again, she used the water to slick her hair back from her face.

'This is supposed to be a sacred place,' Leon said as he approached the water.

'It is.' She stared at him, daring him to point out that she was defiling it.

Instead, he said, 'You come here a lot?'

She held herself in place opposite him, treading water. 'Sometimes. Why? Are you going to tell the Archon?'

He sat down on the edge and took off his shoes. 'Are you going to tell my father?'

'This is my pool, Leon,' she said as he made to take off his tunic. 'This is the only place no one else comes. If you ruin it for me, I'll never forgive you.'

He paused. 'Does that mean you've forgiven me now?'

'I told you back at the house: you haven't done anything wrong.'

'Then stop punishing me.'

'You think this is punishment?'

'What else am I supposed to think? We were close, I thought, and then you just shut me out.'

'You're not entitled to my confidence.'

'No, but I'd value it.'

She looked at him for a moment, then folded. After all, he really had done nothing wrong. 'Fine,' she said, 'but keep your voice down, unless you want us both to be strung up by the acolytes.'

She swam out into the pool to give him some privacy as he stripped and lowered himself into the water.

'How deep is it?' he asked, clinging onto the rocky ledge.

'Deep enough that you have to dive to see the bottom. You can swim, right?'

'Yes,' he said, but he sounded uncertain.

'You can't swim.'

'Well, not much. A little. In the baths.'

'Which come up to your waist.'

'Yes.' His voice had acquired a panicky edge. 'That's about the depth I'm comfortable with.'

'If you're doing this to endear yourself to me, then it's not working.'

'I'm sorry,' he said. His fingers were turning white with the strength of his grip. 'I didn't think this through.'

'I get the feeling you have to say that regularly.'

He smiled. 'Sometimes.'

'Come on,' she said, swimming towards the edge of the waterfall. 'The water's shallower here.'

He looked up dubiously. 'Really?'

'Yes, really. There's a cavern behind the falls.'

'*Really*?'

'Oh, don't be such a baby. You can hold onto the side the whole way.'

She didn't wait for his reply before ducking into the cave. It was cool and dark, but enough of the midday light filtered through the water to illuminate it. She was about to go looking for Leon when he followed her, standing chest-high in the water.

'There are boulders under the surface,' she called to him, raising her voice above the thundering of the falls, 'so watch your step.'

He promptly swore, having stubbed his toe.

'I did warn you,' she said.

'I think I'll just stay here for now.' He sat down on the offending rock.

She smiled and drew her knees up to her chest, spinning her hands in the water so she balanced upright.

'What?' he said.

'Oh, nothing. It's just funny seeing you out of your element.'

'It's funny seeing you in yours.'

She looked at the light playing in the water, a kaleidoscope of light and colour. She never would have invited anyone here by choice, not even Melissa, but Leon's presence didn't seem to impinge on her enjoyment of it. In fact, it was satisfying to share the majesty of the place with someone.

He said something, but his voice was drowned out by the water. Rather than shouting, she gestured at him to wait while she found a rock next to his to perch on. It was only just tall enough to push the curves of her shoulders above the surface, so he had to lean down to her a little to make himself heard.

'I said I can see why you like it here.'

'It's peaceful.'

He looked unconvinced. 'In a loud way.'

'Peace isn't about volume. It's about being yourself.'

That seemed to confuse him. 'I'm always myself.'

'I know.'

'Are you not?'

'You really do have a remarkable lack of empathy. Everyone thinks my parents should have abandoned me when I got sick. My life isn't worth anything here. Can you imagine how that feels?'

'Not really.'

'Like I said: no empathy.'

'But you don't care about what people think, do you? You can do what you want. Isn't that liberating?'

She stared at him for a blink while irritation scratched under her skin. He didn't understand.

'I can do what I want as long as I don't bother anyone,' she said. 'You upset people all the time, and you're untouchable, but if I did that then one day I'd just disappear, like Daos's brother. I don't matter.'

He gave her a look. She should have seen it coming. 'You matter to me.'

'Don't start with that again, Leon.'

'Do you really think that what happened to you is all you are?'

'It doesn't matter what I think. That's the point. It's what everyone else thinks that's the problem.'

'Well, I don't care about your leg.'

She lifted her knee up out of the water, straightening it as far as she could so her foot rose into the air. 'Look at it, then. Tell me you don't care.'

He ran his eyes along its length, then his fingers, lingering at the soft skin behind her knee.

'I don't,' he said. 'It doesn't make you any less beautiful, Kala.'

Her skin felt too warm for the water to cool it. She rasped out an awkward laugh and drew her leg out of his grip, sliding it back beneath the water.

'The Lykos thought my name was a wonderful joke. Oh, how he laughed.' The heat blooming over her cheeks could have been rage, but it felt like shame.

'Well, he's even more of a monster than my father. He laughs at Lali too, if it makes you feel any better, and she's his own granddaughter.'

'What? Why?'

'*Eulalia*. You know.' The name meant 'sweet-voiced'.

'She doesn't sing, then?' Kala asked.

'Not very well, I'm afraid. Her name's a bit of a burden. Anyway, I don't expect he'll be laughing much longer.'

'Oh?'

'They're an ambitious tribe, and he's stubbornly refusing to die and cede the Dekocracy. He's also intensely unlikeable, as you saw. No one would miss him.'

Nikos was still in line, but he had a brother and sister, both older than him. If the Lykos were to die, assisted or otherwise, then his brother Anatolios would take the title. He'd probably been plotting for years.

'Lovely family you come from,' Kala said.

'They're powerful. When that's all you care about...' He shrugged.

'And you don't?'

'I never wanted that. My father says I have a responsibility, so I try to be as irresponsible as possible.' He grinned.

Kala rolled her eyes.

'I love it when you're exasperated with me,' he said. 'You flare your nostrils, you know. Yes, just like that.'

Without thinking, she splashed him. His grin widened in his dripping face.

'This game again?' he said, his voice low and playful.

'No, Leon, I didn't–'

The water went straight up her nose. She was laughing despite herself as she spluttered, all set for a rerun of their water fight at the baths, but he didn't give her a chance to retaliate. Instead, he wrapped his fingers around her wrists and pulled them against his chest, drawing her through the water towards him. Her face was inches away from his, both of her hands held in one of his. He reached up with the other and pushed a drip away from her cheek.

'Kala,' he whispered, and the name sounded different on his lips.

In a moment, those lips were on hers, kissing her as though he meant it. A bubble of emotion rose in her chest. It was almost desperation. Still, she let him bring her close. He loosed her hands and they found their way up his chest and around his neck, hanging her from his shoulders as their kisses chased them higher until they were standing, not floating, the water forgotten as their bodies pulled together.

But she had to push back.

'Leon,' she said against his lips. Her voice was full of regret as she dragged herself away.

'Don't,' he said.

But she was already gone. She swam from the cave, past the waterfall and out into the pool. He came after her, clutching the edge.

'Kala, please. If this isn't what you want–'

'It's not about what I want, though, is it?'

'And if it's what I want too?'

'You can do what you like, Leon, and suffer no consequences at all. You have the luxury of irresponsibility. Scandal only enhances your reputation, but it could have me turned out of my home, or worse. Did you even think about that?'

As she spoke she realised how irrelevant it was. She was leaving. Nothing could condemn her more than that in the eyes of the city. She'd been avoiding Leon for a reason, and she'd let herself forget what it was. She just had to get through the next couple of weeks without drawing attention to herself, then she could disappear with Melissa.

Lissa.

She headed for the side where she'd stashed her things.

'Kala, this isn't some sordid fling.'

'What else could it possibly be? Did you forget that you're promised at the Proaulia this year?' She pulled herself from the pool and shrugged her dress over her head. All she could think of was getting away, but she had nowhere left to hide. He'd found all her boltholes and broken them open.

He followed her out of the water, grabbing his tunic from amongst the weeds.

'The bargain with Elaphos won't hold, like Lali says. I can choose whomever I wish.'

'So, what, you see yourself as my redeemer? The charitable man prepared to take on Glauks's cripple?' She flung his grandfather's insult at him like spitting fat, and he recoiled from it.

'How can you ask that?'

'What does it matter?' she asked, slipping her feet unsteadily into her sandals. 'We both know you'll choose whomever your father wishes, or he'll disown you.'

'There are worse things.'

'He'll kill me. Is that worse?'

He started to protest, but she could see the hopelessness of it overwhelming him, like whitewash pouring down his face, wiping out his colour. It was for the best.

'Give up, Leon,' she said, then she snatched up her cane and started the long walk back to Glauks.

None of this mattered. In a fortnight, she'd be gone.

She diverted her course into the woods and hauled herself up into one of the elms until she had a clear view of the path back to the city. If she didn't give Leon a chance to overtake her, then he'd only catch her up on the walk.

It didn't take him long to go past. He was practically running, his hair dishevelled and his shoes untied. She watched his back as he raced towards the city, the muscles moving under the wet cloth, and remembered how they had felt under her hands.

She should never have let herself get drawn into this, not when there was so much at stake. A scandal was the last thing she needed. Right now, she needed to remain as she always had been: invisible.

After waiting a few moments to give Leon a head start, she slipped down from the branches and onto the soft earth of the forest floor. It must have rained in the night, because the ground was soggy underfoot and the leaf litter was stuck together in damp clumps. There were mushrooms here and there, scattered over fallen branches and decaying stumps. Since she had nothing else to do that afternoon, she decided she might as well gather some for Melissa. Maybe it was because she felt guilty, but she tried not to dwell on that as she looped her cloak into a makeshift basket, then spent a pleasant couple of hours foraging through the woods.

She was about to turn back when she heard someone call her name. Her first thought was that it must be Leon, still searching for her after he'd failed to find her on the road, but the voice didn't sound like his.

'There you are,' Neophytos said as he rounded the edge of a laurel. 'I thought it was you. No one else but Theodora has hair like that, and I just left her up at the temple.'

He wasn't an imposing man, but nonetheless his sudden appearance was discomfiting. Kala was otherwise alone in the forest, and she'd wandered a decent distance from the path as she followed the mushrooms into darker corners.

'Hello,' she said uncertainly. 'What are you doing here?'

He brandished a loose bag that was slung over his shoulder. Greenery poked out of its top. 'With the festival coming up,' he said, 'we're already drying herbs.'

'Ah.' She didn't know what else to say.

There was an awkward pause. Neophytos looked a little panicked. Conversation clearly didn't come easily to him.

'Are you heading back up to the temple?' Kala volunteered.

'Yes.' He brandished the bag again. 'All full up.'

'Well, I'm going back to the path now too. Shall we walk that way together?'

'Yes. I mean, yes, that would be good. Nice, I mean.'

Kala tried to get him talking as they made their way back through the forest, but starting a dialogue with him was like steering a skittish pony through a pack of wolves. He was so jumpy that he needed to start every sentence three times before he could finish it.

'Are you all right?' she asked eventually.

He nodded, his head jerking as though it were on a string. 'A little jittery these days, you know.'

'The escape?'

He looked around before answering, as though he expected hordes of eavesdroppers to be hiding behind every tree. 'Yes,' he whispered. 'It didn't seem real to start with, but now...'

'Are you coming with us?' Uncharitable though it was, she prayed that the answer would be 'no'. He was starting to seem like a liability.

'Yes,' he said, but as he spoke his face screwed up in a way that suggested he wasn't happy about it either. 'That wall, well, there's no other choice, is there? And I go where Theodora goes.'

Silence descended again, and Kala groped for a change of subject. She only half succeeded.

'Do you know how long the wall's been there?' she asked. 'It must have been hundreds of years.'

He snatched the lifeline. 'Not necessarily. The texts indicate that it was built at the first founding of the city, although of course we don't know when that was. It was brick first, you know. The stone is a relatively new addition.

Underneath all the marble, there's a lower wall or walls of clay brick.'

Kala knew all of this already. It was detailed in the Kleitos scroll she had read with her father so many times: the separation of the land, the building of the wall and the founding of the temple. But Neophytos seemed more comfortable surrounded by his scripture, so Kala just smiled and let him paraphrase the lore at her until they finally parted on the road.

It made her uneasy that he seemed to believe in those stories more than he believed in the truth they had seen behind the wall. He must have seen it himself, she supposed, although she hadn't wanted to risk his nerves by asking. Yet he spoke of the first deaths in the city and of the shades they had unleashed on the land as though they were real, as though he truly believed the wall had been put in place to separate the living from the dead.

They knew that was a lie. It seemed such an obvious falsehood that she couldn't now understand why she hadn't seen it before, but Neophytos still couldn't see it, not really. He knew it was true in his head, but not in his heart.

She had a growing suspicion that he was going to be a problem.

It was late afternoon by the time Kala crept back into the house. She was home earlier than she would normally choose to be, earlier than was safe for avoiding Nikos, but there was little point in bringing the mushrooms if she didn't arrive with them until after dinner.

She found Melissa alone in the kitchen.

'What's this?' Melissa asked as Kala emptied the contents of her cloak onto the table.

'I found them in the woods under the temple. There are hundreds of them.'

'Yes,' Melissa said, apparently unimpressed, 'because no one except the acolytes is supposed to go there. I thought we agreed that you'd be careful until we leave'

'It was fine. I had an escort.'

'Oh?' she asked as she sorted through the mushrooms. They all looked the same to Kala, but Melissa was something of an expert. It was the one thing she had chosen to learn from Eirene.

'I saw Neophytos,' Kala said.

That caught her attention.

'He's coming too,' she continued.

'I assumed he would. Didn't you?'

'But he's scared, Lissa. He was practically shaking with it. I'm not sure he'll be able to hold it together. And at the same time, it's almost as though he doesn't believe in the Water. He was quoting Kleitos at me–'

'A man after your own heart.' She laid a few of the choicest mushrooms aside.

'No, I mean he was quoting it like he still believes it, all that stuff about the wall and the dead. I just don't know if we can trust him.'

'Do we have a choice?'

A couple of the kitchen girls joined them then, so there was no more that could be said. In any case, there was little to discuss. Melissa was right: they had no choice.

Kala helped Melissa make a dish with mushrooms, garlic and sheep's cheese, her eyes on the pot at all times. This was how they prepared food now, watchfully and together if possible, but they ate alone. It was safer that way.

Kala took the meal to her room. It felt as though her chewing lasted forever, her eyes focussing into nothingness in the absence of any distraction.

A moon ago, she would have eaten with her father. If he were here now, they would have laughed at her sneaking into the sacred grove to steal the mushrooms. He would have told her to be more careful, but secret pride would have filled his eyes. Maybe he would have told her the truth, finally, about how he came to be in this place and how he planned to leave: everything he should have told her moons ago, when he first found Theodora. Why hadn't he trusted her with that?

Belatedly, Kala realised that she hadn't looked through his papers. If he really was intending to leave at the harvest festival, there should have been some trace of it in his notes. He had been scrupulous about keeping them, although they were not easily understood through his shorthand. Whether it was in his accounts, a list of provisions, or some sort of communication, there should be something.

Kala pushed away her meal as a more urgent thought hit her: he would have left a will. Not everyone in Kepos did, but her father would have. Never mind that the new Glauks would inherit the title, the house and the land, he still would have left a document to set out the distribution of his personal effects. There was his library of scrolls, for starters. Nothing would be left to Kala, since women couldn't own property in Kepos, but he would have wanted his rarer texts to go to those who would treasure them.

Grabbing her oil lamp, she made her way across the house to the library, her mind turning over every possible hiding place. The corridors were quiet now, the slaves tucked away in the kitchen eating their own dinner as the night drew in. She slipped into the library unseen and closed the door softly behind her.

The oil had burned down low by the time she finally located the correct scroll. The will hadn't been in her father's accounts, or in any of the more obvious books that discussed death and testamentary affairs, but was instead wrapped in a second version of Kleitos's history, a scroll Kala couldn't remember seeing before. It was at the back of one of the top shelves, tucked away beyond the scope of a casual search. It looked much older than the copy she had already taken from the library, the parchment curled and stiff with age. When she unrolled it over the desk, fragments flaked off the sides and littered the wood with dust.

The will was a single sheet, with a single sentence: *I leave my library and my daughter to the care of the Delphis,* and then her father's name beneath.

The sight of his handwriting crushed her, but she had to conclude that the will itself was irrelevant. The Delphis couldn't protect her, any more than he could protect her father's library from the tons of seawater that would rot his scrolls away. Khosrow must have known they were a legacy he would have to abandon.

She spread the scroll wide, trying not to cause more damage than was necessary, and slipped the will into the embrace of its coil. But as she was starting to roll it back together, a section of the text caught her eye.

The city had celebrated its hundredth year when the western sea began to breach its shore, she read. *The Archon had noted the passage of the tide and spake to the people, telling them to cease their slaughter of the dolphins and other fish, for the god of Delphis was angered that they plundered his larder. And so the people of the valley withdrew from civilisation and shut themselves away behind the fear of their gods. The boats of Kepos were no longer seen on the western sea and no longer visited the shores of the Plain, and a great wall was built as a barrier to the sea and dedicated to Ampheres, that he might guard the frontier.*

It was a passage she had never read before. She recognised phrases here and there, but the words had been rearranged to tell a very different story from the one she knew. Or rather, she realised, the words in the version she knew had been distorted from this original. The entire history of her world had been rewritten to erase the truth of the Water, and her father had found the proof.

This was the second scroll that would hold the last, coveted place in her travelling pack.

This was what she needed to save.

She was about to leave the library with it when she heard a noise out in the corridor. She couldn't let the scroll be discovered. It felt like a weight of delicate snowflakes in her hands, fragile but vital, a self-destructive burden that was her responsibility to protect. She stashed it back where she had found it and, as if she hoped to draw attention away from its hiding place, walked out of the room. She should have blown out her lamp and stayed in the library in the dark, but she didn't think of that until it was already too late.

There was another light at the end of the corridor. It was moving unsteadily, as though it were wobbling in a breeze, but there was no draught that Kala could feel. She took a step away from it, towards her own rooms, but the clack of her cane on the tiles betrayed her presence.

'Wait,' he called. The tone was authoritative, so despite the darkness she knew who it was. There was only one man in the house who would expect her obedience.

'Come here,' Nikos demanded, setting his lamp on a nearby ledge.

Kala didn't have much choice but to do as he asked. Her mind threw up unwanted memories: the blood on the stone, the screams, the cold determination on his face as he swung the axe down. The hemlock in her food.

She just had to survive for two more weeks.

'Still walking with the stick, then,' he said as she moved reluctantly towards him. His words sounded odd. When he slumped to lean against the doorframe to his room, she realised that he was drunk.

The Glauks, the paragon of frugal virtue, was drunk.

She kept her distance.

'Come a little closer,' he slurred.

She took a single step.

'Little more.'

She took another.

'Come on. Don't be shy.'

When she didn't move, he leaned forwards and grabbed her by the wrist. She muffled a shriek, imagining an axe in his other hand, but it was empty. Until, that was, he used it to pin her shoulder against the wall.

'You remind me of your mother, you know,' he drawled against her cheek. His breath was sour and stale, reeking of wine and hunger. 'When she was your age, she was so... fresh.'

His fingers slid down her chin, the rough pressure pulling her lips apart, and then his other hand was on her hip, bunching the material of her skirt in his fingers as he drew the hem higher and higher. She flailed with her cane, hoping to break his grip on the material, but he batted it out of her hand.

'I'm the Glauks now,' he said and pushed her hard against the wall so her skull cracked against the stone. His hand found the bare skin of her thigh while her head swam with the impact.

'Really, father?' Leon's voice echoed down the corridor, cool and unconcerned. 'If you have to fuck in the corridors, at least find a girl who isn't too lame to stand and take it.'

His words chilled the fearful sweat on Kala's skin.

'Go to the crows, child,' Nikos growled, but he kept his sights on Kala. 'At least then you'll be of use to someone.'

'Fine. I was only coming to tell you about the horse.'

Nikos looked over his shoulder. 'What horse?'

'The one I lost playing dice with Timon. Our best horse.' Leon smiled. 'Your horse.'

Nikos's hands slipped from Kala's body as he turned, and the sudden release crumpled her to the ground. She felt around on the tiles, searching for her cane.

Everything was still for a moment. Nikos was poised with his back to her, his fists clenching at his sides. She could see Leon beyond him, lounging nonchalantly against the opposite wall. His gaze flicked to her, just for a second, then he forced a grin at his father. It was hard and challenging, halfway between a leer and a grimace.

'You never ride him,' Leon said. 'So I took him out to feel the night air, ended up at the tavern, then when Timon asked me to wager my horse I forgot it was actually *your* horse I was betting. Easy mistake.'

The first blow sent Leon to his knees. The second knocked his face against the tiles, sending something rattling loose along the corridor. Nikos kicked him in the ribs, twice, then grabbed him by his collar and dragged him across the floor so roughly that Kala heard the ripping of the fabric. Leon stumbled into a crawl as his father threw him into his room, then the door slammed shut behind them.

A smear of blood darkened the width of the corridor. Kala wanted to cry, or go after him, or both, but instead she pulled herself to her feet and limped to her room with one shoulder against the wall, her cane lost in the shadows of the stone.

She and Leon were both the Glauks's property, and he would use them as he wished.

VI

πάνθηρ | Panther | Leopard

*The god gifted his sixth son the power to communicate with
the animals of the land.
The wolves heeded his call, the oxen herded at his word,
and all the beasts listened for his voice and obeyed.
The god named him Autochthon, for like the creatures he
ruled he was born of the earth.*

- Kleitos, On the Formation of Kepos

The Lykos died at the end of the harvest. They found him in
his alabaster bathtub, apparently dead from natural causes.
The physician suspected an excitement of his choleric
humour. Kala suspected murder.

It had been a week since the incident in the corridor, and
Leon was still too injured to leave the house. He spent only
hours at a time out of his rooms and passed none of them
with Kala. Nonetheless, he had managed to reclaim his
father's horse from Timon, if indeed he had ever lost it, and
some semblance of peace had returned to Glauks. The news
of his grandfather's demise put an end to that.

The cremation was as quick as that of Kala's father, so
quick that it was almost unseemly. Anatolios had already
taken his father's title. He also made it known that he would
be scouting for a bride at this year's Proaulia, since his
current wife had proved barren. With the ceremony less than
a fortnight away, the cremation would be a courting ground,
just as her father's had been. It turned Kala's stomach,
particularly since Eulalia was to be presented as the prize of
Glauks, Anatolios's own niece.

Kala, of course, was left at home with Leon. It came as
some relief; she couldn't face the reek of another pyre.

Minutes after the rest of the family had left for the cremation, Melissa found Kala in the library. The second Kleitos scroll was already safe in her clothes chest with the first, but she still spent her mornings in the company of her father's books.

'Leon wants to see you.'

'What? Why?' Kala asked, but Melissa didn't know.

Kala hadn't spoken to him since the day at the waterfall, the same day his father had beaten him to a pulp. Part of her knew it would be better if he simply lost interest. That part of her had hoped never to speak to him again. She didn't want to tell him that in just a few days she'd be leaving Kepos, and leaving him behind.

She found him reclining on a couch in his rooms.

'I heard you got the horse back,' she said, taking the couch next to his.

He grinned through the bruises. One of his teeth was missing, at the top and to the side. She hadn't noticed, because she hadn't seen him smile since that day.

'I'm actually not as bad at gambling as you'd think.' His voice was weak and gritty, and there were marks around his throat, as though Nikos had throttled his own son. No wonder he was making Leon stay home.

'I'm sorry I didn't try to help,' she whispered.

He looked outraged. 'Of course you didn't. There's no point in my being heroic if you're just going to throw yourself back to the monster, is there? You were supposed to run.'

'He could have killed you.'

'He *would* have killed you.' His words trailed into a whisper. He made to lean closer, struggling to sit up, but she waved him down and went to sit next to him instead.

'Did he hurt you?' he whispered.

'No.'

'He had his hands on you.'

'You got there in time.'

His relief was physical, uncurling his shoulders and releasing the tendons in his neck. 'I thought…'

She shook her head, denying the tears she wanted to shed. 'You shouldn't care.'

'Why not?'

She could give him at least one good reason, but it wasn't just her secret to share. She couldn't decide to trust him with it, not when that meant deciding on behalf of Melissa, Theodora and Neophytos too.

'What did you want?' she asked.

'Why did you come?'

The apparent non-sequitur pushed her off balance. 'What?'

'You didn't have to. You came because you wanted to see me.' The grin was back.

'I thought I owed you a visit, at least.'

'At least? So you think you owe me more? Tell me: what else have I earned with my gallant behaviour?'

'Leon…' Her tone was discouraging, but she wished she had his resilience. Still making jokes, even through his broken teeth.

'Can I expect hymns in my honour?' he asked. 'Or would you like me to pose for a portrait? My ribs are all bound up, but from the waist down I'll be a perfect model.'

He was such an unlikely subject, cut and beaten, that she couldn't help but laugh, and then she was crying with the pity of it, her nose running as all the horror hit home.

'It's all right,' he whispered, pulling her into his arms and leaning back, so they both lay along the couch, her head pillowed on his chest. 'Just mind the ribs.'

He held her close, wrapping her in the warmth of him. He smelled of spice and herbs, probably from the tinctures applied to his breaks and bruises, and it sank soothingly into her lungs.

'I'm sorry,' she murmured. 'And thank you.'

'You should come to visit more often.'

'I don't think that's a good idea.' She shouldn't be in his arms right now. She shouldn't be enjoying the feeling of his body against hers, the smell of his skin, the taste of his breath.

He gently lifted her chin so she was looking into his eyes. 'I'm not my father, Kala.'

'Is that what it was all about? You think you have to prove that?'

'I could kill him,' he whispered.

She jerked away. 'Leon, no. If you wanted to turn into him, then that's a good way to start.'

'But then we could do what we wanted.' He pushed a lock of hair away from her face. Despite knowing it was a bad idea, she leaned into his hand for a weak second.

'That's not how Kepos works, is it?' She got to her feet awkwardly, wrangling her cane, and made to leave. 'You said it yourself: you don't get to choose.'

'Don't go.' There was no hope in his expression.

'I don't have any choice.'

By breakfast the next morning, the old Lykos was dust.

Eulalia didn't like to sit in the courtyard these days, so she and Kala ate in the garden instead. Melissa had made them sesame seed pancakes, drizzled with honey. The syrup melted on the hot cakes, pooling in Kala's bowl so liberally that it was difficult to soak it all up. By the time she had finished, her hands were sticky with sugary residue. Had she been in polite company then she might have restrained herself from licking it off so exuberantly, but Lali was family now.

'So,' Kala said as she sucked her fingers clean, 'how did it go?'

'Awful. Ariston was there, and so was Timon. Father spoke to the Elaphos, but I don't think any decisions were made. And then there's my uncle, so who knows what will happen at the Proaulia?'

'He wouldn't marry his own niece, surely?'

Eulalia shrugged. 'It happens, more in Tauros and Lykos than elsewhere.'

'Really?'

'They're precious about their bloodlines.'

Kala pushed her plate away. 'Gods, I'm so sorry.'

'There's time yet. Anything could happen.'

Either way, Kala wouldn't be there to see it. 'Was my mother all right?'

'Fine, I think. Why?'

'You don't think she's been acting a little strangely?'

'Her husband just died. I wouldn't say she's been acting any more strangely than you.'

'How have I been acting strangely?'

'You both keep to your rooms, or you go off on your own to gods know where. You spend a lot of time giving lingering looks to pieces of furniture. It's only to be expected. You're both a little haunted.'

Kala turned the empty plate between her hands. 'I miss him,' she said.

'I miss my mother.'

Kala smiled a little. 'Leon says the same.'

As though their words had summoned him, he came out to join them.

'It was cholera,' Eulalia was saying, 'a few months ago.'

'It wasn't cholera,' Leon said. 'It was him.'

He sat on the bench next to Kala. He was close, so close that his leg touched hers.

'You don't know that,' said Eulalia.

'I do. She was Tauros, but she had no influence in her tribe. That's all he cares about.'

Hoofbeats clattered down the street at the side of the house and the garden gate was flung open. They turned to watch as a messenger scrambled through, half-falling in his haste to deliver his missive. Eulalia got to her feet.

'Sosias?' she said.

The messenger hesitated on his way to the courtyard. 'Miss Eulalia.'

'What is it?'

But they weren't the only ones whose attention had been drawn by the commotion. Several of the slaves came out into the garden, followed by Nikos himself.

'What's this racket?' he asked. For a man inclined to amputate limbs when slaves displeased him, his reaction was remarkably calm.

'Glauks, Sir,' Sosias said, 'I regret to inform you that your brother is dead.'

'Anatolios is dead?' He raised his eyebrows theatrically. 'How?'

'He seemed to overindulge in his cups last night, Sir. Went to bed fine, slurring and wobbling a bit, but never woke up.'

The symptoms sounded coldly familiar to Kala.

Perhaps it had been the wine. But it might also have been hemlock, the same herb that had been used in the attempt to poison Kala.

She looked at Nikos. She hadn't meant to let her eyes stray in his direction, but once they did he caught them in his gaze until she couldn't look away. He had done this, she knew in that moment, and now he knew that she had worked it out.

His eyes narrowed for a second in calculation, but then he laughed once, sharply, like a dog. Or a wolf.

There was nothing anyone could do to stop him, least of all the little cripple of Glauks.

'Poor old Anatolios,' he said. 'He never could hold his drink. Arrange the cremation immediately, and then it seems I have a decision to make. You may as well stay here this time, Eulalia.'

With that, he turned and walked back into the house. The messenger hurried out of the garden the way he had come, and the slaves did the same shortly afterwards. The three of them were left alone at their table.

'Well,' Leon said, 'I think that's proved my point.'

'It's something of a relief, if I'm honest,' said Eulalia, but she looked shaken.

Kala reached across the table and took her hand.

'So, what happens now?'

'More fuel for the pyre,' said Leon.

Eulalia flicked water at him from her cup. 'That's not a very nice way to talk about Uncle Anatolios.'

'Well, he wasn't a very nice person.'

'I meant,' Kala said, raising her voice over the siblings, 'what happens to Lykos?'

'Our aunt isn't married,' Eulalia said, 'so unless she decides to take a husband, I suppose Father becomes the Lykos, but he can't be the Lykos and the Glauks…'

'Hence the decision,' Kala finished.

'Exactly,' said Leon. 'Frankly, if she has any sense then old Aunt Eumelia will choose to remain single to the end of her days. She'd only make herself a target.'

'Then there's no decision to make,' Kala said. 'Who would choose Glauks over the riches of Lykos?'

'I would,' Leon said softly. 'Any day.' He reached under the table and took her hand.

'Your father doesn't see it like you do.'

'No.'

'Will you and your mother come with us?' Eulalia asked.

Only one person knew the answer to that question. Nikos would decree as he wished. Either way, she didn't care. Whatever he wanted, he couldn't control her anymore. She would be gone in just a few days, free, and after that none of this would matter. It didn't matter now, but the shape of Leon's hand wrapped around her own had made her forget that.

She pulled loose and, with a tight smile, left the siblings to plan their return.

Once their parents had left for the cremation, Eulalia came to Kala in her rooms. She'd realised that the return to Lykos meant her betrothal to Timon was back on. Ariston was slipping through her fingers.

She wept in Kala's lap for an hour.

Looking for something to distract her, Kala suggested that they go for a ride. Leon had a beautiful piebald stallion, far too fast and flighty for Kala, but perfect for Eulalia. With Leon still too injured to ride, they decided his horse could do with the exercise.

They left within the hour, heading out across the city and into the meadows to the east.

'Have you ever been to the sea?' Kala asked.

'No. I've never been beyond the temple.'

'Really?'

'I'm too delicate, apparently.' Eulalia snorted, and her horse mimicked the sound, to their great delight.

'I see he's got Leon's sense of humour.'

'And decorum.' Eulalia smiled. The motion of the canter had shaken her hair from its pins, and the curls bounced as she rode. Kala had never seen her so unbound.

'I'm not really supposed to leave the house on my own,' she continued. 'There's a reason I don't have a horse.'

'Well, you're not on your own.'

'I don't think you count. Not in my father's eyes.'

'Well, that's certainly true,' Kala said, but then she remembered the poison, and his hand on the naked skin of her thigh. He had looked at her then.

'Anyway,' she continued quickly, quashing the memory, 'it doesn't matter because he'll never know. So, do you want to go to the sea today?'

The light in Eulalia's eyes made a response unnecessary.

They raced to the river and watered the horses, preparing for the long ride. Kala would feel bruised tomorrow, but it was worth it for one last glimpse of the eastern sea, for one last afternoon with Eulalia. It was a good thing that their parents would be drinking into the night at the house of Lykos, because it would take them until dark to get to the coast and back.

But as they made to set off again, Kala's attention was caught by a wide column of smoke rising from the direction of the temple.

'Look,' she said, pointing.

Eulalia stared for a few seconds. 'Is that coming from the grove? Or from the temple storehouses?'

The storehouses sat at the foot of the temple outcropping, close to the woods. If the flames spread to the trees, the whole sacred grove could be lost.

Kala hesitated for only a second before kicking Hypatia into action, fording the river in a few easy strides.

'Come on,' she called over her shoulder. Eulalia followed close behind.

By the time they reached the woods, the acrid taste of smoke had filled the air. They galloped out from between the trees to see that one of the warehouses was aflame. Fire was already licking through the roof beams and along the outer sides of the walls. Acolytes were carrying buckets of water from the pool, but it was too late. The dry wood was going up as though it were drenched in oil. All they could do was soak the surrounding buildings and trees with water in the hope of saving them. There was quite a crowd; they had clearly run out of receptacles to fill.

Kala spotted Straton standing close by, anxiously watching the bucket chain. They left the horses by the pool and made their way towards him.

'Hierophant,' Kala greeted him. 'Is there anything to be done?'

'Sadly not.' He clasped the folds of his robe in his fist, scrunching the material between his fingers. 'We're trying to save one of the acolytes who was caught in the blaze, but…'

It was obvious that no one was walking out of that fire. A sick premonition stole over Kala.

'Which acolyte?' she asked, praying that Theodora's plans hadn't been discovered. She was the only one who knew the way out of the valley.

'A young man, very promising. Very sad. A young acolyte named Neophytos.'

Something must have shown on Kala's face, because he asked, 'You knew him?'

'Vaguely.' Her mouth was so dry that she struggled to get the words out. The back of her tongue tingled with the promise of nausea. 'We had a discussion once about Kleitos.'

Eulalia slipped her hand into Kala's. She smiled her thanks for the support, but felt like a fraud for accepting it. Horrible though it was, her anguish was not over his death, but rather over what it might mean for her escape.

'You spoke about Kleitos?' the Hierophant asked, his attention sharpening.

'Yes. Particularly the building of the wall, and what it was designed to separate us from.'

Kala watched his hands move faster as she spoke: crumple, release. The man was nervous, but in the circumstances that was hardly surprising.

'An important text,' he said.

'What happened?' Eulalia asked. 'How did the acolyte become trapped?'

'One of the dogs was in the loft. The boy went in after him, but the fire took hold so quickly.'

It seemed out of character for the anxious acolyte, but perhaps he'd been more complicated than she'd realised. The guilty weight in her stomach increased.

'Well, you should get home,' the Hierophant said. 'There's nothing you can do here.'

Kala looked along the line of faces until she found the one she was looking for: Theodora. She was on the ground, her knees pressed into the stones and her hands scratching at her cheeks. She looked so small.

They found they didn't have the appetite for a long ride after that, so they turned around and made their way back to the city. Eulalia would never see the rolling hills of the valley beyond the temple, the huts of the fishermen, or the sandy shores of the eastern sea.

Soon it would all be gone.

Kala slept in Melissa's arms that night. She needed the comfort. First her attempted poisoning, then Neophytos's death; it seemed like too much of a coincidence to ignore. They were increasingly convinced that someone knew of their plan, so the safest thing they could do was stay together.

Kala expected some sort of announcement the following day. She waited for Nikos to gather the household together, but she waited in vain. In the meantime, she passed her morning in the library comparing the two Kleitos scrolls and relearning everything she thought she had known.

The old god had made Kepos and split its dominion between his ten sons, who became the gods of the valley; that much remained the same. Kala already knew of the discrepancies in the reasons for building the wall, and much of the subsequent text was similar to the story she knew. The account of the construction of the wall, the annual additions to it and its consecration were all familiar too. What differed most substantially was the tone, twisted in the rewriting.

Where the Kleitos she knew had praised the beauty of the valley, respected the power of the Dekocrats and revered the priesthood, this new Kleitos was all bewilderment and contempt. It spoke of a backward civilisation that had been walled away from the world to preserve the wealth of greedy men. It spoke of squabbling aristocrats, brutal in the pursuit of power that was meaningless beyond the anthill of the city. It spoke of a culture mired in mediocrity, unable to grow as it was unable to learn.

Every word resonated.

It broke Kala's heart and hardened her resolve. They needed to leave; not just her and Melissa, but everyone. The priesthood could drown in their hubris for all she cared, but shouldn't the rest of the city be told? What about Eulalia? What about Leon?

The problem was they wouldn't believe her, and she had no authority to convince them.

There was a knock at the library door and Eulalia walked in, fresh from the baths. She hesitated on the threshold, and that was the moment when Kala knew the decision had been made. Her stomach dropped as she got to her feet.

'So?' she asked.

'We're leaving tonight.' She didn't meet Kala's eye.

'We?'

'Father, me, Leon, your mother. Most of the house slaves.'

'Not me?'

Eulalia looked up at her. 'No.'

So they were leaving her behind. She had expected it. Nikos would have to adopt Kala to take her to Lykos, and the thought of being his daughter was as laughable as it was disturbing.

'Melissa?' Kala asked.

'She stays. I badmouthed her to make sure of it. I hope she won't mind.'

'Well, at least I won't be alone. Who else?'

'Daos, and the older woman who thinks she's in charge—'

'Hagne,' Kala supplied.

'Yes, her, and the twins.'

'Wise to leave Daos behind.' He would never serve Nikos.

Other than Daos and Melissa, the new Lykos was taking every able-bodied slave with him. He was stripping the house of valuables, Kala realised. He'd leave her with nothing.

'I'm so sorry,' Eulalia said, tears starting down her cheeks as she spoke.

'Don't be,' Kala replied. 'This is probably what I would have chosen anyway, if it had been my choice. Except I wouldn't have chosen to leave my mother. Promise me you'll look after her.'

'I'm not sure there's much I can do.'

'I know I have no right to ask. I just... I haven't been a very good daughter to her. I thought you might do better.'

'I'll do my best,' Eulalia said, her tone gentle, 'but she chose this. She chose him, Kala. It's not like me and Timon. She could have chosen whomever she wanted. He's what she wants.'

Kala didn't want to believe it. She couldn't believe that her mother would ever choose a man like Nikos.

'She's not herself.'

'Well, I don't know about that. Anyway, her slave's coming with us–'

'Agathe,' Kala said impatiently.

'Yes, Agathe. I'll keep an eye on her, all right? But Kala, Father's the Lykos now. Not the son of the Lykos, or the Glauks, but the Lykos. If something goes wrong, what can I do?'

It was a fair question.

'Just be a friend to her, please,' Kala said. 'For my sake.'

Eulalia smiled uncomfortably, as though she regretted the burden, but she accepted it nonetheless. 'I will,' she said. 'I promise, by your god and mine.'

'Thank you.'

'Will you be all right?'

'I'll be fine,' Kala said, sitting down in her father's chair. She stroked the armrests, feeling the history in its cuts and curves. She'd have to say goodbye soon, and she wanted to remember it all.

'I'm the last of the line, Lali,' she continued. 'Glauks is mine.'

'It'll be your husband's,' Eulalia pointed out.

She was right, of course. The title and ownership of Glauks would be in limbo until Kala, as the sole Glauks heir, took a husband.

'If I go to the Proaulia at all,' Kala whispered.

'What do you mean? Of course you'll go to the Proaulia. The Dekocracy won't let you do anything else.'

Kala hovered on the edge of the truth, on the verge of telling Eulalia everything, but then she remembered Neophytos. Theodora had cared for him, had confided in him, and now he was dead.

Her secrets were dangerous to share.

'Yes,' Kala said eventually, 'I'll be there.'

'And you'll have your pick of them all,' Eulalia said, with gentle envy in her tone.

Of course, Eulalia had no choice at all; her father would see to that. Timon would marry Eulalia and Leon would marry Sophia, just as Nikos had always planned.

But if Kala were staying, she would have had no one to dictate her choice. If she were staying, then the prize of the title of Glauks would have made her valuable despite her twisted leg. She might have had whomever she wished, except the one who was promised to another.

'What a prize I shall be,' she murmured.

But she wouldn't have to see the Proaulia. She wouldn't have to line up in the temple while the suitors assessed her against their other prey. She wouldn't have to see the marriages at the wall, Sophia and Leon bound hand to hand.

It brought her some comfort to know that, as the nearest thing to an heir that Charis would have left, Leon would become the new Glauks when she was gone. He'd get to come back, to leave Lykos, just as he wished. He'd start his new family with Sophia here, for as long as the wall held. For his sake, she hoped Theodora was wrong about the Water.

But it wasn't her concern. This wasn't her city anymore. In a couple of days, she'd be free of the valley forever.

While the new Lykos piled the wealth of Glauks into his carts, Kala made her own preparations. She packed her bag with the two Kleitos scrolls, a couple of bladders of watered wine and as much barley bread as would fit. Other than that, she would take only her cloak, her cane and her Lissa.

Then there was nothing to do but sit in the courtyard as her home was emptied of its treasures. Slaves carried furniture, fabrics, platters, sculpture and papers from the house, but they didn't touch the library. For someone so ruthlessly practical, Nikos certainly seemed superstitious about the room. Maybe he just didn't care for books.

When the slaves had finished in her wing of the house, it was barer than she could ever remember it being. They'd left behind everything she needed, certainly enough to see her through the next couple of days, but it felt empty. Hall tables and tapestries were gone, leaving the corridors echoing with the steps of the deserting family. Familiar sculptures were gone from the courtyard, and the dining rooms were bereft of their painted wares. Her home had not just been invaded; now it had been looted too.

She wanted to run away to the waterfall so she wouldn't have to see it, but that felt cowardly. This tribe was hers now, for the next two days anyway. She had a responsibility to witness this. If her presence might even slightly deter the Lykos's rapacious urges, then it was worth staying, so she sat in the courtyard and watched as her home was gutted.

Clouds made the day dark and cold. Melissa fetched Kala's cloak, but she didn't linger, as though she knew that it made Kala feel more helpless to watch the pillaging with an audience.

She should be doing something, but there was nothing to be done. She was a woman; she owned nothing. She had no claim to this property.

She wrapped the cloak tightly around herself, tucking the edges under her arms to keep it snug. When the rain began to fall, she moved to sit under the colonnade and watched from there as it splashed into the central pool. It was heavy, dropping on the water with loud slaps that reminded Kala of the day she had found her father dead, her mother in the courtyard with the bloody rag in her hand.

Slap, splash, slap.

That had been what had broken her mother's mind. She'd clawed at him, bloodied and ripped her nails as she tried to drag his mouth open. Kala couldn't imagine it.

She didn't notice Leon until he took a seat beside her.

'I'll miss you,' he said.

'I'll miss my father's dining couch.' She watched it being carried from the house. 'The rain will ruin the upholstery.'

'Then at least my father won't get to enjoy it.'

'I suppose not.'

They sat spectating as the slaves finished moving the last of the spoils and said their goodbyes. They'd all grown up in this house, families and friends, and now they were being separated. It didn't seem fair.

'That's it, then,' Kala said. 'I'd better say farewell to Mother.'

Leon looked at his hands. 'She's already gone. He sent her and Eulalia ahead.'

'What? When?'

'Last watch.'

'They didn't say.'

'I don't think they were given the opportunity. It's just you and me now. Father rode off a moment ago.'

It didn't feel real.

Seeing the house picked apart like carrion left her feeling as empty as its walls. Her old life didn't exist anymore. There was little here for her now, and soon that would be washed away too, if Theodora were to be believed.

'I need to get going,' Leon said. 'I don't want to leave Lali alone.'

'No, of course, you must go.' Kala felt dazed, as though she were a long distance from herself.

'I'll miss you,' he said again, but as though he meant something else by it. Whatever he was trying to impart, Kala couldn't decipher it.

'I'll see you at the festival, the day after tomorrow,' she said.

'And you'll be at the Proaulia after that, yes?'

She wouldn't. She'd be miles away, she hoped, but she looked him in the eye and lied.

'Yes, I will.'

Leon's brow creased. 'You're doing it again, pushing me away. What is it you're not telling me, Kala?'

'You're the one leaving,' she said.

He took her hand in his. 'I don't want to go.'

'You have to.'

'But I'll see you at the Proaulia?'

His insistence, and his uncanny intuition, made her irritable. 'I said yes, didn't I?'

'You did,' he said, but it was clear he wasn't entirely satisfied. 'Glauks is in your gift now,' he continued. 'Choose better than your mother did.'

'I will,' she said, and this time it was the truth.

She had chosen him. When she left, they would make Leon the Glauks, and for as long as the wall held he'd be a true successor to her father. He'd look after her home, her lands and her people. He'd be kind like her father was, and not cruel like his own. If only he could keep himself away from the taverns, he might be a half-decent Dekocrat.

He stood to take his leave.

'Goodbye, brother,' she said as she used her cane to lever herself to her feet.

He smiled unhappily. 'I'm not your brother, Kala.'

'Not anymore, I suppose.'

'No,' he said, stepping closer, 'you were right. I never was.'

He brushed a kiss across her cheek, then with a last rueful smile he turned and made his way towards the stables, towards his beautiful piebald stallion, and back to Lykos.

Not much had changed in Kala's own rooms, because there hadn't been much worth taking. A few of the prettier ornaments had gone, but most of her things were right where she had left them. She probably had Melissa to thank for that.

With Nikos gone, Melissa moved her paltry belongings into Kala's rooms. It would only be for two nights, but Kala needed her close.

'You didn't tell him?' Melissa asked as they sat on the bed together, Melissa cross-legged as she brushed Kala's hair.

'No,' Kala said.

'He could come with us. They could both come with us.'

'It's too dangerous to tell them, Lissa. If everything goes well, maybe we could come back for them. Maybe we could come back for all of them, if the valley really is going to flood.'

'You still don't believe it.' She jerked through a particularly tough tangle, dragging Kala's head back. Kala turned to face her and took the comb from her hands.

'You've seen the wall,' Kala said. 'You've seen how massive it is. I suppose I just don't see it falling down that easily.'

Melissa held Kala's wrist with one hand and prised the comb from her fingers with the other, then used Kala's shoulder to spin her back around so she could reach her hair again.

'I'll be gentler,' she promised.

'I could just cut it all off when we leave,' Kala said. 'I could cut it short like a boy and not have to worry about braids or hairpins ever again.'

'I'm sure they have them in the Plain too.'

'Maybe we should just stay here then. We might drown, but at least if I were dead I wouldn't have to endure this scalp torture anymore.'

'I love your hair,' Melissa said, and as she spoke she gathered a handful of it and held it to her lips. 'So dark and thick. It slips through my fingers like a waterfall.'

Kala snorted. 'You could have fooled me. It seems to stick and tangle in your fingers like it's covered in honey.'

'Only because you don't sit still.'

Melissa brushed in silence for a few minutes, each of them afraid to voice their own anxieties about the trip. Kala broke first.

'Do you think we'll make it?' she asked.

'It'll be a hard journey. I've packed as much rope as I could find. We'll just have to hope it's enough to get us to the top.'

'No, I mean do you think we'll make it to the harvest festival? We're one companion down, and someone's already tried to kill me once.'

'But that was Nikos, you said yourself, and he has no reason to kill you now. He used the hemlock on his brother, so he must have been the one who slipped it into your food.'

'Hemlock isn't hard to find. And anyway, who says he has no reason to kill me?'

Melissa stopped combing.

'What do you mean?' she asked. Her face was pale.

Kala sighed, wishing she'd not said anything. They had enough to be worried about without Kala heaping more on her.

'Who becomes Glauks if I die before I marry?'

'Well,' Melissa said, 'the line would go back to your mother. So I suppose it would be Leon, as her eldest...' She trailed off as the truth hit her.

'Killing me would make Nikos's son the Glauks.'

It was the simplest way for Nikos to control both tribes. Maybe that had been the plan all along. Maybe he had planned for Kala to die before Anatolios, so Leon would have inherited today, when Nikos moved back to Lykos.

'But couldn't he just make you marry Leon?' Melissa asked. 'Why wouldn't he just wait until the Proaulia? Why kill you?'

'And have his son married to a cripple? Better to make him Glauks and let him have his choice of bride.'

Melissa's voice was soft as she replied, 'You are his choice, Kala.'

Kala laughed, but her tone was brittle at the corners. She wanted it to be true, but she was suspended between two worlds: Kepos and the Plain. In neither was it possible that she would marry Leon. He could only be Glauks if she were no longer here.

'Nikos will marry Leon off to Sophia, just like he and the Elaphos had planned. I wouldn't be surprised if he intended to kill me before then, just to lock Leon in as the Glauks before the Proaulia.'

'Well, good thing we'll be gone before he gets the chance.'

But Kala was still uneasy. Nikos seemed like the most rational agent for the attempt on her life, particularly given the use of hemlock. But if he really was the one who had tried to poison her, then why hadn't he tried again? He'd had ample opportunity, not least on that drunken night in the corridor, so why had there been no second attempt? What had changed?

The hemlock had been put in her food in the frantic days after the wedding, when the household was still in turmoil. In the calmer weeks that followed, when the Lykos presence had been a constant in the house, there had been no recurrence.

Now that she was on her own, she couldn't help but feel that she was a bigger target. If the poisoner was anyone other than Nikos, her new solitude might provide just the opening he was waiting for.

The next morning, Melissa declared that they were in need of a distraction. She suggested that they go to the quarry to fetch another marble block, so they could decorate it on behalf of the new Glauks family. Which was just Kala, now.

Kala saw no reason to refuse. A distraction would be welcome, especially since her anxiety had prevented her from getting much sleep the night before. In the end, Melissa had moved to the couch so she could have some respite from Kala's restlessness, so Kala owed her something in return.

She hadn't left the city since the day she and Eulalia had seen the temple warehouse burn. It had only been the day before yesterday. She dragged her eyes away from the temple on the northern cliff as they travelled south and east. They were travelling in a smaller cart this time, the larger one having caught Nikos's eye, but with only one block to collect it was more than ample. One of the field slaves was with them, as was Daos.

Kala had tried to tell him to stay at home, that he didn't need to return to the scene of his brother's accident, but he'd just given her a strange look and said that he passed through the courtyard every day. The quarry could be no worse than the haunted corners of what had once been their home.

When they arrived, everything was in a much more orderly state than it had been during their last visit. While the air was still white with dust, it wasn't so dense as to block Kala's view of the quarrying operations. The scope of it, the height and depth of the cuts scored into the landscape, was greater than Kala remembered from her visits as a child.

Melissa borrowed Hypatia so she could make a quick visit to Eirene while Kala watched the slaves loading up the block. It was only after Melissa had left that Kala realised she should have gone with her, but she returned within the hour, so no harm was done.

'We need to speak,' she said to Kala as she slipped down from Hypatia's back.

She must have heard something from Eirene. From the look on Melissa's face, the news was not good. Her lips were pinched with worry in a way that filled Kala with trepidation.

'Here?' she asked.

'Back at the house.'

The long ride to Kepos felt like days rather than hours as Kala's imagination buzzed with speculation. She couldn't help but fixate on the worst possibilities. There was one in particular that plagued her: had something happened to Theodora?

When they finally got back to the house, it took an age for the slaves to carry the marble block into the courtyard and mix the paints. Entire watches had passed before she and Melissa were alone, by which time the tension had wound itself into a throbbing mass at the base of Kala's skull.

'So?' she whispered to Melissa.

They were sitting on the ground on opposite sides of the stone, fingers dripping with colour as they smeared it across the porous surface. Their shapes were nothing like as graceful as Eulalia's, and Kala had a particularly terrible eye for colour, but at least they weren't spattered with blood. There was something redemptive in this small act, and Kala was grateful to Melissa for it, even if her current reticence was giving her a headache.

'There's news from the temple,' Melissa said.

Kala made an impatient gesture that flicked mismatched colours onto the tiles. She didn't care.

'They sent the slaves in when the warehouse had cooled,' Melissa said. 'They wanted to see if anything could be saved, but of course none of it could. It was the poorest warehouse. Did you know?'

'They didn't keep anything in it?'

'They did, just nothing valuable. Broken tools, things that might be useful for fixing other things. Nothing important. The warehouse was practically falling down even before the fire.'

'And the dog?'

'In the loft, with a rope around its neck. They found a knot on the rafters. It was tethered there.'

'Deliberately?'

'That's what they told Eirene.' Melissa looked unsure, but Kala knew she wouldn't have said anything at all if she didn't think the source was reliable. Eirene was an informer, not an idle gossip.

'And Neophytos?' Kala asked.

'They dragged his body out.' Melissa hesitated, apparently unwilling to go on.

'What?'

'There was an arrow in his back. The shaft was burned down by the fire, but there was enough of it left in the wound to tell.'

Neophytos had been murdered.

'Gods,' Kala said. 'Whoever did it must have hoped the body would be burned away. Did anyone see?'

'Plenty of people saw him go in. No one saw the arrow fly. Too much smoke, too much panic.'

There was only one reason Kala could imagine that someone would kill Neophytos, and that was because of the escape. If they knew about Neophytos, then doubtless they also knew about Theodora, but did they know about her and Melissa too?

'We're in trouble, aren't we?' Kala said.

'It's just one more day.'

'Then I need you by my side for every second of it. We don't separate, we don't drop our guard for a second.'

So they planned as they painted, talking through each step. The harvest festival would start with Kala, as the representative of Glauks, escorting all the stones of the Glauks tribe to the wall in the opening procession. It wouldn't just be the stone they were painting today, but every stone of every tenant and non-tenant family in the tribe. There would be dozens of carts in their convoy alone.

After her would come Ophis and Onos, then all the other tribes in reverse order until they reached Lykos and Tauros. Finally, the Archon would process with the stones painted by the acolytes themselves, one from each of them.

By then, all the acolytes would be at the wall and the temple would be empty, but Kala wouldn't be able to leave. Not until after the festival itself.

'That'll be the easiest part of the day,' Kala said. 'After the Hierophants have led the sacrifices at their sancta, and before the feast. There'll be dancing, hymns and every kind of bustle for us to get lost in.'

'I've never seen it,' Melissa said, a little awed.

'You'll love it, but don't forget why we're going. We'll have to stay together. We can slip away as everyone makes their way back to the sancta after the celebrations. No one will miss me at the feast, and if anyone asks we can say I'm ill.'

'And your pack?'

'I'll stash it in the library and collect it on our way to the temple. We'll have to be quick, so we'll take Hypatia. It'll be a louder exit, but there'll be no one left in the city to hear us anyway. We'll meet Theodora at the bottom of the temple steps, and the rest is easy.'

'Climbing up the slope to the temple will not be easy,' Melissa said.

'After the wall, it'll be a breeze. Don't worry about me.'

'Of course I'll worry.' She drew a lazy line of ochre across the top of the marble. 'We'll come back for him,' she said.

'Lissa—'

'You don't want to leave him behind. I don't want you to leave him behind.'

'I don't want to leave either of them behind. They've been kind to me, despite everything.'

'They had no reason to be unkind to you.'

Kala laughed. 'No one does, but that doesn't seem to stop them. They chose to be kind. I wish we could take them with us.'

'We could.'

Kala smiled ruefully. 'Not now. It's too dangerous. Besides, it's Theodora's secret too.'

She thought of the crumpled figure on the gravel by the warehouses, her face streaked with ash, tear-tracks and scratches from her own fingernails. Kala's greatest fear wasn't that something would go wrong at the festival; she was ready for that. Her greatest fear was that Theodora would let them down. She had prepared for every possible obstacle, but if Theodora changed her mind there was nothing they could do. It was out of Kala's control.

'I think that's as good as it's going to get,' she said as she got to her feet.

They regarded the multicoloured block of masonry with an uneasy mixture of pride and disappointment. They'd finished it, but it wasn't quite what they'd hoped for. It seemed an appropriate epitaph to her life in Kepos: colourful, messy and full, but fundamentally misconceived.

VII
ἵππος | Hippos | Horse

To his seventh son, the god gave the great plains surrounding the garden.
He filled them with horses and gave him the knowledge of breaking them,
so that he might travel swiftly over all the lands of the god with news of his people.
Because he was thus blessed the god named him Elasippus, the horse-driver.

- Kleitos, On the Formation of Kepos

It had all started with the pirates, Straton thought. If they had never found the channel between the cliffs, never left the girl there, then none of this would be happening. They had a lot to answer for. They were the reason that Kepos had been rediscovered, and now everything had gone wrong.

Straton found himself at the Glauks sanctum once again, conducting his augury while he waited for his niece to make her appearance with the first of the stones. If only Nikos had taken her with him to Lykos, everything would have been so much easier. There would have been no opposition at all. He could have taken his birthright, finally allying the power of a Hierophant with the influence of a Dekocrat. Then things would have changed. He might even have been Archon.

She was the only thing in his way.

The wall loomed large behind him, the dawn light picking out its multi-coloured hues. This year's building works would stabilise it for the next decade, filling in the cracks. He'd seen the rising tide, but there would be more than enough stone to exceed its highest reaches. The pirates would bring their slaves with bricks and mortar, and between them the secret of the Water would be safe for another year. Kepos was a valuable monopoly, an investment worth protecting.

If it were Straton's choice, he wouldn't share it with thieves.

He could see the first carts on the horizon, pouring out of the city. It would take all morning for them to arrive, each splitting off to their tribe's sanctum.

All the travellers were bundled in layers against the chill, but the wind was fierce enough to cut straight through the cloth. Driving the cart at the head of the convoy, Kala and Melissa were getting the brunt of it.

After another sleepless night, Kala shivered with cold and exhaustion as she drove Hypatia on. The reins trembled in her hands.

Most of the carts held a few stones, as each household often contained many families, but Kala and Melissa's block sat alone. They hadn't had time to seal it after the paint had dried, so when the drizzle fell it drew rivers of murky colour down the sides of the stone. If anything, that improved the design.

'I hope the rain clears up before the festival,' Melissa said.

'It can rain all day for all I care, as long as it clears up before we have to climb the cliff face,' Kala said, but she instantly regretted her tone. This was a chance for Melissa to see a part of Kepian life she'd never been allowed to experience, and she was excited. 'Anyway,' Kala went on quickly, 'I shouldn't think it'll make much difference to the entertainers. They'll carry on whatever the weather.'

'Do you think?'

'I'm sure. They always carry on, even in a downpour.'

'Nonetheless,' Melissa said, 'I pray for good weather.'

In the time it took the carts to make their way to the sancta, her prayer had been answered. The sun had made its reappearance, and their rain-marbled stone had dried in a puddle of colour. They drove it over to the edge of the

Glauks sanctum, where slaves waited to drag the stones from the carts. From there, the blocks would be pulled up the staircase by the acolytes on a laborious system of planks and ropes. It would take them days to finish the job. After seeing the weight of water that pushed on the wall from the other side, Kala wished they could work more quickly.

Once their cart was unloaded, Kala left it by the cliff and released Hypatia so she could graze in the meadows. When she and Melissa made it back to the sanctum, Straton was waiting at the altar, his hands already bathed in blood. There were no acolytes to assist him; they were miles behind, bringing their own stones. It would be hours before she could see Theodora and know that all was well. Until then, she would worry.

The fires lit up across the sacred precinct as each tribe finished its sacrifices and prepared its spits. Glauks was the first to send up its flame, and a second fire answered only moments later from Ophis on the opposite end of the wall. Next was Onos, closest to Glauks, and then nothing.

Kala's anxiety made her restless. She spun the cane in her hands, digging a hole into the turf of the sacred space. It was all she could do to keep herself calm. The higher tribes were still arriving, and hadn't even begun their sacrifices. They were bigger, too, and richer, with more tenants who had brought greater offerings, so the whole process took hours.

Rather than occupying herself in prayer, as she should have done, Kala watched over her shoulder as the entertainments were arranged. The ground was muddy and churned from the passage of so many carts, but that didn't seem to deter the slaves and freedmen who marked out the edges of their stalls with tables and banners, then soaked up the puddles with sawdust and straw. There was so much colour in their decorations that they rivalled the wall itself. Between the colours of the stalls and the bright blue of the sky, the day had become a truly beautiful one.

Kala remembered the festivals of her youth: hand in hand with her father, eating sticky cakes and nuts while they watched archers competing by the Delphis sanctum. One year they had watched acrobats jumping onto each other's shoulders, another year they'd drunk honeyed wine while they played hoopla in a vain attempt to win an orichalcum ring for her mother. The festival had always been a happy place for her. She started to think she might actually enjoy the afternoon, if she could only see Theodora.

It was midday before the fires of Tauros finally blazed into life in the central sanctum, joining the line of flames from Glauks to Ophis. By then, Kala and Melissa had watched as wine shops, bakeries, games of horseshoes, a running track, a theatre and a wrestling ring were assembled in the fields bounding the sancta. By then, the Archon had arrived with the acolytes. As always, theirs were the prettiest of the stones. They were lined up with the rest behind the sanctum. The thought of the acolytes' creations sitting next to her own sad specimen gave Kala pangs of inadequacy. But then they'd had a whole year to work on their designs, and she'd only had a day.

The stones were followed to the sanctum by the acolytes themselves and there, finally, was Theodora. Kala saw her only briefly, and the girl didn't acknowledge her presence. There was too much at stake to give it all away now with an incautious glance, but Kala longed to look, to study her expression for any sign that her resolve might be wavering. Instead, she kept her eyes fixed on the bloody altar.

It wasn't long before the acolytes turned to their task: the wall. They would have no opportunity to enjoy the festival.

The Archon climbed halfway up the first staircase, so he stood in the centre of the wall facing the Tauros sanctum, and declared the festival open. A mounting cheer rose from the sancta at his words, echoing off the sides of the valley.

That was the boring bit done. Now they could go and have fun. One last hurrah.

* * *

Kala was stiff from sitting still for so long, and cold. Although the day was now bright and sunny, the loss of cloud cover seemed to put an edge on the autumnal weather. It took a while for her to get her leg to cooperate. She tried not to dwell on it, because it didn't bode well for the evening's adventure, but it was clear from the expression on Melissa's face that she was worried.

'I'll be fine,' Kala assured her as Melissa helped her to her feet.

She didn't look convinced, but when she saw that they were the only ones left behind, she let Kala lead her out of the sanctum and into the colourful bustle that had transformed the fields.

'What do you want to see first?' Kala asked, holding on to Melissa's arm.

'Will they serve me?'

Everything was given freely at the festival, as everything was provided by the Dekocrats as a gift to their people, but only to the aristocrats and tenants. The festival was no holiday for slaves.

'Don't worry,' Kala said. 'I'm the last of the house of Glauks. They'll serve me whatever I want, and if I want to share it with you then what business of theirs is that?'

She'd said it simply to reassure Melissa, and was surprised when it turned out to be an understatement.

The first stall Melissa chose was selling hot wine and cakes. They were still ten paces away when the stall holder greeted them.

'Miss Kala, good day to you and your friend! Let me fill your cups.'

Kala and Melissa exchanged glances. It was unusual for a tenant to acknowledge a slave so openly. It seemed that word of Melissa was already getting around, probably as a result of Kala's sudden shift in status.

'Thank you,' Kala said.

Melissa fished their wooden mugs from her bag and handed them to the man.

'The finest spiced wine in all the valley,' he said merrily as he filled them. 'The best cakes too, if I can interest you ladies? Courtesy of my wife, best cook in all of Onos.' He didn't wait for their answer before taking two little nut-studded cakes from beside the fire.

'Try them, Misses,' he said, holding one out to each of them. 'Tell me they're not the best you've ever eaten.'

Kala was slightly intimidated by his patter, worried that the product wouldn't live up to the hype, but one bite was enough to prove his confidence was justified. The outside of the cake was crisp like fresh bread crust, but inside it was all soft, sweet nuttiness.

'See?' he said with a grin. 'She's a genius with a cake, my wife is.'

'She is indeed. You're Onos tenants?' Kala asked as she passed Melissa a cup and took her own. She was enveloped in the aroma of cinnamon and alcohol. The warmth seeped through the wood into her fingers, easing the cold in her joints.

'That's right, Miss. We're in the east of the city, the tavern by the fountain. Come and see us when you're out that way.'

'I might just do that. Thank you.'

He smiled warmly. 'You enjoy the festival now, Misses.'

They walked on slowly through the crowds, careful not to spill their wine. Between that and the cake, Kala was already enjoying herself. Melissa seemed to be as well, if the awed expression on her face was anything to go by.

'Look,' she said, tugging gently at Kala's cane arm to direct her towards an excited huddle of people. 'What's that?'

An obscene amount of grunting was emanating from the centre of the gathering. It parted as they approached, making a pathway so they could see the focus of attention: a wrestling match.

'Gods,' Melissa said, a little breathlessly.

In Kepos, all exercise was undertaken in the nude. The two opponents currently in the makeshift palaestra were already covered with mud and sawdust from previous fights. They appeared well-matched, both of them heavily-muscled but quick. The spectators surrounded them with a cacophony of cheers and jeers as their bodies slammed together into the first hold.

'You wonder that they don't injure themselves,' Kala said.

Melissa tilted her head to one side as she considered the fighters. 'They're certainly very energetic.'

One of the wrestlers got his arm around the other's leg and, pulling it from behind as he kept his own body low, toppled him down onto his back. The volume of the crowd increased.

'A noble display of athletic prowess,' Kala declared.

'Mm-hmm,' was Melissa's only reply.

They watched three more matches while they finished their wine, then moved gently back into the flow of the festival.

'Where next?' Kala asked.

'We shouldn't go too far.'

'Why not?' They had hours before the feast yet, hours before they had to leave.

'Well, I don't want to miss anything,' Melissa said. 'Why don't we look around here?'

But before they could decide on their next destination, they were joined by a young man about Kala's age. He inclined his head in greeting.

'Kala of Glauks, my name is Drakon of Ophis.'

'Oh?' She didn't know him, nor could she think of any reason for him to approach her.

He looked at her uncertainly, as though he were unsure what to do next.

'Yes?' Kala said, trying to be encouraging.

He cleared his throat. 'Would you like to… um…' The pause went on for several seconds while he struggled to find the words he wanted.

Kala raised an eyebrow at him.

'Walk?' he finished, eventually.

'That's very kind of you…' Kala's mind was blank. 'I'm sorry, what was your name again?'

'Drakon.'

'That's very kind of you, Drakon, but as you can see, I already have a companion.'

He eyed Melissa, clearly surprised that Kala had rejected his company for hers.

'Oh, I, er–'

He was interrupted by a pretty young woman of about thirteen, who neatly blocked Drakon by stepping in front of him.

'My name is Pelagia,' she said, 'of Hippos. I wonder, Miss Kala, whether you have met my brother Hilarion.' As she spoke, she presented a young man of perhaps eighteen. He had strikingly handsome features, but was plagued by acne.

'I haven't, no,' Kala said. She didn't want to, either.

'Greetings, fair Kala,' he intoned. Melissa stifled a laugh and the little lord cut her a filthy look.

'This is my dearest friend, Melissa,' Kala said in a threatening tone. 'I can honestly think of no one in the world more precious to me than her.'

Melissa smiled, but looked like she wanted to roll her eyes. However, the transformation in the boy's demeanour was instant.

'Charming to meet you,' he said, taking Melissa's hand in his. The gesture caused a stir of interest in the surrounding crowd. Hilarion was clearly an aristocrat of some standing, and he was taking a slave's hand as though she were an equal.

They were starting to become the centre of attention, and that made Kala uncomfortable. It would make it so much more difficult to slip away later if everyone was watching them.

'Look, it's lovely to meet all of you,' she said, 'but we really must be moving on. Lots to see, you know.'

Drakon drifted off, but Hilarion wasn't giving up so easily.

'Perhaps I could escort you both, then,' he said. 'There's a play starting shortly near the Panther sanctum, if you'd care to join me?'

'Thank you, but we'll be quite all right on our own.'

A tiny wrinkle of frustration appeared between his brows. 'It's no inconvenience, I assure you.'

'Thank you,' Kala said forcefully, 'but no.'

He opened his mouth to protest further, but a more familiar rogue came to the rescue.

'Hilarion, you shit-eater,' Leon said. 'What are you doing harassing my favourite girl who isn't my sister? Shouldn't you be off picking the lice out of your hair?'

The indignation was clear on the lordling's face. 'I was simply offering her an escort to the theatre.'

'What, are you a whore now? Anyway, she's got me to take her wherever she wants, so push off.'

Hilarion scowled at him then ambled away with bad grace, towing his sister behind him.

Once he had made sure they were gone, Leon turned back to Kala and Melissa with a gap-toothed grin. His bruises were much better, so faded now that Kala wouldn't have noticed them had she not been looking for their traces.

'Hello, Kala,' he said. His eyes lingered on hers just a little too long for comfort. The air seemed to get stuck in her lungs, swelling as he held her gaze. The feeling was almost nostalgic, despite the brief time they had known one another.

'And lovely Lissa,' he said, leaning forward to kiss the slave's cheek. She startled a little at the gesture, but the smile she gave him was one of genuine pleasure.

'Sir,' she said.

'Oh,' he replied with a dismissive wave, 'let's not start that again. It's just Leon. Have you been looking after our girl?'

'As much as she lets me.'

Kala looked between the two of them. The fact that they were this chummy was a revelation to her.

'Well,' Leon said, 'I'm glad to see some attempt is being made to keep her from the clutches of the rabble. Rapacious bastards.'

'Excuse me,' Kala interrupted, 'but what exactly is going on here?'

Leon grinned guilelessly, but the guilt was written all over Melissa's face.

'Lissa…'

'Oh, stop being so suspicious,' Leon said. 'I just wanted to make sure that we'd find each other today, and Melissa agreed to help.'

'Well, if we're not waiting for anyone else, then shall we go and see the rest of the festival? Or do we have to stay in sight of the Glauks sanctum all day?'

'Come on, then.' Leon offered her his arm.

Kala ignored it, preferring to keep hold of Melissa's, but Melissa had other ideas. She dropped Kala's arm and gently pushed her towards Leon.

'I'm right beside you,' she whispered, slipping around to Kala's cane side.

Leon smiled widely and said, 'Ready, then? I saw something this way that I think you'll love.'

The stall wasn't much to look at. It sat away from the main thoroughfare, and unlike those that surrounded it, it boasted no banners or flags. It didn't even have a table, just two stools next to a small campfire. On one of them sat an old man holding a tray made from a single slice of wood. Behind him, a ramshackle tent had been erected.

'What's this?' Kala whispered to Leon.

'You'll see.'

Despite its humble appearance, there was a line of people waiting to speak to the man, though they kept their distance from the fire. As the three of them approached, he looked towards the line as if to invite his next guest, but then he saw Kala. With an enthusiasm that was starting to feel inevitable, he beckoned her forwards.

'What is this, Leon?'

He smiled. 'Humour me.'

They stepped past the queue and up to the fire, where the man greeted them.

'Kala of Glauks,' he said, 'and, if I'm not mistaken, Leon of Lykos. Care to hear your fortunes?' He'd lost so many teeth that his words were difficult to decipher, spitting and sucking through his cheeks as he spoke.

'A seer, Leon?' Kala said. 'Really?'

'Come on,' he said, letting the man lead him into the tent. 'Don't you want to know the future?'

Kala looked to Melissa for support, but it was obvious that she was just as excited as Leon. He ushered Melissa in while Kala hesitated outside, trying to find an excuse to leave. Eventually, she followed them into the tiny space. It smelled musky and damp, like wet dog and fox, but there was something pleasant about it nonetheless. There was a base note of exotic oils that sweetened the air, a perfume Kala recognised but couldn't place.

The man sat on a stool, but it was the only one in the tent. With Melissa and Leon already sitting on the sheepskins that covered the ground, there was hardly any room left for Kala. Seeing her predicament, Leon shuffled backwards and pulled her down in front of him. She was practically sitting in his lap. She tried to keep some distance between them, but it was a losing battle.

'Relax,' he whispered in her ear. 'This is hardly the most compromising position we've ever been in.'

She elbowed him in the stomach to shut him up.

'So,' the man said, setting the tray over his lap, 'who would like to go first?'

Leon looked at Kala, then at Melissa. Kala wasn't going to validate this adventure by volunteering. Melissa looked as though she wanted to, but something was holding her back.

'I'll go first, shall I?' Leon said.

The man nodded and put a hand into his pocket, bringing out a pile of knucklebones and offering them up on his palm. When Leon reached forwards to take them, his chest pushed up close against Kala's back. His warmth drew her irresistibly closer, so that when he leaned back again she moved with him, letting her head rest against his shoulder. After all, what did it matter now? They were leaving in a few hours.

Leon held his closed fist in front of them both. The man held out the tray underneath his hand. Kala could see now that its construction wasn't as simple as she had first thought; there was a raised lip running all around the edge.

'Drop,' the man said.

Leon did, and eight bones rattled across the surface of the wood until they came to rest. The man drew the tray back onto his lap with an ambiguous grunt.

'Is it good?' Leon asked.

The man stared at the bones for a moment longer before leaning down with the tray.

'These sheep knuckle bones,' he said, pointing to the larger four, 'they show the gods. And these,' he pointed to the smaller four, 'human wrist bones, they show the garden.'

'So?'

'See the way these four are all on different sides?' the man asked, pointing to the smaller bones. 'The Delphis throw. Very lucky. But these,' he pointed to the bigger ones, 'are all on one side, the fattest side. The easiest throw. Very unlucky.'

'What does that mean?' He leaned forwards, curling more tightly around Kala's frame.

'Means you have luck with people, but not with the gods. People love you, they help you, you marry well, have many children, but the gods will shit on you every chance they get.'

Leon looked thoughtful for a moment then laughed. 'Sounds about right,' he said cheerfully. 'Your turn, Lissa.'

The man handed her the bones, which she dropped with some ceremony. Kala thought she saw her eyes flicker closed for just a second, as though in prayer.

The man was quicker about his assessment this time.

'Good luck,' he pronounced, 'but bad luck too. Two bones on each of the four sides, but not all human bones on different sides, not all sheep bones on different sides. Means you'll have good luck, but not when it's useful. Bad luck when you most need it to be good. But overall, a good life. A happy life, but not the life you'd ask for.'

A moment of disappointed silence followed his pronouncement.

'Oh well,' Leon said to Melissa. 'At least you won't get shat on by the gods.'

She laughed, and Kala's chest clenched. She couldn't remember the last time she had heard that sound. When had Melissa last been happy? But she was happy here, sitting in this stinking tent as Leon wrapped himself around Kala, on the day that they would leave Kepos forever.

Kala hoped their departure was the reason for her levity. They couldn't stay.

'You, Miss?' the man asked, holding the bones out to Kala.

'If you insist.'

'We certainly do,' Leon said.

As she dropped the bones, she thought of all the things she wanted in life: freedom, love, a purpose, a home. Melissa's laughter. Leon.

'Very lucky,' the man said as he pulled the tray back onto his lap. 'Very lucky throw.'

'I thought you said it was bad when they landed on their fattest side?' Kala asked.

'Normally,' he said, holding up a finger, 'normally yes. But this throw… a very special throw. Very prophetic. It says you marry this year. Very special husband. And you'll meet him today. This bone here? Means he's tall. This bone here? Means green eyes. This bone here? Means a bit blind in one–'

'Hang on,' Leon interrupted, 'are you from Panther?'

'I might be,' the man said shiftily, but with a good-natured smile.

'That's Thales,' Leon said, 'one of the Panther's grandsons.'

'Good boy, he is. Strong boy. He'll give you lots of strong babies,' he said to Kala, with a cheeky grin.

'Well, you can both go to the crows.' Leon hauled Kala to her feet and handed up her cane. He had to dig around in the sheepskins, but he found it eventually. 'Come on, Melissa,' he said. 'Pig-shagging charlatans, the lot of them.'

When Kala looked back at the man, he just grinned contentedly. She smiled too, despite his trick.

'Yours is a hard life,' he said to her, 'but happy soon. You'll see.' He tapped his heart with his finger, and then Leon was ushering her out of the tent.

He was practically spitting with enthusiastic anger as they walked away. Unfortunately, Thales didn't know that things hadn't quite gone to plan. The boy was waiting for them, ostensibly watching a footrace taking place opposite the Panther sanctum. When he saw the expression on Leon's face, he looked like he might bolt.

'I'd join the race if I were you,' Leon called to him, 'because if I catch you then you're never going to run again.'

He didn't wait to be told twice.

'Gods, Kala,' Leon said, 'fending off your suitors is harder work than listening to Lali talk about her hair. Can't you just marry me and get it over with?'

It sounded like a joke, so Kala decided to ignore it.

'How is your sister?' she asked.

'Fine, I think. She spends a lot of time with your mother. Your doing, I gather.'

'I was worried.'

'I know, but there's not much Lali can do. There's not much any of us can do.'

'I know.'

They wandered on through the stalls and contests, Kala's spare arm looped through Melissa's once more. Leon walked on her other side, gazing idly at the entertainments until the next distraction caught his eye. They played horseshoes, ate pastries, drank wine and watched the acrobats, gradually making their way towards the centre of the festival. When they drew level with the Delphis sanctum, Leon started scanning the crowds.

'What?' Kala asked him.

'Ariston should be around here somewhere,' he said. 'I told him I'd find him… Ah, there he is. Back in a moment.'

He left Kala and Melissa to watch a juggler while he went to speak to Ariston.

'Are you not going to tell him?' Melissa asked when he was out of earshot.

'Tell him what?'

Melissa gave her a frank look. 'You know what.'

Kala had thought about it. She couldn't stop thinking about it, in fact. She could tell him now. She could tell him all about the wall and the Water, about the Plain and the city that waited for them there. He might even come with them, if she asked.

'Do you want me to tell him?' Kala said.

'I would if I were you. He might be useful.'

'I don't know about that.'

Melissa looked puzzled. 'Don't you trust him?' she asked.

'It's not that, it's just… You've seen him, Lissa. He's impulsive, and he's loud. I'm not sure he knows what subtlety is.'

'Do you want him to come with us?' Melissa asked.

'We can come back for him, and Eulalia, and Ariston. And Eirene,' she added.

'That's not what I asked.'

Kala glanced over to where Leon stood with Ariston, his face unusually serious as they plotted together. Ariston waved. Leon looked up and caught her eye. There was that grin again, chasing the darkness from his face.

'Yes,' Kala whispered, 'I want him to come with us.'

'That's settled then.'

'And what if he says no?' she said.

Melissa smiled and reached up to take Kala's face in her hands. 'He won't say no, Kallista. Believe me. He'll say yes.'

Ariston had promised to meet them at the Delphis sanctum in time for the archery contest, so they loitered around the stalls in that area while they waited. The archery butts were set up out in the meadows, away from the festival, but all the action would be here, where the archers would stand to take their shots.

Kala had hoped that she might have the opportunity to speak to Leon privately while they waited, but they were so close to the Lykos sanctum that he was never short of friends, relatives or tenants eager for a moment of his time. He offered her a helpless look, but she couldn't save him from their attentions. He was the heir of Lykos now, and that role brought with it all the political responsibilities he had tried so hard to avoid.

The first archers were already lining up when Ariston made his appearance, with Eulalia in tow.

'Kala,' she said, pulling her into a hug. 'I'm so sorry that I left without saying goodbye. Father...'

'I know,' Kala said. 'Don't worry. And thank you for looking after my mother.'

'Of course,' she said.

Eulalia looked over at the archers as she moved to stand closer to Ariston. It could have been an accident that they were now so close that their fingers were almost entwined. Almost. The distance looked painful, as though it were using every bit of their strength to keep empty air between them.

'So,' Leon said as he barrelled towards the group, 'shall we go and watch, then?' He kept looking over his shoulder, as though he might be waylaid by another petitioner at any moment. His expression pinched into desperation. 'Now? Please?'

There were benches set up in rows along the sides of the range. The space was raucous. Kepians weren't quiet spectators, nor respectful ones. As one row stood to cheer for their favourites, those in the row behind shouted them back down to their seats. One fight had broken out already, and cups of wine went flying as a bench tipped over backwards, taking its occupants with it.

Ariston had sent a few slaves ahead to keep some good seats for them near the front. The young men vacated with some relief. Seeing how the other slaves saving seats were being berated by those looking to oust them, Kala could understand why.

Ariston took the lead as they slipped into the row, with Eulalia close behind. Kala ushered Melissa in next before taking her own seat, with Leon at the end. Everything smelled of wet turf and sawdust. The benches were new enough that splinters caught at the fabric of Kala's dress, but they were comfortable. Still, Melissa shifted restlessly.

'Are you sure this is all right?' she whispered to Kala. Kala just smiled and took her hand. They had seen enough deference to Melissa today to reassure her that they had nothing to worry about.

Unfortunately, the same couldn't be said for Eulalia and Ariston. During the first few rounds of archers, they had inched so close to each other that there was now a wide gap between Melissa and Eulalia, and no gap at all between Eulalia and Ariston. As Ariston tentatively put his arm around her shoulders, one of the men in the front row looked back over his shoulder. They realised too late that it was

Nikos, sitting with a few of the other Dekocrats. His eyes locked quickly onto Eulalia's, and then he was on his feet.

'Balls,' Leon muttered, getting ready to intervene.

But Nikos didn't come for Eulalia. Instead, he threw his wine cup to the ground and strode towards another occupant in the front row. Pulling him to his feet by the front of his tunic, Nikos pointed back at where Ariston and Eulalia sat, now with a clear foot of air between them.

'You condone this?' he shouted into the man's face. It was Zotikos, Ariston's grandfather. His eyes swivelled towards them.

Kala leaned across Melissa and asked Eulalia, 'Does the Delphis know?'

She shook her head, her eyes fixed in horror on the scene in front of them. The cacophony from the surrounding benches had stilled as they waited for a response from Zotikos. Even the competitors had fallen silent, their bows hanging loosely at their sides. Apparently, this was more entertaining than archery.

Zotikos said nothing, calm despite Nikos's rage.

'You keep that little bastard away from my daughter,' Nikos spat.

The older man laughed in his face, then said pleasantly, 'Did you forget, Lykos, that he's *your* little bastard?'

Kala looked at Ariston. In fact, everyone was staring at him. She could see it, now that she knew: the hard line of his jaw, jutting into a chin that was a duplicate of Nikos's, and the soft curve of his cheek that sank into almost-dimples, just like Charis's. He was their lost child, the one everyone had said was stillborn.

Nikos's initial anger was nothing in comparison with his fury now. He shoved Zotikos down into the grass, muscles taut with the anticipation of violence, and if the other Dekocrats hadn't intervened there might have been a new Delphis that day. Thwarted, Nikos pulled his tunic straight and stalked off alone, towards the Lykos sanctum.

Kala looked at Leon. Ariston shared a parent with each of them. The realisation stole slowly over Eulalia until it settled as despair in her eyes, until she couldn't even look at him. Shame coloured her cheeks.

Everyone was watching them.

'I think it's time for us to leave,' Leon said. He reached across the others to take Eulalia's hand and drew her past them until she was tucked safely under his arm.

'Come on, brother,' he said to Ariston, a little bitterly.

'Leon,' Kala rebuked.

Ariston was in no state to respond for himself. The boy's face was snow-white, his jaw shaking and his eyes glazed. Kala took his arm and led him out of the benches, following Melissa and the others into the main festival. They turned away from the Lykos sanctum and walked in the direction of the carts.

There was a long moment of nothingness before anyone spoke again.

'So, you're Father and Charis's son then,' Leon said. 'We're just one, big, happy family.'

Eulalia hiccupped out a sob.

Kala gave him a look. 'You're not helping.'

'I knew I was adopted,' Ariston murmured. 'But I thought I was Delphis. I thought my parents were dead. I didn't know…'

Tears were pouring down Eulalia's face, but she said nothing.

'You're right,' Leon said to Kala, 'I'm not helping, so I'm going to take Lali home. We'll see you at the Proaulia.'

Eulalia turned her face to cry into his shoulder, her breath hitching at the back of her throat.

'Really, Leon?' Kala whispered on a sigh. It was hardly tactful to mention the Proaulia just after his sister had found out that the love of her life was their brother.

He closed his eyes at his own stupidity. 'Gods, Lali,' he said, 'I'm sorry. I'm a thoughtless burden to the earth. Farewell, you three.'

'Farewell,' Ariston muttered, but they were already walking away. He took his own leave a moment later, with a tight and joyless smile.

So Kala and Melissa were alone, too quickly for Kala to realise that it had been the last time she'd see the others. She'd never had a chance to ask them to leave with her, or to say the things she wanted to say to each of them in parting.

The abruptness of it left her breathless, but there was no time to mourn for her lost friends. The sun was already dipping below the wall, so they needed to make a move.

'No wonder Nikos was so eager to marry her off to Timon,' she said as they made their way back to the Glauks sanctum.

'Perhaps this is kinder,' Melissa said.

'What?'

'Nikos would have made her marry Timon anyway. Maybe it's better that they know the reason why. Maybe it'll be easier.'

Kala tried to imagine it. If Leon were her brother, truly her brother in blood rather than just brief circumstance, would she feel less pain in leaving him?

'I think it might be worse,' she said.

She might never see him again, but at least she could remember the time they had spent together fondly. There was no corruption there, no new knowledge to sully her memories.

Poor Eulalia.

The Tauros Hierophant was calling his tribe to the feast when they reached the Glauks sanctum, but they didn't stop there. Instead, they walked back to the place where they had left the cart, where even now Hypatia stood waiting. It was as though she had known she was needed. Either that, or she'd remembered the bag of carrots Kala had hidden in the box that formed the driver's seat. Given how avidly the horse was snuffling at its edges, Kala guessed the latter was true.

She looked up at the wall, towering like a black monolith above them. It blocked out the sunset in a straight line across the sky. There were torches placed here and there up its height to help the acolytes in their labours, but it wouldn't be long before they'd have to stop for the night. It was simply too dangerous to work in the dark, too easy for open flames to bite at the ropes that tethered the stones in place.

It might work, she supposed. This latest effort to fortify the wall could succeed, but it was too late for her and Melissa. They couldn't live in its shadow, knowing it was a lie.

'We'll come back for them,' Melissa said as she helped Kala onto the cart. 'When we know it's safe, we'll come back for them all.'

'If it's safe.'

'It can't be much more dangerous than Kepos.'

'I suppose not.' But Kala knew Kepos, and she knew where the threats were centred. There were no pirates here, no exotic and dangerous animals, and she knew the city's greatest intrigue. In the Plain, she would be walking in blind, albeit with their lost princess. That might make their arrival more welcome, she supposed.

Theirs was the only cart leaving the festival. They could see horses across the meadows, which Kala assumed carried Leon and Eulalia, but they were moving fast and would reach the city far ahead of Kala and Melissa.

They put the wall to their backs, turning away from the sound of the Hierophants calling their tribes to the feast. The heavy scent of fat was in the air once more. Kala was glad to leave it behind them. The darkness wrapped a chill around her shoulders, shrugging itself onto her cloak until she sat shivering with the reins in her hands. Melissa shifted closer so they were pressed side to side and slung her own cloak over them both.

'You should eat,' she said. 'We won't have time to stop.'

'I'm not hungry.'

Kala's stomach still churned with the emotions of the afternoon: joy at the discovery of a lost brother, grief at leaving, trepidation for their journey, horror for Eulalia and, most of all, a bitter warmth in the pit of her stomach when she thought of Leon's chest pressed into her back as they crouched together in the foetid tent.

'You should still eat.'

Melissa had squirrelled away an extra cake or bread from most of the stalls they had visited. She brought them out now.

'There are more,' she continued, patting her bag. 'I'm taking them with us for the climb.'

Kala looked at the array in disbelief. 'How did you manage this?'

Melissa smiled. 'People were keen to win your favour today.'

'What would I do without you?'

'You'll never have to find out,' she said, breaking apart a cheese bread for the two of them to share. It was still warm in its centre, a perfect antidote for the evening's chill.

This was enough, she told herself. If she could take only one person with her, then Melissa was enough.

It was dark when they reached the city. The streets were deserted. There were a few slaves sweeping doorsteps and watering plants, but every shop and kitchen was closed. Kala had never seen the city this empty. Usually she would have been down in the sancta with everyone else.

The hollow darkness of the markets made it easy to imagine an end to this place. Now that there were no canopies, no trestle tables and no wares, she could picture the alleys filled with water rather than people. It would be this dark. It would be this calm and quiet if it were under water, as quiet as the refuge Kala sought in the depths under the waterfall. Fish would swim around the pillars of the council house. The waves would break open the doors and gates of even the most elite houses, and weed would replace the green in their gardens. Everything would be washed clean.

It might have a kind of beauty.

'I'll wait here with Hypatia,' Melissa said as they reached the stables. 'I have everything I need in my bag.'

She was already unharnessing the horse when Kala slid down to the ground.

'I'll be as quick as I can,' said Kala, then made her way through the house to the library to collect her own pack.

Her cane tapping along the stones had clearly announced her presence, because as she reached the library she saw a light suddenly extinguished through the crack in the door, which stood ajar.

'Who's there?' she called.

She shouldn't have lingered. Her bag was right inside the door, just next to her foot. She should have grabbed it and left, but someone was in the library, her library, her father's library. It shouldn't have mattered, because this was the last time she would ever see it, and yet…

'I saw the light,' she said, pushing open the door, 'so show yourself.'

Movement in the darkness washed the odour of wine over her, together with a ranker scent that had the metallic tang of blood. She took a step backwards, but too late. A hand fixed around her throat, pulling her into the dark room and cutting off her voice.

'I saw you there today,' he whispered as he eased the door shut and pinned her to its back. 'I saw you leave.'

The sourness of Nikos's breath filled her nostrils, mingling with the coppery odour that was now so much closer. His fingers were sticky on her skin, and something was dripping steadily onto her chest. She panicked, wriggling as she tried to break free, but every movement just forced his hand tighter around her throat.

'I saw my son, too.' Another sticky hand was on her leg now, pulling her dress up from the ground in a movement that brought old terror screaming back from the halls of her memory.

But this time, she didn't drop her cane. This time, she brought just one hand to her neck to pull at his fingers. This time, she wasn't going to lose her only weapon.

'Do you think you love him?' he mocked, his hand on her naked thigh. 'Do you think he loves you? Just like your mother. There's no kind of love that can make Glauks worth Lykos's time.'

His fingers were spread on her hip now, rubbing viscous liquid across it. She could feel it cooling and constricting the skin as it dried. It was still warm.

There was no Leon to save her this time. No one except Melissa even knew she was here, and she was starting to feel faint, gasping against the hand at her throat.

She had been so close.

His grip loosened for a moment and then disappeared entirely. He was drunk again, fumbling in the dark, and seemed to think a hand on her hip was enough to keep her restrained. She took her chance, stepping in closer until her body pressed against his. He made a surprised noise, and she took advantage of his confusion to bring her knee up hard between his legs.

Diaprepes was smiling on her, and her aim was true.

When he curled forwards with a squeak, his head dipping onto her shoulder, she stepped to the side and brought the pommel of her cane down on his skull as hard as she could. There was hot blood under her fingers, but she didn't pause. She scooped up her pack and hauled the door open with a jerk that slammed it into his body, and then she stumbled down the corridor as fast as her limp would allow.

There were footsteps behind her when she reached the garden gate.

'Quick!' she yelled at Melissa.

'Gods, Kala, what happened?'

'We have to go, now.'

Melissa boosted Kala up into the saddle then hauled herself up behind. Kala was already urging Hypatia into a canter when Nikos burst through the gate.

'You little whore!' he shouted after them, clutching his head.

'Go to the crows, you shit-eating sadist!' Kala yelled over her shoulder, because now she could. They were never coming back. They were free.

Hypatia's hooves clattered over the cobbled streets as they raced eastwards.

'Are you all right?' Melissa asked.

'Yes,' Kala said, 'I'm fine.'

'So this isn't your blood?'

She looked down and saw the stains in the moonlight: smeared across her hands, dripped down her front. She must look a complete state.

'Some of it's Nikos's,' she said. 'The rest, I don't know. He was in the library, and it smelt of death, but it was dark and I didn't see.'

'One of the other slaves?' Melissa asked.

'I don't know.'

She hadn't had time to stop and look. She hadn't even had time to think that she should, that there was someone who might need her help. The identity of that someone was a mystery that would haunt her.

She was crying, she realised. The wind was pushing the tears into her hairline.

'Why would he be in the house at all?' Melissa asked. 'And why would he be in the library, when he avoided it the whole time he lived there?'

'Maybe because it's my place.'

'You mean he came to kill you?'

Kala shuddered at the memory of his hands, and decided not to tell Melissa the whole truth.

'Who knows?' she said. 'It doesn't matter now.'

They were free of it. She closed her eyes for a second and pushed the memory down. When she opened them again, all she could see was the moon and the stars and the darkness. She rubbed at her thigh, at her hip, at the blood congealing beneath the fabric. There was so much already on her fingers that she didn't feel it when it soaked through.

She'd wash at the pool. There would be time for her to wash it clean. She could take the time.

But right now she couldn't seem to relax her muscles, and Hypatia's motion had her body rocking strangely with its tension. Her anxiety wasn't helped by what they found on the road. They hadn't expected to see anyone once they'd cleared the boundary of the city, but there was a steady stream of acolytes leading carts from the temple. This was hardly the deserted scene that Theodora had anticipated.

'What are they doing?' Kala whispered. 'They should all be at the wall.'

When they drew closer, they could see the carts were filled with marble blocks and bricks, all the same uniform shape. There must have been hundreds more here. Together with those already at the sancta, there would be enough to pave the heights of the wall several times over.

Kala greeted the first acolyte they passed, but he seemed unhappy to see them. No one was supposed to witness this, Kala realised. No one was supposed to know just how much stone was being added this year.

'We need to go around,' Melissa said once the cart was out of earshot. 'We're going to have to circle through the woods then wait till it's clear, or they'll see us coming a mile off.'

'We'll be late,' Kala said.

'She'll wait.'

'If she comes at all.'

But there was no other option, so once they'd crossed the river they swung wide towards the tree line. The going became more difficult as entered the woods, with the canopy blocking out the moonlight. They relied on Hypatia to find her way forwards, avoiding roots as she picked her way through the trees. Thank Diaprepes they'd decided to bring her, instead of one of the faster horses.

Every step took them closer to the temple, closer to the steps, and closer to their escape. Kala tried to focus her mind on the task ahead, to prepare herself for the climb, but she couldn't clear her head. All she could think of were the hands she was fleeing, and the friends she was leaving behind. She was abandoning them to the Water. She was abandoning them to Nikos. She could only hope that they'd survive long enough for her to return for them.

As it transpired, they were not the friends who needed her concern.

VIII
ὄνος | Onos | Donkey

The god's eighth son had no domain of land or sea or sky,
but the god gave to him the afterlife, that he might collect
and contain the shades of the dead.
In time his subjects would outnumber those of the garden by
many factors,
and test the bounds of his domain, and thus the god named
him Mestor, which means 'replete'.

- Kleitos, On the Formation of Kepos

They found her by the water.

Her arm had fallen over the edge of the pool, so her fingers draped into the darkness. The current played with them, batting her hand to and fro as the water swirled away from the falls. She was facedown, but there was no mistaking that dark spread of straight hair.

Melissa jumped from the horse and ran to the body, but Kala was more leisurely in her descent. There was no point in rushing; the acolyte was obviously dead.

Kala hitched Hypatia's reins to a nearby tree, then quietly came to stand beside Melissa.

'She can't be dead,' the slave whispered.

Kala crouched down and put her hand on Theodora's shoulder in an attempt to turn her over, but her limbs seemed to have lost their integrity, the bones shattered. When she pushed the joint, there was no resistance. It was like prodding a bladder loosely filled with water. In the end, she had to use both hands to flip the body.

Her face was broken, but it was still recognisably Theodora. The green stone shone in the moonlight against her collarbone.

Kala looked up at the temple perched on the outcrop above them, then back down at the body.

'You think she fell?' Melissa asked, blinking back tears.

'Was pushed, more likely.'

There was blood on the rock where her body had lain, but less than Kala would have expected for a fall from that height. It was still warm, despite the cool of the evening.

'This just happened,' Kala said, looking up again at the temple. It was too dark to see much, and it might just have been the foliage, but there was definitely some movement up there.

'So she wasn't waiting for us?'

'Not here,' Kala said. 'Maybe she was waiting until she could see us coming before walking down, or maybe she was late, but whatever happened we need to get out of here before someone sees us.'

'We're not leaving Kepos?' Melissa's despair at that prospect was far more acute than it had been on seeing Theodora dead. She grasped Kala's hand, begging with her touch.

'We can't go up there, Lissa. Someone pushed her off. They might be waiting for us. It's dark, and we don't know the way.'

Panic suffused Melissa's features. 'But we have to,' she said. 'What about Nikos?'

She was right, of course. There was no way he would let Kala live, not after this evening. She'd sworn at him. She'd hit him. She'd made him bleed.

There was a noise off to one side, from the direction of the city. A cart was approaching. Kala snatched the necklace from Theodora's throat on impulse, then drew Melissa back into the trees. There was nothing they could do for Theodora now. She untied Hypatia and led them both into the shadows of the woods, out of sight.

'We'll come back at dawn, when it's light,' Kala said. 'We can hide in the grove until then.'

'They'll all be back by dawn.'

'I know,' Kala said.

They wouldn't get up to the temple at dawn, or on any other day while the acolytes were bustling from here to the wall. Their only chance would be at night, but that was assuming they'd have a guide. Without Theodora, they'd be lost.

Kala knew they'd missed their chance to escape, but she wasn't prepared to give up and return to Glauks yet, not in the darkness where Nikos could be waiting.

The evening was cold now, and a light drizzle had started to fall. The branches above them offered some protection from the rain, but not from the chill it brought with it. A fire would have solved all their problems, but smoke would soon be spotted in the sacred grove. There were no open flames permitted in these woods.

They didn't go far into the trees. If Kala climbed up into the elm next to their camp, she could still see the dark shape of Theodora's body by the water. She hoped that someone would come for her soon.

'First Neophytos,' Melissa said as she tethered Hypatia in the grove, 'then Theodora. Do you think they know about us too?'

'What does it matter?' Kala said. 'They've stopped us from leaving Kepos.'

She was shaking now, her nerves frayed by everything that had happened since they had left the festival. She wanted nothing more than the warmth of a fire and the dry comfort of her bed. Instead, the leaf litter was soggy underfoot and everything smelled of mould and rain. Water seeped under the straps of her sandals and between her toes until she could no longer feel them.

'We're going to try again, though,' Melissa said. It sounded like a plea.

'We don't know the way.'

'She said there was a pulley lift. If we can just find that, we can do it alone.'

'Have you ever been up there, to the temple?' Kala said.

'No.' Melissa's voice was small. Of course she hadn't been to the temple; she was just a slave.

'I've only been once or twice myself,' Kala said in a conciliatory tone, 'but it's like a maze up there. From down here, you'd think it's just the temple on a little rock, but it's a big space. All the acolytes live up there. There are hundreds of buildings all clustered back against the cliff with alleys winding through them. We don't stand a chance unless we know where we're going.'

'So we're giving up?'

'No. We just have to find another way.'

'And in the meantime?'

Kala took a deep breath. 'We go back,' she said. There was nothing else they could do; they couldn't stay here. They had to maintain the illusion that everything was normal. It was the only way. They had to go back to the city.

'The Proaulia's just over a week away,' Melissa said.

'I know.'

'And there's Nikos.'

'I know.'

Kala unfastened her pack from Hypatia's side and pulled out a large blanket. 'Do you have the rope?' she asked.

Kala set to making a hammock for the two of them, rather messily. When her knots failed on the third attempt, Melissa took it gently from her hands. She had it secured on her first try.

'What happened tonight?' Melissa asked as she tied off the final hitch. 'If we're going back...'

'He said he saw me and Leon,' she said, 'and he wasn't happy about it.' Kala thought back to Nikos's words earlier this evening, trying to decipher their meaning.

'You think he meant to kill you?'

'I don't know.'

His hand on her thigh, her hip. His sour breath on her cheek. The blood.

Her voice was ragged when she spoke again. 'I don't think so. He wanted to scare me. He wants me to stay away from Leon, I think.'

'He doesn't want Leon to be the Glauks, then.'

There's no kind of love that can make Glauks worth Lykos's time.

'No,' Kala said, but it didn't make sense to her. Why would he have courted her mother as a teenager if he thought Glauks was so far beneath him? 'I don't know,' she said. 'He was drunk.'

Melissa was quiet for a moment before she replied. 'It's going to be dangerous,' she said.

'There's nowhere else for us to go. At least this way, I'll get up to the temple at the Proaulia. Maybe I can slip away and scout it out… I don't know.'

Kala sat down into the hammock. It swung between the trees.

'You could just go,' Melissa said as she dropped down next to her. 'At the Proaulia, you could just leave.'

'Not without you.' Kala took Melissa's hand and pulled her close, resting her head in the crook of Melissa's neck. 'Anyway,' she continued with a hollow laugh, 'I'm never going to make it up the last stretch on my own. Not with my leg.'

'You're stronger than you think.'

'Maybe, but I'm not as strong as *you* think.'

The wind was picking up, shaking the branches above them so occasional fat drops of rain rattled down from the canopy. In the protection of the thick foliage that surrounded them, there was just a slight breeze. The only other movement was the swaying of their makeshift bed, creaking as the rope chafed against the bark.

'It had to be one of the priests,' Kala said. 'No one else would be up there tonight.'

'Theodora did say the Water is the Archon's secret. If anyone wanted to protect it, it would be him.'

'He would have been at the wall when it happened, at the feast.'

'So?' Melissa said as she reached into her pack. 'One of the acolytes would have done it for him, no doubt.'

She pulled out the rest of the cakes, along with a bladder of wine. The sweet honey confections went some way to pushing away the frost that had crept under their skin, so they ate them all. They had no reason to ration them now.

Once they had eaten, they curled up for the night, tucking their cloaks around each other so they could share their warmth, skin to skin.

'Until tomorrow, then,' Melissa said.

They would return to Glauks tomorrow. Kala would open the library and read the horror of its dark shelves. She would be back within Nikos's reach.

'Tomorrow,' Kala said.

For all her bravado, the word felt like a whimper.

Kala slept poorly, waking again and again in the cold only to find that it was still dark, and that Melissa was still asleep beside her. Shortly after she closed her eyes for the final time that morning, there was a shout from the direction of the waterfall.

She tried to slip from the hammock without disturbing Melissa, but that was an impossible task.

'What is it?' Melissa murmured as Kala started to climb the elm.

'I think they've found her.'

The day became lighter as she made her way out of the densest branches, light enough for her to see the scene by the pool. There were four acolytes surrounding Theodora, and more were running down the steps from the temple outcropping. The Archon was amongst them, his shining robes picking up the first light of the dawn.

There was nothing more Kala could do here. It was time for them to head back to the city, and back to Glauks.

There was no one out on the road this early, but when they reached the city the market stalls were already doing a brisk morning trade. Kala pulled her cloak tight around her to cover her clothes; she still hadn't washed the blood away.

The Onos tavern keeper they'd met at the festival rushed out to press fresh cakes into Melissa's hands as they passed the fountain. From his wife, he said, on behalf of the Onos suitor. Kala didn't bother to remember the boy's name. Doubtless he would be calling on her before the Proaulia.

'Are you sure you want to do this?' Melissa asked.

'Of course I don't, but I have to go to the Proaulia to scout for our escape, and I have to pretend everything's fine if I want to go to the Proaulia.' She'd thought it through from every angle during the night, and she still couldn't think of a better plan.

'We could go and stay with Eirene.'

'For how long? No, this is the only way.'

When they arrived, everything was just as they had left it. Apparently, their absence had gone completely unremarked. One of the field slaves saw them on their way past, but he didn't flinch at the blood staining Kala's clothes. That complacency, even more than the emptied halls, was an indication of how Nikos's tenure as Glauks had fractured the place's spirit.

They took Hypatia to the stable together. Kala knew the library was her next destination, and she didn't want to go in there alone. Instead, she washed her hands clean then helped Melissa rub down the horse and clean her gear. She polished everything to a shine, taking more care than usual with the task.

'You can't put it off forever,' Melissa said gently.

Kala put the tack aside with a sigh. 'Come on, then.'

There was blood smeared across the door to the library. Dark drops patterned the flagstones at their feet, fatter at the point where the door stood ajar. The shutters were closed so there was no light coming from within, just a ripe odour that made Kala regret the cake she had eaten on their ride. The door swung easily on its hinges when she pushed, releasing another waft that had her running to open the windows wide. She didn't look at the shape in the centre of the room, not until the light was streaming in from every direction.

It was Daos. She recognised him by the tattoo on his wrist, Nikos's first punishment for his disobedience. It seemed that the mark alone hadn't been enough to satisfy the new Lykos.

Daos's face was caved in, but there were no weapons that Kala could see in the room. She remembered Nikos's hands, so slick with blood that it spread over her skin. She remembered his fingers, clumsy at her hips, and his wine-soured breath. He had beaten the slave until his fists ran with blood.

'Was this meant for you?' Melissa asked. She looked like she was rethinking their return to the city.

'For Zotikos, I think. Nikos could hardly do this to the Delphis.'

'Why not? He killed his own father, his own brother.'

'We assume.'

Melissa looked at Daos's body. 'I think we know.'

'You saw him yesterday. He was too far gone. He was looking for a target.'

'He wouldn't have come all this way just to find a slave to beat, Kala.'

She was right, but Kala couldn't tell her the rest. She wanted to forget it, to push it away and never think about it again. Twice now he'd trapped her, but she could only admit that to herself. It was bad enough that Leon had seen it once. Admitting it to Melissa would make it real, and that was a shame she didn't want to feel. Her vulnerability made her weak.

And now death had invaded her safest spaces. The waterfall was defiled, and the air of the library was rich with decay once more. Brown-red gore sprayed the scrolls like age spots and clogged in drips from the edges of the shelves.

Daos's head was split open on the floor, leaking out onto the place that Linos had once occupied at her father's feet.

She had nowhere left to hide.

Hagne laid the body out while Melissa and Kala scrubbed the library clean. With the household so diminished, she had no other choice but to pitch in, but she would have done it anyway. She owed Daos that much.

They set the pyre by the pond, so his soul was released in the same spot as his brother's.

It had taken them all day to finish cleaning up the library, and even then they'd simply had to turn some of the scrolls around to hide the marks. They'd paused for nothing, not even to eat or wash themselves, but it was still dark by the time they put a taper to the bier. There were no acolytes here for Daos, no mourners other than his household, and no prayers other than those Kala could muster for Diaprepes to guide his steps. There was no mention of justice or retribution. There was none to be had, not for a slave, and not when Nikos was the closest he'd had to a master. Kala didn't count, of course.

She was the only one who lingered as the wood burned down, lowering the body to the ground as the ashes crumpled under its crackling weight. They hadn't known how to build the pyre to hold the limbs in place as the priests did, so Daos's body contorted strangely as it disassembled itself. She couldn't escape the scent of the meat.

The blood Nikos had smeared on her throat, her thigh, her hip, it tied her to Daos. She could almost feel his blood burning on her skin.

It was her duty to sit here in her blood-spattered dress and watch him go.

She heard the garden gate swing hard into its frame and turned to see Leon striding across the grass towards her. When he saw her face in the firelight, he broke into a run.

'You're all right,' he said as he dropped to his knees at her side and folded her into his arms. 'Thank the gods, you're all right.'

He pressed a kiss into her dishevelled hair. She was too stunned by the events of the day, and by his sudden appearance, to respond. She had so little energy left.

'What happened?' he asked.

She looked away, struggling to find an answer that would satisfy him.

'Did he hurt you?' he said. 'They just found him in his rooms, his head bleeding and his hands broken open like he'd been punching a wall. He's been locked in there all day with half the wine cellar. He was saying your name.'

'My name?'

'Over and over.'

He remembered what she'd done. When he recovered his faculties, he'd have her whipped, or worse. Maybe Melissa was right. Maybe they should have stayed in the woods.

'You have blood all over you,' he said.

'It's not mine. He killed Daos.' She pulled away and looked into the flames. 'This is his pyre.'

'Did he hurt you?'

She shrugged one shoulder. 'I hit him on the head with my cane. The rest was Daos, I think.'

'So you're all right?'

'Yes,' she said, but not without hesitation.

'Then why won't you look at me? Kala?'

That was the moment when her exhaustion found her. She could no longer hold it back.

'I'm not supposed to be here,' she said. Her voice was barely a whisper. 'We were supposed to have left last night. We were going to leave Kepos, but now we're still here, and he's still here. I just don't know if we'll ever be free.'

'You were leaving?' Leon said. The crack in his voice finally pulled her gaze to his. 'You were going to leave, and you didn't say anything?'

'I wanted to tell you yesterday.'

He took her shoulders in his hands. 'I'll come with you. If you want to go, then we can find somewhere. We can hide in the forest, or maybe on the coast. I'll keep you safe, Melissa too.'

That was how small their world was: he couldn't think beyond the eastern sea. Had she ever been like that, she wondered, or had her father's stories always pulled her out beyond the cliffs? She could no longer remember how she had viewed the world before his death.

'I'm not staying in the valley, Leon,' she said. 'I'm getting out.'

'Out?'

'Yes, out. Up there,' she said, pointing to the clifftops she knew lurked beyond the darkness. 'I'm not just leaving the city, I'm leaving this whole place.'

'But… where?'

So she told him. She told him about her father and the palace on the Plain. She told him about the Water, about Neophytos and, finally, about Theodora.

He was silent for a long time after she finished talking.

'I never would have seen you again,' he said eventually, 'and you said nothing.'

'That's what you're upset about? I just told you the valley is about to be destroyed by the sea, and you're angry because I was going to leave without saying goodbye?'

'I'm angry because you didn't trust me. I'm angry because every time I get close to you, you push me away. I'm angry because–'

'It wasn't safe to tell you,' she said. 'Two acolytes are already dead, Leon. Would you want to put Eulalia in danger? We were going to come back when we knew it was safe.'

'And who says it was safe for you?'

'Nothing's safe for me,' she said, her voice rising. 'I'm in danger whatever I do. Don't you understand that? I've had a target on my back ever since the day my father died. Someone tried to poison me, my friends keep being murdered, and your shit-eating drunkard of a father can't keep his hands or his fists to himself. How am I any safer here?'

'Someone really tried to poison you?'

'The leaf in my food that night. It was hemlock. The same thing that killed your uncle, and probably your grandfather too.'

Leon's face darkened. 'You think my father–'

'I don't know. Maybe. If he wasn't trying to kill me before last night then he will be now, that's for sure.'

'If you'd just let me kill him then it'd solve all of our problems.' His voice was oddly calm, as though he contemplated the task regularly.

'No, it wouldn't,' she said. 'The only safe place for me is out there. The only safe place for any of us is out there.'

They sat side by side, watching the flames in a silence that wasn't altogether comfortable. There was little left of the body now. It would burn through the night until the last bones fell apart. There would be no one to collect the ashes. All Daos's family were dead now.

'How's Eulalia?' Kala asked, to break the tension.

'She hasn't left her room, and I don't know what to say to her. I keep getting it wrong, and that just upsets her more. Everything I think of seems trite.'

'You both have a new brother, at least,' Kala said, proving his point.

'So do you,' he said. 'I hope that doesn't change things between us, though. You know, the extended family thing.'

'Why would it? There's nothing between us to change.'

'Now you're just lying to yourself.' He reached out and stroked his thumb across her cheek, rubbing the flakes of dried blood from her skin. His next words were a whisper. 'Don't leave me behind next time, Kallista.'

The endearment threw her off balance. She'd only heard it from Melissa before, but hearing it from his lips unspooled her emotions in a way she couldn't control. She didn't want to control it. She leaned in to meet him halfway, but then he put his hand on her hip, on the spot stained in Daos's blood. His father's voice filled her head.

There's no kind of love that can make Glauks worth Lykos's time.

She knew the tribes didn't matter. They'd mean nothing up on the Plain, when she eventually reached it. But in that moment, sitting by the pyre in the garden of her ancestors, they seemed to run in the blood.

She pulled back before their lips touched.

'What's wrong?' he asked.

'Nothing,' she said quickly, pushing her hair behind her ears. 'I'm just feeling… unwell.'

It wasn't entirely a lie.

'I'll take you inside.' He climbed quickly to his feet and helped her up, then called for Melissa to prepare a bath for her. It was a rare luxury, but when Kala raised her eyebrows at the extravagance he said, 'You're the mistress of this house now, aren't you?'

She was longing for the hot water so she didn't protest too hard. She might have been more stubborn had she realised that he would be the one helping her into it.

'I don't mind at all,' he said when Melissa asked if he would stay.

'Well, I do!' Kala said.

But there was no arguing with Melissa. She shut the door pointedly as she left them in Kala's chambers with the steaming tub.

'Turn around,' Kala said once they were alone.

Leon grinned. 'You weren't this shy last time. In fact, if I recall correctly, you told me you had no reason to be ashamed of your nudity. Very accurately, as it happens.'

'Just turn around.'

He held his hands up in surrender and turned his back to her. She was no more prudish than the rest of Kepos, for whom running around naked in public was part of daily life at the gymnasium, but she didn't want Leon to see the bloody marks his father had left on her skin. She intended to wash them off quickly with a cloth, so she could enjoy her bath without the shadows of the past day colouring its water.

Unfortunately, her tired body was unwilling to cooperate. After a night in a hammock and a day's hard scrubbing, she was too stiff to pull her dress off over her head.

Leon caught her as she wobbled. The material fell back into its proper place, but not before he'd seen the bloody fingerprints on her skin. She tensed, prepared for him to rage against his father, but the anger never came. Instead, he picked up a cloth and, dipping it in the hot water, knelt at her feet.

He didn't say anything, because nothing needed to be said. All that was needed was a look from him: half offer, half entreaty. She lifted her skirt to bare her side up to her hip and, with the softest of strokes, he cleaned away the mess his father had made.

He was back the next day, popping in on his way to the baths to bring her a bunch of flowers. The day after it was fruit pastries, then wine, but he never stayed. On the fourth day, when he turned up bearing some familiar nut cakes, she worked out what was going on and dragged him into the house.

'You're courting me,' she said.

'What if I am?' His gap-toothed grin was back on display this morning.

'With other people's gifts.'

The grin turned shifty. 'What makes you say that?'

'These are cakes from Onos, Leon. The tavern keeper has been giving them to me at every opportunity so I'll look kindly on the Onos suitor. So why would *you* give me them?'

He opened his mouth, then closed it again. 'It's like this...' he started, but again found himself without an explanation.

'The truth, please.'

'All right, all right,' he said. 'The suitors have split up the days until the Proaulia, so they each have a chance to court you. I've been acting as a sort of go-between on their behalves.'

'A very poor one.'

'Well, yes,' he grinned again, 'but they don't know that. I thought it would keep them at bay, and if it swung the odds in my favour, then I wouldn't have complained.'

'What odds?' She threw up her hands. 'You know that the Proaulia is irrelevant. I'll choose the best of them for the sake of appearances, but I'm not planning a long marriage. You know I'm leaving.'

'You want me to keep up the pretence that you're not, though, don't you?'

'How is dismissing all my suitors helping with that? I wouldn't do that, not if I were staying.'

'No, but it's exactly what I'd be doing.' He stepped closer. 'And anyway, you're still here.'

'For the time being.'

'Then so am I.' His hand was on her waist now, his thumb stroking the fabric of her dress. 'I'll be at the Proaulia.'

'Where you'll choose Sophia, just like your father has arranged.'

He laughed. 'When have I ever done what he wanted?'

'Leon…'

'All right, you're leaving. I know. But would it be so awful to spend your time with me, just until you do?'

She stared at him as understanding dawned.

'You don't believe me,' she said, pushing him away.

'I didn't say that.'

'You don't, though, do you? You think I won't leave.'

'I believe you want to.'

'But you don't think I can.'

Emotions cascaded across his face: desperation, hope, resolve.

'I think you could be happy here,' he said, 'if you gave it a chance.'

'You didn't understand a word I said the other night, did you?' She shook her head incredulously. 'You keep telling me I'm pushing you away, but you don't believe me when I let you in.'

'Then explain it to me.'

'What is there to explain? I've told you: we'll all die if we stay here.'

'So you believe it all?' Leon said. 'You really believe the city's going to be flooded?'

'I've seen it.' Her frustration made the words sharp, even though she shared his doubts. 'I've seen the water trickling through. It might not be this month, or this year, or this decade even, but that wall is not going to hold forever, and when it falls I fully intend to be elsewhere.'

'On the Plain.'

'Yes, on the Plain.' She touched the pendant at her throat, the green stone Theodora had worn, her last connection to the Empire's Heart.

Leon still looked sceptical. 'In the palace that's up there,' he pointed to the unseen cliffs, 'which you haven't seen, which no one's seen, where there's a whole civilisation we don't know about?'

She sighed and dropped onto one of the courtyard benches, suddenly tired of the whole debate.

'Theodora was right,' she said. 'You have to see the Water to understand it.'

Leon sat down beside her. 'It's not that I don't believe you,' he said. 'It's just a lot to take in, and you're taking a lot on faith yourself. All you have is a story.'

'Then why are Neophytos and Theodora dead? Why would someone kill them if the Plain doesn't exist, if there's nothing for us to find up there?'

He had no answer to that.

'Even if there were no danger in staying here,' she went on, 'and even if the priests hadn't been lying to us all our lives about it, wouldn't you want to see the clifftops for yourself? Wouldn't you at least want to go and look?'

Leon ran his fingers through his hair.

'When are you leaving?' he asked. 'Do you have a plan?'

Her worst fear was that she and Melissa might not get their chance until next year's harvest festival. They might be stuck here for months, fully aware of the threat that was looming over them, and unable to do anything about it. They would be trapped here with Nikos.

'Not yet. Soon, I hope. It won't be until after the Proaulia, anyway.' She didn't mention that she was planning to go scouting. He'd only want to join in, and she'd be less conspicuous on her own.

'Then my plan remains the same.' He spoke with finality.

'No. The best thing you can do is stay out of trouble. I don't want to raise suspicions.'

'Staying out of trouble is about the most suspicious thing I could do.' Somehow his arm was around her waist again, pulling her close. 'So we may as well enjoy ourselves.'

She used her cane to push herself to her feet, stepping out of his embrace. 'Are you incapable of taking anything seriously?' she said. 'This isn't fun to me, Leon. I'm just trying to survive.'

She had raised her voice loudly enough that her guards came running from the corridors around the house. She and Melissa had installed them on the day they had burned Daos's body, pulling field slaves into the house to protect the doors. It had seemed a sensible precaution at the time, but with four of them now watching her argue with Leon, it suddenly felt excessive.

'Everything all right, Mistress?' one of them asked.

'Yes, thank you. Please return to your posts.'

They eyed Leon warily as they retreated, but they didn't linger in the courtyard.

'You're scared,' he said when they had gone.

'Of course I am.'

'Of me?'

'Of your father.' The confession was a whisper. 'He's your blood, Leon.'

'So you still don't trust me.'

'How can you say that after everything I've told you?'

But he wasn't entirely wrong. She'd told him what she knew, and what had happened, but not what she was planning to do. She hadn't told him their route out. She hadn't told him anything that he could use to stop her, in fact, or to help her either.

She hadn't issued an invitation for him to join them.

'You're always holding back,' he said.

'And you hold back too little. We each have our own burdens.'

'Yes, we do,' he said as he came to stand in front of her. 'I'm just offering to share yours.'

'You know you can't. You have Sophia.'

He made a dismissive noise. 'Sophia doesn't have me any more than I have her. I barely know her, and yet you keep dragging her out as an excuse.'

'Fine, then how's this for an excuse: your father will kill me rather than have a cripple in his family. That's what will happen if you push him, Leon. Then you'll be the Glauks, he'll be the Lykos, and I'll be dead, all because you hold back too little.'

It wasn't the first time he had heard this from her, but this time there was more determination in his response. 'I'm not going to let that happen,' he said.

'Neither am I.'

She couldn't afford to provoke Nikos any more than she already had. He had stayed away since her return, but she was still cowering inside for fear of meeting him in the streets. She wouldn't leave the walls of Glauks and the protection of her guards, because one day there would be a reckoning for that dark night in the library. She wasn't going to let Leon force his father's hand.

'Get out of my house,' she said, and then she picked up her cane and walked away, leaving him alone in the courtyard.

'Kala, wait,' he called after her, but the guards hadn't gone far. They were more than happy to help him on his way.

Kala left orders for Leon to be turned away from her door. He still came the next day: morning, noon and night. Each time he shouted her name it dragged across her resolve. She'd rise to her feet, sometimes even getting as far as the courtyard before she remembered all the reasons she couldn't relent.

The hemlock, the axe, his father's fists.

She'd find him after the Proaulia, she promised herself. She'd get them all out of this valley if she could, but until Leon was safely married off she couldn't risk his company.

The guards sent him away.

It wasn't long before the suitors started coming to her door themselves. She had to entertain them. There was no other credible option.

The string of callers reminded her of the Dekocrats on the day of her father's cremation. They were variously kind, avaricious and sneering, although they all made at least some attempt at civility. She smiled and nodded and thanked, half her mind on their conversation and the other half wondering when Nikos would come to her door, and whether her guards would be strong enough to deny him entry.

Drakon and Hilarion were amongst her first visitors, but her final caller on the eve of the Proaulia was neither the one she had expected, nor the one she had feared.

'Ariston?' she said as Melissa showed him in. He was carrying a box of fat dates stuffed with almonds, which Kala eyed apprehensively. It looked like a courting gift.

'Don't worry,' he said quickly. 'I'm here for my brother, not myself.'

'Well, in that case: come, sit.' She patted the bench beside her, and he joined her in the evening sunshine. It was only after he had handed her the gift that she thought properly about his words.

'Wait,' she said, 'which brother?' She'd assumed he'd meant one of his many brothers from Delphis, but now she wasn't so sure.

Ariston twisted his fingers in his lap.

'Oh, gods,' she said. 'Leon sent you, didn't he?'

'He said you wouldn't let him in.'

'And did he tell you why?'

'He said,' Ariston started, pausing to clear his throat. 'He said you were being…'

'Yes?'

'Stubborn.'

She handed him back the dates. 'Then you can tell him where to shove these.'

'Oh, that'll be fun,' he laughed, although he looked a little shocked by her turn of phrase. 'Are you? Being stubborn, I mean?'

'I'm being sensible. I've managed to incur the Lykos's wrath, and Leon's ridiculous overtures are only going to make that worse. Anyway, he's marrying Sophia.'

'He says not.'

'Then you tell me who's being stubborn here. We both know he doesn't have a choice.'

Ariston nodded grimly. She wondered whether he was thinking about Eulalia and Timon.

'Anyway,' she said, keen to lighten the mood, 'enough about him. How are you, brother?'

He smiled at the word. 'Well enough, thank you, sister.'

'I haven't seen you since the festival.'

'Ah, yes. Another display of the Lykos's famous wrath.'

She remembered how Zotikos had laughed in Nikos's face, as though there were nothing intimidating about him. She wished she could do the same.

'Is your grandfather all right?' she asked.

'He's fine. He told me the whole story that night. Half of Delphis is adopted, you know.'

'I didn't.'

'Well,' he laughed, 'neither did I. He's always been one for taking in strays, it seems.'

Her impression of the tribe was a warm one, albeit chaotic. Its mixed heritage explained a lot. It was a family she might easily have made her own.

'You all seem to muddle along together all right,' she said.

'More or less, although I wish he'd spoken to me sooner. It would have saved us some pain.'

She took his hand in hers and held it tight, but there was nothing she could say to make it better.

'What will you do tomorrow?' she asked.

'I don't know.' His eyes were fixed on the ground, and she couldn't read his expression. 'I think I'll still come. I told Grandpa I would, anyway.'

'You can come and keep me entertained,' Kala said with a smile. 'I rather think it's your brotherly duty.'

'I'd be happy to, but I think you'll be entertained enough. Have you decided who you're going to choose yet?'

'No.'

She'd have to pick someone. If she didn't, then the Archon would intervene and choose someone for her. The city had been too long without a Glauks already. He wouldn't allow that situation to continue. She would have nearly a week between the Proaulia and the marriage itself, and she hoped they'd escape the valley during that window. If they couldn't, then she'd rather be stuck with a husband of her own choosing.

'You could do worse than Leon,' Ariston said quietly.

'I'd like to live out the week, so no, thank you. Any other recommendations?'

'I'd also like to survive the week,' he said, 'so I'll only recommend Leon. Don't underestimate him, Kala. He's not playing.'

'Nikos?'

'Leon.'

She laughed. 'Of course he is. Everything's a game to him.'

'Is that what you really think?' he said. 'He might smile through it, but nothing's ever just a game. Don't forget who his father is, or what it must have been like growing up in that house. I thank Euaemon every day that I was saved from that.'

She remembered Leon telling her how he'd become used to the fear, that he'd never known anything else. He'd attracted his father's anger to keep it from Eulalia, and for that he must have paid a price. But the image of him that endured in her mind was not a bleak one. She could only picture his gap-toothed grin, and the way he had laughed despite his broken ribs.

But when he'd said he would kill his father, he had meant it. She was the only thing holding him back.

On the evening before the Proaulia, Kala should have been praying to Diaprepes to send her a husband worthy of the title of Glauks. Instead, she was hiding in her father's library, trying to chase away the ghosts.

She didn't know what to do. She might not be able to leave this place for months, so she should choose someone she could tolerate for that long. She knew whom she wanted to spend that time with, but the knowledge terrified her, and not just because of the threat it would bring with it. Melissa wanted her to take the risk and hope they could avoid Nikos for their remaining time in the valley, but for Kala it felt too dangerous. She was paralysed by the choice, and no option seemed correct.

If only she could choose no husband at all, then Glauks would fall to Leon when she left. If only she could have left the valley at the harvest festival, as they had planned.

There was a knock at the door. 'Mistress?' It was Hagne.

'Come in.'

'Here,' she said, bustling in with a bowl of stew. 'Now, you're not to stay in here all night fretting. Melissa's set your clothes out for the morning, and you'll want to be fresh.'

'I won't be up much longer,' Kala said, wishing the woman would leave her alone. There was enough noise in her own head. Nonetheless, she forced a smile and thanked her for the food, and then she was on her own again.

She ate mechanically, barely tasting what she was putting in her mouth. It was warm and filling, and that was all that mattered. She must have been more exhausted than she had realised, because the next thing she knew she was waking up to find her face pressed against the top of the desk.

Was it morning? Had she slept straight through?

The library was hot and filled with the sound of rustling paper. Kala blinked a few times to clear the fog from her sight, but it didn't work. Then she smelled the smoke. The library was on fire, and she was stuck in the middle of it.

She tried to get up, but found that she couldn't move. She was tied to her father's chair at her wrists and ankles.

Someone was trying to kill her. Again.

She opened her mouth to scream, but the smoke clogged her lungs. She had to get out of the room. The door was blocked by the fire, but one of the windows at the back of the house was open, feeding the flames. She'd be able to wriggle through it if she could just get out of the chair, but there was no way to loosen the knots. She tried to stand awkwardly, hoping to gather up enough momentum to smash the chair beneath her, but instead she just toppled over onto the floor.

Pain shot down her twisted leg. It had been twisted further by the rope, so it was now completely useless.

The fire was running along the bookshelves, eating up their contents. It wouldn't be long before it blocked the window too.

She had to get up.

She tried again, lifting herself to her knees then using the table to pull herself to her feet. She jumped off her good leg, bringing the chair down hard onto the ground.

Please, Diaprepes. Please, let this work.

Her head cracked against the floor, but the chair stayed intact. Her father had been an even better carpenter than she'd given him credit for.

The flames were already creeping around the window frame.

Gods, she was going to die here.

She crawled up to her feet once more, forcing her head into the smoke. It scoured her throat tight and raked at her eyes.

Last jump. Last prayer. Last chance.

Her hip jarred against the wood as she landed, but the chair finally gave way beneath her. She didn't pause to shake the fragments free before scrambling through the window and out into the air of the garden.

It took a few seconds for her to realise she was on fire, and a few more for her to extinguish the flames.

She could hear the bell now, sounding through the house as someone roused the slaves, but she was too tired to move. Despite the heat of the fire, her skin was prickling with cold sweat. When she heard someone calling her name, she croaked quietly back at them.

'Kala!'

'Here.' Her voice was no more than a whisper, but Melissa still managed to find her and drag her farther away from the house.

'Kallista,' she said as she rested her face on Kala's shoulder. 'I thought you were dead.'

'So did I.'

Kala shivered.

Melissa pulled her into her arms.

The two of them sat there, Melissa rocking Kala like a child, while the rest of the slaves bustled around them. Kala could hear the shouting as they shuttled to and from the library, carrying pails of water. After a while the light changed, the strobes through her eyelids diminishing as the blaze was contained. It had a dreamlike quality to it, a fugue from light to darkness.

The water wouldn't be enough to save her father's scrolls. The library would be a charcoal canker in the centre of her home.

Kala opened her eyes as one of the twins crouched down beside her.

'Hagne's gone,' he said. 'One of the horses, too.'

Kala exchanged a glance with Melissa, who mirrored her surprise. What possible reason could Hagne have to want Kala dead?

She raised her hand to wipe her face, and found that the carving from the chair's armrest was still tied to it: the running wolf of Lykos. It was the only animal that had survived the fire.

It was large enough to rest heavily on the palm of her hand, and yet so fragile that she could have broken it in two.

IX
ὄφις | Ophis | Serpent

To his ninth son, the god gave the skies and the sands as his domain,
and he named him Azaes for the dryness of that latter portion.
He gifted him with a leather bag that held the winds, which he unleashed at his will
to chase storms across the land and drive dunes over cities like waves over the shore.

- Kleitos, On the Formation of Kepos

The Proaulia was a midday event, which was just as well. It was already dawn when the slaves conquered the smouldering wreck of the library, and the whole house was coated in damp ash and misery. Kala's cane was the only thing rescued from the rubble. It was practically burned away, but the owl carving was mostly intact. It was a small comfort, but a comfort nonetheless. Along with the Lykos carving and the Kleitos scrolls, it was all she had left of her childhood. Kala stowed it in her bag, which was always packed and ready, just in case.

Then began the laborious preparations for the ceremony. Melissa took her to the baths to wash, since there was no more appetite for fires in the Glauks household that day. Kala's dress had burned through to the skin here and there, blistering into angry red patches that screamed when they hit the water. She didn't care. The pain woke enough determination in her to face another day in Kepos.

When they returned to the house, Melissa tortured her hair into braids, then pinned and piled it high with combs of orichalcum and amethyst. Her dress was of the softest linen, secured at her shoulders with fine brooches and at her waist with a trailing knotted belt, so the fabric fell in pleats and waves down to her feet. A jewelled diadem completed her armour.

She had never felt so overdressed, but Melissa assured her it was not optional.

'Have you decided?' Melissa asked her.

'Yes.'

All her indecision had coalesced into grit in the fire. There was nowhere she could hide, and nowhere she could run. Instead, she would have to stand.

'Good.' Melissa kissed her forehead. 'I'll be waiting for you here.'

She would walk alone, with no slaves to accompany her, because that was what the Proaulia required. The symbolism was that each participant should arrive as an individual and leave as a couple, but it would also have been Kala's choice. This morning, for the last time, she needed to stand on her own.

The walk was long, but not unpleasant despite her aching leg. There was enough of a breeze to keep her cool, but the day was bright and warm. Although slightly bereft without her usual cane, she had to admit that its replacement was kinder on her palm than the one her father had made for her.

The door of the Lykos house was ajar when she passed it on her way out of the city, and shortly afterwards she heard a set of footsteps behind her own. She turned to see Eulalia following closely, although with enough distance between them to keep up the pretence of solitude. Her eyes were red and her cheeks pink, as though she had been crying. Kala didn't ask what was wrong; she already knew. Eulalia's father would be up at the temple when the rest of the men arrived. Only eligible men were allowed inside, but he'd make sure that the one he had selected was the only one who approached his daughter.

It was comforting to have Eulalia's presence behind her as she left the city, but once they had crossed the bridge out in the meadows Kala realised that Eulalia wasn't the only person following her.

She had left home early so she would have plenty of time to scale the steps up to the temple, enough time to compensate for her awkward gait, but the other girls were catching them up now. With each girl leaving a respectful space between herself and the girl in front, Kala found herself leading dozens of young women in a slow and silent convoy across the valley. Although she was confident that they wouldn't be late, she still felt the urge to rush her steps so she wouldn't force them all to walk at her pace. Her panic confused her feet and slowed her still further, until she resigned herself to being the enemy of all her peers. When she finally relaxed, her strides fell back into their usual rhythm.

Her nerves returned as they walked past the temple warehouses, as she approached the steps that would take them to the outcropping above. She had climbed this way before, though. She had scaled the wall, up and down. She had walked all across the valley in this past month, and that experience gave her strength.

She knew she could conquer this.

She was sweating and exhausted by the time she reached the top of the promontory, her diadem slipping down onto her forehead, but she was more or less presentable.

'Kala of Glauks,' the Archon greeted her as she staggered up the last steps.

She squinted against the glare of his robes. Immediately in front of her was the temple itself, with yet more steps leading up to its columned entrance. She could see the statue of the great god glittering beyond the doorway, with the animals of the gods circling it. Behind the temple, mud brick buildings crawled up the cliff face in a wide swathe of multiple tiers, clustered around narrow openings that had no discernible pattern. They filled the entire width of the space.

Kala could see nothing of the pulley lift on which Theodora had pinned their hopes. She wouldn't even know where to start looking.

'You lead the procession this morning, I see,' the Archon said, dragging her attention back to him. 'Appropriate, is it not? After all, it is your next decision that will shape the future of the city.' The statement was too ambiguous for Kala's liking.

'Why is that, Archon?' she asked.

'You control Glauks now, child,' he said. 'Today you gift it to another.' The 'or else' was implied.

'Yes,' she said firmly. 'I shall.'

He directed her towards the altar at the foot of the steps, where the Glauks acolytes were waiting with the Hierophant. As she was the only bride from her tribe, she would have their entire attention.

She adjusted her diadem and went to greet Straton. He didn't look happy, but his hands were calm at his sides today, stroking his robes rather than clutching at them. Kala took that as a good sign.

'Kala of Glauks,' he said.

'Hierophant.'

'If you'll come with me, then we'll perform the purification before you enter the temple.'

She followed him to the altar at the foot of the temple steps, surrounded by Glauks acolytes. She couldn't help but notice the two who were missing, the only two she'd known. The other young brides would have the acolytes of their tribes shared between them, and only the most important ones would receive the attentions of their tribe's Hierophant. Kala didn't enjoy her distinguished honour. She felt like a shepherd corralling pious sheep.

They took the cloak from her shoulders so her arms were bared, then washed the dust of the road from her hands and face with water that was perfumed with oils. She looked past them and into the temple as they worked. Although she'd witnessed sacrifices here at the altar, she'd never been inside the temple itself. Its interior glistened darkly in the sunshine, forbidden and seductive.

Melissa had left a single lock of Kala's hair falling loose from the crown of her head, as was the custom for young women at the Proaulia. The Hierophant now wrapped it around his fingers then cut a few inches from its end before laying the strands carefully on the altar. The dark hairs danced a little in the breeze, but the shape of the altar kept them in place. Its top was curved in like a bowl, ready for the blood of the sacrifice that would follow. The men would bring the doomed animal with them when they made their own pilgrimage.

'Come,' Straton said, offering her his hand.

Her fingers were still slick from their anointment, so she rested them only gently on his. He clearly had in mind that their ascent of the temple steps would open the Proaulia with gracious dignity, but he hadn't counted on Kala's limp. Her cane clacked into the reverent silence, the noise echoing around them as they crossed the threshold.

What she had seen from the altar was nothing compared with how the temple looked from the inside. The walls were painted in a riot of colourful frescos, coursing around the large room from tribe to tribe as they told their stories. In the middle of the back wall was a huge mural of the bull of Tauros, head high and proud. To either side were the wolf of Lykos and the deer of Elaphos, with the lesser tribes filling the walls back towards where they stood. Glauks's owl was painted just to her left, close to the door. A pedestal stood in front of each of the tribal frescos, flanked by braziers and by the columns that held the roof above them. On the Glauks pedestal was a decorative table next to a single, lonely stool: Kala's seat for the duration. Straton led her to it through the smoke of fire and incense, and then she was on her own. The thick air burned her eyes.

Eulalia was brought in by the Lykos Hierophant shortly afterwards, but her pedestal was at the other end of the temple. Kala couldn't even see her once she was settled, because the pillars barred her view. In fact, between the central statue and the thick columns, she could see none of the other pedestals. That must have been intentional, to avoid them seeing who else was approached by their suitors, but it was isolating.

Kala started to fiddle with her cane, but stilled her hand as the tapping echoed around the walls. There were no tapestries to absorb it here, no furnishings to temper the emptiness of the space.

More young women were escorted into the temple in no particular order, until finally they were all seated. The acolytes shut the temple doors, closing them in.

By then, Kala had already traced every detail of the statues that filled her line of sight: the orichalcum animals chasing each other around the base of the towering god. The animals of the tribes were represented out of their usual order here; Glauks glinted between Lykos and Delphis, the owl flying above the wolf and dolphin. It was a satisfying rearrangement. The figure of the great god stretched so high above them that his head was lost in the smoky fug that had collected near the ceiling. She never saw his face.

The screams of the sacrifice outside filtered through the doors. A young bull, Kala guessed, and a sheep. The noise grated down her spine and raised a sweat beneath the oils coating her arms. She felt their desperation.

She had been drawn in by the decadence of the sculptures, but in the flickering firelight they took on a threatening aspect. She was trapped in this dark, silent space, filled with the anticipation of her companions, listening to the slaughter outside the walls. This was not what she had expected. She had been told that the Proaulia was a time of celebration and joy for the young women of Kepos. The atmosphere should have been one of excitement.

Instead, the air tasted like fear.

When the doors finally did open, there was moment of held breath before anyone stepped forwards.

The youngest son of the Tauros was first through. The women may not have entered the temple in order, but the men would keep to their hierarchy. Leon should have been next, but he was nowhere to be seen. Instead, Kala recognised two of his cousins, and then a cluster of men from Elaphos. That group brought the first of her suitors, and she soon lost track of the crowds coming in.

'Kala of Glauks,' the boy said, and he was indeed a boy. He couldn't have been more than thirteen.

'Er, hello,' she said.

'I'm Phaidros of Elaphos.'

He handed her his token, a wooden ring burned with his name and a tiny deer, before moving on to the next pedestal. Apparently, his name was all he was prepared to offer her.

The next suitor was Drakon, again. He told her in intricate detail how he had carved the courting ring he gave her, how he had found its shape in the raw wood, and how he had burned the serpent around its edge. She was suppressing a yawn when Ariston came to save her.

'You're doing well, then,' Ariston said, nodding at the two rings that now sat in her lap.

'I'd rather not be here at all. Where's your new brother?'

He sighed. 'I think he has it in mind to make a statement.'

'Oh gods. What kind of statement?'

'One he thinks is romantic, probably.'

Kala couldn't reconcile Leon with the idea of romance. The problem was that he made up his own rituals, instead of following everyone else's.

'I dread to imagine,' she said.

Ariston laughed, but the echoing space sucked the warmth from the sound.

'Here.' He held out a glass cup ornamented with orichalcum foil. 'Grandfather thought you'd need something to display all the tokens you'll be collecting today.'

She turned it in the light of the braziers.

'It's beautiful. Please thank him for me.' The wooden rings clunked softly against the glass as she dropped them in and placed the glass on the table beside her. 'Do you have sisters here today?'

'None except you. Do you want me to stay?'

'Yes, but you shouldn't. Besides, you have your own tokens to distribute.'

'I only made one,' he said ruefully.

She reached out and squeezed his hand. 'Choose wisely then, brother.'

'And you, sister.'

She smiled as he left her. 'I will.'

She'd made up her mind. They'd face the danger together, or not at all.

He still made her wait. There were ten more tokens in her cup before Leon finally made his appearance, the very last of the men to enter the temple. He didn't look at all himself. His usual swagger was entirely absent, as was his grin. When he eyed the glass full of rings, his mood only darkened further.

'As statements go,' she said as he approached her pedestal, 'turning up late isn't going to win you much favour.'

'Not late,' he said. 'In my proper place, according to my tribe.'

'Your proper place was second through the door, with your cousins.'

'Not anymore. I denounced him.'

It took Kala a moment to understand what he was telling her. She knew it was possible, but she'd never heard of it happening. If he really had denounced his father, then he'd revert to his mother's tribe or, since he'd once been a member of another tribe…

'I'm not Lykos anymore,' he said. 'I'm Glauks.'

But that wasn't all.

'You mean you're *the* Glauks,' she said. '*The* Glauks, Leon.'

He was older than she, and he was now the only aristocratic man in the tribe. There was no contest. She'd planned to give the title to him anyway, but he'd clearly become tired of waiting.

Anger rushed to her cheeks.

'So this is what it was all about?' she continued, her voice rising. 'All this time, you just wanted your own little slice of power, and when you couldn't get it from me you decided to take it for yourself. Is that it?'

He looked pained. 'That's how little you think of me? That's how little you think of yourself, Kala?'

'What am I supposed to think?'

'That I'm not going to leave you unprotected anymore, you or Lali. I heard about the fire. I'm going to keep you safe, for however long you stay.'

'So, what?' she said sceptically. 'This is you just being a good friend?'

He looked away, his jaw clenching. 'No,' he said quietly. 'I'm not any kind of friend to you. I don't want to be your friend, Kala. I'm in love with you. Don't you know that? Don't you feel that?'

His voice was cracking under the words, but Kala's mind was emptied by them. She couldn't think of a thing to say.

He stepped onto her pedestal and crouched beside her, drawing her hand into his.

'Every time you send me away, it feels like I might never see you again, and I can't take that. I can't let you slip away from me. Tell yourself this is about Glauks, if that's what you want to believe. Tell yourself I just want the title and the land, and if that's all you want to give me then I won't ask for more. Just please, Kala, don't accept anyone else.'

He folded a small object into her hand then started to walk away. It was a wooden ring like the others, and yet completely different. It had a wolf and Leon's name on one side, but on the other side an owl had been burned next to another name, her own name.

It had been made for her, and her alone.

'Leon, wait.'

There was no hope in his eyes as he returned to her.

She held up the ring. 'I have one condition,' she said.

The corner of his mouth twitched, as though he wanted to smile but was afraid of what she might say next. 'Which is?'

'You come with me when I leave.'

His hazel eyes sparkled as their mischief returned. 'Then I have a condition of my own.'

'You think you're in a position to make demands?'

'Marry me before we go.'

That would mean five more days in Kepos. She could think of a way to dissuade him from waiting that long.

'Only if you'll come to the wall tomorrow and see the Water for yourself,' she said.

'That's two conditions now. You can't just go adding more conditions to your list. That's hardly fair.' But he was grinning as he came back to her. He held her gaze for a long moment. 'Are you sure?'

'Yes,' she said, handing him the ring.

He slid it onto her finger, finding one it fitted on his second attempt, then clasped her hand tightly.

'Kallista,' he murmured, leaning close to press a kiss to her cheek.

Despite the smoke surrounding them, she could smell the sunshine on his skin.

'Are you ready to get out of here?' he said.

'Definitely.'

There was no reason to stay in the temple any longer; she'd made her choice. Now they would have to deal with the consequences.

When they turned to leave, they had a small audience.

'Well?' Leon said to her would-be suitors. 'What are you lot hanging around for? The lady's declared herself. Go spend your tokens elsewhere.'

Hilarion stepped towards her. 'Surely not, Miss Kala.'

'You may as well throw your tokens off the cliff,' Leon said to him. 'None of these beauties are likely to stoop to your pig-shagging level.'

'Apparently only the damaged ones will stoop to yours.'

Leon growled. 'I can drop *you* off the cliff too, if you like.'

'Come on,' Kala interrupted, resting her arm on his to pull him towards the door. He was entirely too fond of fighting. 'There's something I need you to do for me.'

'Oh? Yet another condition?' He grinned. 'Now you're just pushing your luck.'

'Well, the old seer at the festival did say I was very lucky.'

'Because he wanted you to marry Thales, of all people. I know I'm missing the odd tooth, but *Thales*? Really?'

'Hey,' a voice from the crowd complained. Thales himself, presumably.

'Come on,' Kala said, and then they were out in the fresh air. She only had time for a few breaths before the consequences found them.

'So this is why you turned your back on your family?' Nikos was striding towards them. 'You denounce me for this cripple whore?'

'No,' Leon said as he tucked Kala behind him. 'I denounced you for me and Lali, so we could be free from you and from Lykos.'

Kala wouldn't have thought it possible, but Nikos's expression became more furious still. 'You're telling me you've corrupted your sister, too?'

'If that's what you call me putting myself in front of your fists to keep them from her. If you think saving her from you is corruption, then yes, I've corrupted her, because she's denouncing you too.'

Nikos stared at Leon for a long moment then raged up the temple steps, but the acolytes barred his way.

'You may not enter the sacred space, Lykos,' the Archon said. 'You know this.'

'Eulalia!' he called past the barricade of priests. 'Eulalia, get out here!'

'How much more of your family do you need to poison before you're satisfied?' Leon shouted at him, loudly enough for the whole plateau to hear. 'How long would Lali and I have been safe under your roof, when you have so little conscience that you'd murder your father and brother for the title you now hold?'

The precinct was silent as Nikos turned slowly to face his son. 'You may come to regret those words, boy.'

'Do you think they don't know you for the savage you are?' Leon said quietly. 'There's not a single man here who wouldn't support me in protecting my family from you.'

As if to prove his point, the Dekocrats waiting by the altar had gathered close around Leon and Kala as he spoke. Nikos's gaze flitted amongst them, trying and failing to find an ally.

'So a man no longer has dominion over his own family in Kepos,' he yelled at them. 'Is that right?'

'Of course he does,' the Delphis replied jovially. 'This young man is now the Glauks, I believe, and his family is his to do with as he wishes. A family that includes his bride, of course, and his sister. I see nothing inconsistent with our laws here. Don't you agree, Tauros?'

All eyes turned to the man who thought he ruled the valley. Eulalia was visible behind the wall of acolytes now, peeking out from between their shoulders. Kala sent her a nervous smile as they waited for the Tauros to speak.

'That seems correct to me, Delphis. Archon?'

The high priest turned to Nikos. 'You are overruled,' he decreed. 'Kindly return to the city, Lykos. You have no children here today.'

He didn't fight it, but his sharp eyes marked the men who'd denied him. With one final glance at Kala, filled with the promise of violence, he left the plateau. They watched him go.

Relief drew laughter from the crowd as the acolytes abandoned their formation, releasing the Proaulia participants from the temple. Most of the young women stayed inside, still awaiting their matches, but Eulalia hurried out of the temple with Ariston in tow. The cluster of Dekocrats dispersed at the same time.

Kala didn't miss the look the Tauros gave to Leon. It was a clear message that he expected repayment for his support. Leon accepted the debt with a nod.

The only Dekocrat who hung around, other than Leon of course, was the Delphis. Kala turned to him, pressing her hand to her heart.

'Thank you, Zotikos,' she said.

'Oh, think nothing of it, my dear.' His smile creased his eyes into a gorgeous mess of wrinkles. 'The man's a brute, but I'm afraid that shan't be the last of it. Nevertheless, well done,' he said, taking Leon's hand in his own, 'and felicitations to you both on your excellent match.'

'It is rather, isn't it?' Leon said with a grin.

Eulalia and Ariston joined them then, so elated by events that they seemed to have forgotten their heartbreak, for the moment at least.

'Ah, my boy,' Zotikos said to Ariston. 'Any luck?'

His face turned grim. 'Not this year, I think.'

'Well, yes, very wise, I'm sure. There's time enough,' he said, patting Ariston's hand. 'No rush. And how are you, Miss Eulalia?' he said. 'I can't apologise enough for the mix up. I do hope you'll forgive me. I was a silly old fool not to say something sooner. I just didn't realise that it had become relevant. I am truly sorry.'

She managed a smile for him. 'I don't blame you, Delphis.'

'That's very kind of you, my dear, but I shall still hold myself accountable. Anyway, you don't want to waste your time with a blathering old man. I shall leave you to enjoy the rest of the day. I wish good fortune to your new family in Glauks.'

They all thanked him again, and then the four of them were alone.

Leon's gap-toothed grin appeared to be a permanent fixture now, but the others were less confident with their smiles.

'We're really free?' asked Eulalia.

'Better than that,' Leon said, pulling her into a rough hug, 'we're Glauks. We're going back tonight. If that's all right with my bride, of course.'

'Of course,' Kala said as he kissed her cheek.

'So you finally said yes,' Eulalia said. She smiled and took Kala's hand in her own. 'I was starting to worry that you'd never put him out of his misery. I mean, it's been weeks.'

Leon raised an eyebrow. 'How did you even know, Lali?'

'As if you've ever managed to keep a secret from me,' she said, returning the eyebrow with interest. 'Speaking of which,' she said to Kala, 'what's going on with you?'

'What do you mean?'

'That day at the temple warehouses, and again at the festival with you and Melissa. Something's up.'

'Annoyingly perceptive, isn't she?' Leon said to Kala.

Ariston and Eulalia looked at her expectantly, and the realisation hit hard: along with Melissa, this was her family. How had she ever thought to leave them behind?

'Come back to Glauks,' she said. 'There's a lot we need to discuss. But first, I need a favour.'

Ariston was a terrible actor. Fortunately, everyone was so panicked when he tipped over the brazier that they didn't notice it wasn't an accident.

While their attention was on the hot coals skittering across the ground, Eulalia untied the goats that were awaiting their fate at the side of the temple and let them loose amongst the crowd. It created complete pandemonium, sufficient to cover Kala and Leon as they slipped away.

Kala scanned the cliff face as they hurried towards the brick buildings, looking for any sign of the pulley lift, but they were swallowed up by the first tier of houses before she had worked out where they should aim their path. The alleys were so narrow that the buildings crowded over their heads, blocking their view.

'What are we looking for?' Leon asked.

'Marks on the cliff, or ropes. Anything to indicate there's a way up.'

'Is there?'

'That's what Theodora told us.'

They were whispering, but there was little need for discretion now they'd reached the squalid settlement. All the acolytes who weren't at the temple would still be working on the wall. The only priests who would be in their homes were those too ill or decrepit to leave their beds, and they had nothing to fear from them.

'We need to get closer,' Leon said, 'and higher.'

They pressed on through the twisting passageways until they were in the shade of the cliff's overhang, and then they started to look for a building they could climb.

'Here,' Kala said.

The house was three storeys of rickety mud and wood, but it had an external staircase that went straight up to the roof. Leon led the way, testing each step carefully before trusting it with his weight, but it was secure enough to hold them.

There were planks up here leading from rooftop to rooftop, so they could bypass the maze of warrens beneath them if they watched their step. That was harder for Kala than it was for Leon, since they didn't often find plank bridges wide enough that she could use her cane effectively.

'Can I help?' he asked her.

She wanted to say no. She was used to saying no.

'I'm practically your husband, Kala,' he said. 'You don't have to struggle on for my sake. I'm not going to think any less of you.'

He had managed to persuade her into piggybacking over the bridges by the time they finally found the pulley lift, hidden in the folds of the landscape by the waterfall. It wasn't a very dignified mode of travel, but it was efficient, and it felt right. Comfortable. It had the added benefit of putting Kala's head close to his neck, so she was enveloped in the warm smell of his skin. His nearness settled the strangling clamour in her stomach. She was starting to think of him as hers, she realised. He smelled like home.

'What now?' he asked as Kala slid from his back.

There was a crease in the rock face, a narrow gulley into which the lift had been fixed. It went up as far as Kala could see, beyond the point at which the cliff sloped backwards to its crest, but she couldn't see where the path of the lift ended. The platform itself sat at the bottom of the gulley on a rooftop against the cliff.

'We need to get to that building,' she said, 'then track back to the temple through the alleys on the ground.'

They followed a staircase down into the street they were aiming for, but then they heard voices. Leon grabbed Kala's hand and pulled her into a side passage. She was starting to think they'd been hearing things when the voices started up again.

'Every year, this happens,' a male voice said. 'Every year I say: how about I help with the Proaulia? And then every year I just get stuck here.'

'Twice,' a second voice interrupted.

'What?'

'Twice. You were at the Proaulia the year before last. I'm the one who's done four years in a row.'

'Look, it's not a competition.'

'Yes, but if it was, then I clearly lost it, didn't I?' the second man said. 'Drop the incense one time, and this is where you end up: guarding a bit of rope. Petty, I call that.'

There was a pause, but a clicking noise filled the silence. Kala peered cautiously around the corner and saw that the two men were sitting on the steps of the building playing chequers. Both were acolytes, but they were older than those she was used to seeing, perhaps in their forties.

'You did drop it on his foot, though,' the first one said.

'What?'

'I said you did drop it on the Archon's foot, the incense.'

The pieces clicked on the board.

'Well,' came the reply, 'it's not my fault he's got such big feet. They're hard to avoid.'

Kala pulled back into the passage and shook her head at Leon. They couldn't get any closer without being seen. Instead, they headed away from the wall and found a surprisingly direct route back to the temple.

'I hope they're not always guarding it,' Kala said.

'I hope they are. They seemed pretty easy to outwit. We could just climb across from the roof next door, and I doubt they'd even notice.'

'I don't think it'll be that simple. We'll only be able to get back here at night, and it'll be different then, when all the acolytes are home.'

'Well, at least we know where we're going.'

They were in sight of the temple now. Its colourful frieze was a beacon through the mud brick.

'Do you think they'll come?' Kala asked.

'What?'

'Ariston and Eulalia. Do you think they'll want to come with us?'

'Lali, yes. Ariston…' Leon shrugged. 'We'll see.'

When they emerged back onto the plateau Kala marked the alleyway carefully in her mind. It was easy to spot because someone had made a small garden of potted herbs at its entrance. The splash of green in the muddy landscape was hard to miss.

It didn't take them long to walk back to the temple, using its bulk to block the sight of their return from the crowds at its front. As far as anyone else knew, they had never left.

'So,' Leon said with a grin as he laced his fingers into Kala's, 'are you going to take me back to your place?'

She laughed. 'Well, since you're the Glauks now, it's your place too.'

His grin slipped. 'I'm going to have to be responsible, aren't I? I'll have to go to meetings. I'll have people knocking on the door, wanting things. Gods, what a nightmare.'

'I'm sure you'll rise to the challenge. Anyway, we won't be here long.'

'How soon, Kala?' Leon asked. His expression was ambivalent: desperate to leave yet longing to stay. What did he feel he would be leaving behind? There was nothing Kala wanted beyond the people who were coming with her.

'We'll go to the wall tomorrow,' she said. 'Then you can decide.'

A spot of colour by the edge of the plateau caught her eye. It was off to one side of the temple, right on the brink of the drop. She knew what it was without going any closer, but she couldn't walk by.

'Kala?' Leon said.

'I'll wait for you here,' she said, moving towards the monument. 'You go and find the others.'

He hesitated for a moment, but he didn't argue.

'Don't wander off,' he said. 'Between you and the goats, we'd be rounding up strays all afternoon.'

She was only vaguely aware of him leaving as she approached the cliff edge, her cane scuffing in the dust. Stubby trees had taken root in the rock face, growing back up towards the plateau. They were adorned with ribbons of every colour, crowning the collection of items below: wilting flowers, honey cakes, oil lamps, and two small portraits painted on pieces of tree bark: Neophytos and Theodora. Although the likenesses were good, their eyes were dull and glazed. There was no mistaking these for paintings of the living.

Theodora had looked so like Kala in life, but she couldn't see anything of herself in the portrait. It was all Theodora. She had known the two acolytes so briefly that there was little impact in seeing their features rendered on wood, but they had clearly been missed enough to merit the expense of the painter. The esteem in which they had been held was evident in other ways too; there were more than standard memorials here. There was a small clay ornament, a wooden child's toy, a seashell and several slates carved with prayers.

She knelt in front them, studying the faces of the two acolytes.

This was where Theodora had fallen.

Kala felt the need to contribute her own offering, for the freedom Theodora had offered them. She might not be with them when they left the city, but their escape wouldn't have been possible without her, or without Kala's father.

She wished he were here. He would have liked Leon.

She pulled an orichalcum comb from her hair and added it to the monument with a silent prayer, then pushed herself awkwardly to her feet with her cane.

Before she could turn away from the cliff, an impact to the base of her skull tipped her forwards. Her weight pulled her onto her toes as she tried to recover her balance, but the blow had been too strong and she had been too close to the edge. She crouched low in a last attempt to bring herself back, grasping with her fingers, but her knees dipped down beyond the level of the ground and out into nothingness.

When she fell, she took the memorials with her.

She dropped headfirst towards the rocky basin of the pool below, but then there was a sharp tug around her hips and she watched the offerings fall past her. She was the right way up now, her belt pulling tight against her ribs. There was a crack in her chest. For a moment all she could do was gasp for breath while she swung against the stone of the cliff face.

She couldn't bear to look down, so she looked up instead.

The end of her knotted belt was impaled on one of the scraggly trees. She was dangling from it, spinning gently from the branch where it had snagged. When she reached up, she could just hook her fingers over the edge of the plateau, but with no purchase for her feet she didn't have the strength to pull herself up. Her ribs and head were both agony.

Someone had thrown something at her. Someone had wanted her to tumble off this ledge.

Her hands shook as they took her weight. She wanted to shout, to draw as much attention to herself as possible so that someone would find her. But what if her would-be murderer was close by? They might already be walking this way to finish her off.

She could hear footsteps now. Leather crunched softly into the dusty surface of the plateau.

She couldn't just wait, so she tried to rescue herself. The rocks grazed her fingertips bloody as she levered desperately with the tiny joints, but there wasn't enough strength in them. She sagged against her belt, gasping for air as it pinched her ribs.

'Kala?' The voice was feminine and soft, and it sent relief rushing through her.

'Here!' she yelled. 'Over here!'

The footsteps sped up, rushing towards her, but paused a small distance from the cliff edge.

'Down here,' she said, then she saw Eulalia's face. It paled immediately.

'Ariston!' she yelled over her shoulder, lying down on the ground to take hold of Kala's wrists. 'Run, Ariston!' Her voice softened as she turned back to Kala. 'It's all right,' she said soothingly. 'He's on his way. We'll get you up.'

'Where's Leon?'

'He's coming. Just hang on.'

Eulalia managed to haul Kala up enough that she could get her elbows onto the edge, by which point Ariston had arrived. Between them they helped her the rest of the way. She rolled gratefully away from the drop and lay on her back, with as much of her body touching the ground as possible. Her head and ribs were throbbing.

'Are you all right?' Eulalia asked.

'Yes,' Kala whispered. 'Thanks to you both.'

They sat next to her, waiting for her to pull herself together. That was how Leon found them. When he saw the blood dripping from Kala's scalp, he pushed Ariston aside.

'What happened?' His fingers fussed over her skin, checking her face and neck then gently probing the edges of her injury.

'Mind the ribs,' she squeaked.

His face was pale. 'Gods, Kala,' he said. 'I only left you for a few minutes.'

'I'm fine,' she said, sitting up, but Leon wasn't calming down.

'What happened?' he asked again.

'Something hit me in the back of the head, and I went over.'

'Over?'

'The cliff.'

'The cliff. You went over the cliff?'

'Yes.'

He put his head in his hands, running his fingers through his hair.

'Well, it wasn't my fault,' she said. 'Someone threw something at me.'

'And you were standing where, exactly?'

She pointed to where the offerings had once been stacked. All that was left now were the coloured streamers caught in the branches of the stunted trees. Everything else was probably smashed down on the rocks by the pool, just like poor Theodora.

Kala could see him processing the implications, and she regretted it. Today had been such a triumph for him, but denouncing Nikos wasn't going to solve all their problems. Nikos was just another battle. Their war was against something bigger, a force that penned them in this valley despite its dangers, and that was prepared to kill to ensure its secrets were kept from the rest of Kepos.

They still didn't know who they were fighting. Kala was willing to bet it was the Archon, or one of the Hierophants. Who else could have targeted Theodora and Neophytos?

'I'm sorry,' she said to Leon, 'but it's not over yet.'

They didn't hang around to see the end of the Proaulia. Leon helped Kala up onto his piebald stallion, and then the two of them were riding back towards the city. Ariston and Eulalia weren't far behind on Ariston's chestnut mare.

'Are you comfortable?' Leon asked.

His words were warm against her cheek. He was sitting behind her, one hand on the reins and the other carefully cradling her against him.

'As comfortable as I can be,' she said. 'I think I broke a rib or two.'

'I'm just glad that's all you broke.'

Her stomach lurched as she remembered the feeling of her knees hitting nothing but air.

'I nearly lost you,' he went on. 'Just when you'd finally said yes, you were nearly gone.'

It must have felt like that to him, but Kala knew she'd been on borrowed time ever since her father died. How ironic that his death had turned out to be accidental, when her suspicion of it had been the only thing that had saved her from being poisoned.

'Three times,' she murmured, her voice lost under the thud of the horse's hooves.

'What?'

'Three times,' she said, 'someone's come for me. First the hemlock, then the fire last night, and now today. Hagne's the only person who could have told me why, and now she's gone.'

She must still be somewhere in the valley, Kala thought. Melissa had intended to ask around today in their absence, but Kala didn't hold out much hope that the old slave would be found. She wondered how Melissa would react to their news of today's events.

'Well, what do you think?' Leon asked her. 'Why do you think someone's targeting you?'

'With Theodora and Neophytos dead too,' she said, 'it has to be about the Water. They'll probably come for all of us now.'

'And you'd rather face it alone,' he said. It wasn't a question.

'Shouldn't I? Do you really want to involve your sister in this?' she asked. 'Ariston too?'

'You can't make that decision for them.'

'Oh,' she bristled, 'like you made the decision to take Glauks from me?'

He must have known she wouldn't just let it go.

'All right, I know,' he said. 'It was overbearing, but you wouldn't speak to me. If you shut people out then sometimes they're going to be pig-headed enough to force their way in.' He leaned forwards and pressed a kiss to her neck. 'Especially if they're in love.'

She should have said something, but she couldn't find the words. How did she feel? She found him magnetic, but she couldn't explain why. She enjoyed his company, but they spent most of their time arguing. She wanted his arms around her, but she couldn't seem to open hers to him.

Maybe she was as broken as her mother.

By the time she found her voice, he had already leaned away.

'Leon, please don't,' she said, clasping his free hand in her own. 'It's not that I don't feel—'

'I know. You have your Lissa.'

'No,' she said, turning in her seat to look at him over her shoulder. It was a mistake: the pain in her ribs flared from the torsion and she had to turn back around, holding her side. Suddenly the motion of the horse beneath them was torture. It took a moment for the sharpness of the pain to slide away.

'Are you all right?' he asked, his tone mellowed with concern.

'It'll pass. Stop making a fuss.'

'You're my bride. I'm allowed to fuss over you, especially when you've got broken bones and a head wound.'

Leon's bride. It was a shame she didn't intend for them to stay in Kepos long enough to get married. She could almost imagine enjoying it.

'What Lissa and I have,' she said, 'it's different. She lost her husband, then she lost her child. I had no one except my father. We found each other. We love each other.'

'And you don't love me,' he said. His voice was disappointed, but resigned. He had expected this.

'Leon, no–'

'It's all right. I don't mind. Well, of course I mind, but I meant what I said in the temple. If this is going to be a marriage in name only, then I won't ask for more. I won't get between you and Lissa.'

'Will you let me finish?' she said. 'That's not what I meant. It doesn't mean I love Lissa any less, but this, with you…' The heat of his body sang across her skin. 'It's different.'

'Oh?'

'Yes.' She might not be able to articulate it, but she could feel it in the squeeze of her chest when he looked at her, and in every touch of his fingertips on her skin. It tingled like citrus on her tongue.

'I wish we weren't on a horse right now,' she said, resting her head back against his shoulder.

'Why?'

'I'll show you later.'

'I'll hold you to that promise.'

He was more relaxed for the rest of the ride. He held her closer, fitting himself to her rather than making a cage of his arms to hold her in place.

Melissa met them by the garden gate. She smiled to see them together, but the smile slipped as she saw how carefully Leon was handling her.

'Glauks,' she said with a respectful nod. She had heard, then.

'Oh, you're definitely not calling me that.' Leon reined his piebald stallion to a halt. 'It's still just Leon.'

'Is she all right?' Melissa asked.

'My hearing's fine, thanks Lissa,' Kala said, 'and I'm fine too.'

'She's not fine,' Leon said as he slid down from the horse. 'Someone chucked a rock at her head, and she fell off the cliff. Her belt caught her, but she thinks she's broken a rib.'

'I'm still right here.'

'Well,' Leon said, turning back to her, 'apparently you're not to be trusted for an accurate assessment of your condition, are you?'

The fact that she was still sitting on the horse made it easy to look down her nose at him. 'You're making such a big deal of it,' she said. 'Anyone would think I'd really fallen off the cliff.'

'Because you did,' he said reasonably. 'You fell off the cliff, Kala.'

'You know what I mean.' She waved a hand dismissively. 'It's just a bump on the head and a sore chest. Stop being such an old woman and get me down from this horse.'

Ariston and Eulalia had arrived during the bickering, so Ariston and Leon helped Kala down to the ground. They stabled the horses while Melissa saw to her injuries.

'He knows what he's doing,' Melissa said when the two of them were alone in Kala's rooms.

'He certainly thinks so,' Kala said.

Melissa smiled and reached out to feel the finish of the wooden ring, turning it around Kala's finger as she followed the design.

'He's does,' Melissa said. 'He's capable.'

'It's a good carving.'

'That's not what I meant.'

Kala looked at her.

'It was a clever move, denouncing the Lykos. Stopped you from wavering too, didn't it?'

'He's worried about you,' Kala said.

'About me?'

'About us.'

Melissa crouched next to Kala's chair and pressed a kiss to her hand. 'We've both always known what this was,' she said. 'I wouldn't have pushed you at him if I were jealous.'

'I know.' Kala stroked her cheek. 'I do love you, Lissa.'

'And I love you, but we're not in love. He is.'

'He said,' Kala confessed, looking down at the ring on her finger. It was such a beautiful thing.

'And you said…?'

'Nothing.'

Melissa stood to wash the blood from Kala's scalp. 'No wonder he's worried.'

'We found the pulley lift,' Kala said, keen to change the subject. 'It should be easy to find again.'

'You told them all?'

'No, just Leon, but Eulalia and Ariston should know what's going on. I'm going to speak to them tonight.'

'Good. It's about time.'

Kala sucked air through her teeth as Melissa dabbed at the wound. 'How bad is it?'

'It's a good thing I plaited up your hair. If I hadn't, there would've been nothing to soften the blow. What happened?'

She tried to think back to any detail she might have missed, but there was nothing. One moment she had been kneeling by the memorials, and the next she had been dropping into nothing.

'I don't know,' she said. 'I was at the edge, and then I was hit. I saw nothing. Did you hear anything about Hagne?'

'No. No one's seen her, and there's no one she'd run to. Not that we know of, anyway.' Melissa's movements were more confident as she cleaned the last traces of blood away from Kala's hair. 'It's actually only a small cut,' she said.

'Does that mean you'll take the braids out now?'

She sighed. 'Just this once, but only if you'll let me bind your ribs.'

Kala smiled. 'Deal.'

It was late by the time they joined the others in the family dining room. It had been months since it had been used properly, not since Kala's father had died. Seeing it repopulated, even in its looted state, brought her unexpected pleasure. It was a shame the whole house still stank of smoke.

'I'll go and fetch dinner,' Melissa said once Kala was safely ensconced.

'We'll help,' Eulalia said, waving Ariston up from his seat. Leon winked at his sister as they left, and Kala's stomach flipped. They were leaving her and Leon alone. She could feel her pulse racing against the bindings around her chest.

'How are you feeling?' Leon asked her.

'Fine,' she said.

He was smiling, but there was a twist of disquiet in his expression.

'What?' she asked.

'I need to ask the question.'

'What question?'

He moved to sit beside her. 'Whatever your answer,' he said, 'I need to know what to expect from this marriage.'

His hazel eyes were darker in the lamplight, intent on hers.

Instead of trying to find the right words to express what she couldn't, she tentatively reached out to cup his jaw in her hand. Rough points of stubble caught on her fingertips, but they were fair and few. She looked into his eyes, then put her other hand to his neck. He was so warm.

'I said I'd show you,' she whispered.

She leaned towards him and, very gently, kissed his lips.

He groaned softly from the back of his throat, so she kissed him again. This time, his hands snaked around her waist and pulled her closer as he kissed her, this man who would be her husband. The kiss became deeper, and she couldn't stop her fingers from running through his hair.

'Leon,' she murmured against his lips.

'No,' he said, holding her closer, 'not this time. Don't leave me this time.'

'I won't.' She watched his eyes transform with his smile. 'I'm not going anywhere,' she said, and then he was kissing her again.

'Well,' said Eulalia from the doorway, 'that's a bit of a disappointment. Melissa was just telling us that we have to get out of the valley before Kepos is flooded into oblivion.'

Kala pulled back and tried to rearrange herself to retain some semblance of decency, but Leon wouldn't let her go. His arms were locked around her waist, and he was kissing her neck.

'Stop that,' she said, swatting at his arm.

'It's only Lali,' he said, but he relented and let her go. To compensate, he moved to sit so close that she either had to rest her body against him or risk falling onto the floor.

She glared and pretended to be irritated, but couldn't stop her lips from twitching into a smile.

Leon grinned back.

The others were bringing in platters heaped with stews and breads. They didn't waste any time in tucking in.

'You've told them everything?' Kala asked Melissa.

She nodded as she chewed.

'We're coming with you,' said Ariston.

'You're sure?'

'Yes,' said Eulalia.

She wouldn't have to leave any of them behind. She hadn't even had to argue, because Melissa had already convinced them. Thank the gods for Melissa.

'I want to take Leon to the wall tomorrow,' Kala said. 'In Lykos watch, I thought, while it's still quiet.'

'You'll need a plan to get past the acolytes,' Melissa said.

'I'm sure we can work something out,' Leon said mischievously. He was looking at Eulalia and Ariston as he spoke. 'But for now,' he continued, 'I suggest we all get to our beds and get some sleep. Particularly you, my battered bride.'

Kala didn't really want to leave him, but Melissa whisked her away to her room, padding her bed until she was comfortable. She dropped off unusually quickly, wrapped in Melissa's arms.

But Kala's sleep was not uninterrupted.

Charis and Nikos both died that night.

The slaves had found Nikos drunk in his bed with a dagger in his heart. Charis had been the one who put it there.

The slaves had fetched Agathe, who'd arrived just in time to watch Charis slitting her wrists in the bath. She'd held her as the strength sapped from her limbs. She'd heard her confession and carried it back to Kala, waking her in the darkness.

She'd brought the letter for Kala to read by lamplight, with Melissa at her side.

Sometimes, it read, *the strings tying us together unravel. Sometimes they snap apart.*

Mine snapped.

I have been dutiful.

I never wanted to marry Khosrow, but my father thought it was the best match I'd make after my 'disgrace'. I never wanted Nikos either, not back then and not now, but he took what he wanted anyway. In return, I was blessed three times.

Twice, I was permitted to keep my child past infancy. Once to the brink of adulthood.

I didn't want to surrender any of them, but I was given no choice.

They told me my first son was dead.

Then my second son died.

Finally, my husband said he would take my daughter away from me.

I snapped.

I could say that I did not mean to kill him, but in that moment I wanted nothing more than his death. I have had too many children taken. I would not let it happen again, so I did what I had to do. I tried to protect her.

Then I discovered the lie: my first son still lives, and Nikos knew it.

I am still dutiful enough to perform this one last task. I will protect my children. I will carry out the punishment due to my new husband, before he exacts his own against me and mine. Then I will pay my debt to the gods.

Diaprepes, shield my children from my shame. Lead them into the power of people better than those who had power over me.

Kala and Ariston, I am sorry. I love you both more than I have shown you. Take care of each other.

The scrap of paper fell from her fingers.

Charis had killed Leon's father, and Kala's too.

X

γλαῦξ | Glauks | Owl

*The tenth son was the keeper of stories, and so the god gave
to him power over words.*
*He filled his mind with the knowledge of language and
scripture,*
*so all the deeds of the garden might be recorded and known
when it was gone;*
*and he named him Diaprepes, to mark his fame and wisdom
amongst his brothers.*

- Kleitos, On the Formation of Kepos

They rode out at dawn the next morning so they could get to
the wall by Lykos watch: Eulalia riding Hypatia, and Leon
and Kala on his stallion.

Leon remained vague about his plans for getting them
onto the wall, but he seemed so confident in his success that
Kala didn't question him. She trusted him, she realised, but
she couldn't point to the moment when that had changed.

'I'm sorry about your mother,' he said as they rode.

'I'm sorry about your father,' Kala replied.

'Don't be.'

She wasn't, in truth, but she didn't know how to feel
about her mother. Had Khosrow really intended to leave the
valley without Charis? Or had she misunderstood? Kala
would never know now. Her mother had been so broken at
the end, forced into unwanted directions by so many hands
that she had shattered under the pressure. Kala felt hollow
when she contemplated the stark realities of her mother's
life.

Kala wasn't inclined to mourn the woman who had
killed her father, but she found herself doing so nonetheless.

No one else would. A proper cremation would be denied her. Instead, she'd be buried for the worms to feast on her flesh. That would have been Nikos's fate too, had he been a woman.

Women didn't get away with murder in Kepos.

Ariston met them outside the market on his chestnut mare, and from there it was just a short ride to the meadows that led down to the wall. The stretch of ground that the festival had occupied was hard to negotiate because it was still churned up by activity and littered with discarded food. It didn't help that the ground here was extremely wet, so the horses were struggling to place their feet without sinking. The footfall from the festival must have compacted the ground and prevented the recent rains from draining away.

The colours of the wall were sharp in the morning light, but their beauty was marred by the ropes and planks that littered its face. The new stones must all have been placed by now, so why hadn't the trappings been removed? Their continued presence worried Kala. The zigzagging steps near the top were brighter now, but the very top of the wall was the brightest of all, so colourful that it was like a river of paint across the sky. The acolytes must have put hundreds of extra stones on top of the platform for that splash of colour to be so striking. She only hoped that they had placed them well.

'So,' she said as they approached the sancta, 'what's the plan?'

'Just watch,' said Eulalia.

With a nod to Leon, she and Ariston steered their horses towards the Delphis sanctum. They chatted loudly as they hitched the horses there, drawing the attention of the two acolytes at the base of the wall while Leon and Kala rode to the Glauks sanctum.

There was a scream from behind them as they dismounted. It was drawn out and dramatic, and also entirely fake.

'My ankle!' Eulalia cried.

'Gods,' Kala whispered. 'I think she might be even less convincing than Ariston.'

'Just wait until the acolytes see her. It won't matter that she's faking, because they'll do whatever she says anyway.'

'Really?'

Leon raised an eyebrow. 'Did you think Ariston was her only admirer? She's a heartbreaker, my Lali.' He sounded almost proud.

They watched as a figure ran from the Delphis sanctum to the wall. It must have been Ariston. When he came running back the other way, he wasn't alone.

'Is that both of them?' Leon asked, squinting.

'I think so.'

'Then let's go.'

The path to the wall was churned to mud, so Kala's cane was useless. Instead, she had to lean on Leon's arm. He seemed more than happy to oblige, but it did slow them down.

She'd forgotten how daunting it was to have the wall looming over her. She'd also forgotten how high that first step was. They'd need to find the ladder in order to reach it, but that might be tricky, since the ground was covered with a foot of water.

'This doesn't seem like a good thing,' Leon said, kicking his feet through the muddy liquid.

Kala was wading up to her knees, and starting to panic. The tiny trickles of moisture that had once coursed down the face of the wall were now streams, and they had multiplied. They were everywhere she looked, pouring more and more water into the pool at their feet.

'This is definitely a bad thing.'

As she spoke, there was a series of heavy thuds from above them. A marble block had detached from the top of the wall. It crashed its way across every staircase, rolling down the face of the wall until it finally splashed down next to them. The ground seemed to detonate with the force of the impact, spraying them with grimy water and knocking them both off their feet. Kala found herself on her back, looking up into the sky as another block sailed silently through the air towards them.

'Move!' she yelled, rolling out of the way and dragging Leon with her. The wave hit. When Kala opened her eyes again, she saw that the second block had landed just inches away from where she floated in the wash.

Leon helped her to her feet, fishing her cane out of the water. They were both soaked to their skins. There was a narrow waterfall down the surface of the wall now, washing planks and ropes away as it picked up speed in its descent.

'It's really happening,' Leon said as they sloshed quickly backwards.

'So you believe me now?' She could barely believe it herself.

Two more blocks slid from their berths on the top of the wall and thundered down to join the others. The cascade of water widened, and then stone after stone was following it down, picking up companions from the staircases they hit as they fell. In seconds, the breach was as wide as the wall itself, and it was quickly becoming larger as the water pushed at the lower levels.

'I definitely believe you,' he said, 'and I think we need to run.'

'We finally agree on something.'

Kala picked up her sodden skirts and they hurried back towards the horse, Leon half-carrying her to compensate for her limp. Eulalia was still in the Delphis sanctum with Ariston and the acolytes, all four of them staring up at the wall. Eulalia was the first to recover her wits, dragging Ariston back towards the horses. As they mounted up the acolytes ran past, racing towards the city on foot.

Leon boosted Kala up onto his stallion then jumped on behind her. The horse didn't even wait for his command before bolting up into the meadows, where Ariston and Eulalia were waiting for them anxiously.

'What did you do?' Eulalia asked.

'For once,' Leon said, 'I am entirely blameless.'

The water level was rising as they watched, so fast that it was quickly climbing the hill towards them. It split around the valley to either side of the city, flowing along the river bed towards the sea, but there was too much of it and it was coming too quickly to drain away. At this rate, Kepos would be under water in a matter of hours.

'We have to warn them,' Kala said.

'Who?' Leon asked.

'Everyone. We have to get everyone up to the temple, and we have to do it now.' Kala had planned for this, and she knew what needed to be done. 'Ariston, you go to Delphis. Leon and I will go back to Glauks. Just get your family and go, leave everything else behind. Eulalia, go straight to the temple. Warn everyone you see on your way and we'll meet you there.'

Eulalia looked terrified, but determined. Ariston just looked terrified.

'We'll see you soon,' Leon said to them. 'Go.'

The water was starting to paint the hooves of the piebald when they set off again, galloping at full speed towards the city. When they reached the streets they shouted, pointing back towards the wall, telling everyone to go to the temple. Soon, the message was spreading itself without their intervention. The people could see for themselves.

The colourful face of the wall was eclipsed by a mass of dark, foaming water. Soon the whole thing would be washed away, and then there would be nothing to moderate the spread of the ocean across the valley. Everything would fall in its path.

Despite the turmoil in the streets, the house was quiet when they reached Glauks.

Kala didn't wait for Leon to help her down from the horse, because she was desperate to reach Melissa. She fell awkwardly as she dropped, landing on her hands and knees, but the pain didn't slow her down. She pulled herself up again and hobbled into the house as quickly as she could. Leon was close behind.

'Lissa!' Kala called. 'Lissa? Where are you?'

She met them in the courtyard with Kala's bag.

'It's happening, isn't it?' she said.

'Yes,' Kala said as she took the bag. She felt around inside it until she found the top of her old cane, the owl of Glauks carved by her father. Every Glauks tenant would recognise it. She folded it into Melissa's hands.

'Take this,' Kala said. 'Take the horses, take the rest of the slaves, and get yourselves to the temple now. If anyone questions you, show them the owl and say the Glauks sent you.'

'Where are you going?' she asked.

She thought of the fear in Ariston's face. His household was immense. It would take hours to clear them out.

'We'll meet you there after we've got Ariston,' she said. Melissa looked like she was about to argue. 'I promise.'

Apparently satisfied, Melissa took the owl then kissed Kala's cheek.

Kala pulled her into a hug. 'Just don't dawdle, all right? We'll see you at the temple.'

Then Melissa was gone, running into the house to gather the household together.

It was the last time Kala would see the house in which she had grown up. This was the end of the lie they had lived. Leon laced his fingers in hers and tugged her back towards the garden, where they had left the horse.

'Come on,' he said. 'No dawdling for you either.'

Scant seconds later, they were riding north through the city, towards the house of Delphis.

'You don't think Ariston can manage?' Leon asked her.

'Have you seen how many cousins that boy has?'

'I take your point.'

But they needn't have worried. Zotikos was on his horse at the front door when they arrived, ushering the last of the slaves out of the house and into the carts that waited for them.

'The Glauks has arrived,' he shouted to them in greeting. 'If you were hoping to find Ariston, then he's gone on ahead with the rest of the family. Just me and a few miscellaneous grandchildren left.'

'Can you manage?' Kala asked.

'Absolutely,' was his reply. 'Ah, here's the last of them now. Off we go, then.'

Zotikos kicked his horse into a trot as the final slave jumped into the cart. They moved off in convoy, three carts behind Zotikos and four more riders behind them. The streets were full of people scurrying out of the city, but they moved when they heard the carts.

Instead of following with the procession, Leon picked a shortcut through an alley that was barely wide enough for the horse. It would get them ahead of the crowds. At least, it would have done had it not been blocked with furniture stacked thick across its width.

'Balls,' Leon muttered. 'Who tries to take their bed with them when they evacuate? I mean, of all the ridiculous—'

Kala felt his arms go loose around her, and then he was toppling to the ground. A moment later she felt a blow across her shoulders and joined him. A man was leaning out of a window behind them with a length of wood.

The furniture hadn't been left there by accident. It was a trap.

'Much obliged,' the man said. He jumped onto their horse and, turning awkwardly in the narrow space, galloped out of the alley.

Her pack was still strapped to the saddle. She had one final image of it bumping against the horse's flank, carrying away all her treasures, and then it was gone.

She was too winded to shout after him, but in her mind she screamed obscenities. She realised then that she had heard none from Leon. He was out cold, his cheek pressed against the grime of the alley floor.

She shook his shoulder.

'Leon?' she said. 'Leon, wake up.'

'Wuh?'

'Leon, someone's taken the horse. You have to get up.'

How long would it take them to walk from the city to the temple? They'd have to cross the river. It would be more like a lake by now, if the water had continued to pour at the same rate.

They had to hurry.

He sat up and rubbed his face groggily.

'What happened?'

'Someone stole your horse. Are you hurt?'

He felt the back of his head carefully, but there was no blood when he brought his hand away.

'No, I'm fine. What shit-eating whore would steal a man's horse when he's trying to escape a flood?'

'A man just trying to escape the same flood, I assume. We're going to have to run for it.'

Leon's face paled. Try as he might, he couldn't stop his eyes from drifting to Kala's cane. At least the thief hadn't taken that too.

'I know,' she said, 'but it's our only option, so come on.'

She was already climbing over the furniture blockade as she spoke. She moved slowly, but at least she knew how to swim if the worst came to the worst. If they didn't make it to the temple before the floodwater submerged the valley, then Leon would be lost.

'I'm sorry, Kala,' he said as they touched down on the other side of the blockade.

She broke into an awkward run that made her leg scream. It still wasn't much faster than Leon's walking speed, but it was the best she could do.

'What for?'

'I chose to take the shortcut. We should have stayed with Zotikos.'

'Don't worry. We might still catch up.'

They did eventually, but he was in no position to help them.

When they reached the edge of the city, the river was twenty times its usual width, the bridge under water and the plain flooded. There were a few riders picking their way across the submerged bridge, but their horses were neck-deep in the water, so crossing it on foot was out of the question.

They were too late. The crowds rushing out of the city had come to the same realisation, and the three Delphis carts were being inundated.

The riders on the bridge beckoned to Zotikos's caravan, but there was nothing he could do. People were climbing up the sides of the carts and throwing out the slaves to take their places. The cart drivers had drawn their swords, but their threats made no impact on a mob desperate to escape to the safety of the temple.

They had no choice but to cut the horses loose and ride off with all the passengers they could carry, leaving the carts behind.

Some of the crowd were taking their chances in the water, hoping to latch on to one of the horses as they passed, but the rest just stood at the edge and watched them go. There were more people left behind than safely crawled out on the other side.

By the time Kala and Leon reached the water's edge, the bodies had started to surface.

'You go,' Leon said. 'You can make it across.'

'Don't be ridiculous. I'm not going without you.'

'I can't swim,' he whispered. 'Better that you survive than neither of us.'

'I can help you,' she said. Desperation made her voice weak. 'We can make it across together.'

'No. No heroics.'

'Then what are you doing? If you think I'm going to tolerate heroics from you then you're quite mistaken.'

'Kala—'

'Look, Leon, it's very simple: either we both stay here and die or we both swim for it. So which is it to be?'

'Gods, you're impossible.' He kissed her, hard. 'All right,' he said. 'Just tell me what to do.'

Kala strapped her cane to her back by twisting it into her dress, and they waded out. The current was strong. She would have doubted her ability to get across on her own, but with Leon to worry about too, she was more than a little fearful.

'I want you to lie on your back,' she said once the water was chest-high. 'Kick your legs as fast as you can. I'll be behind you keeping your head out of the water, and together we'll make it. All right?'

'All right,' he said, but he didn't look hopeful. He kissed her again, as though every kiss needed to be crammed into this last moment, then he let her take his chin in her hand.

She took a deep breath and pushed off from the ground, then everything went wrong.

A piece of debris got caught in Kala's dress and dragged them downriver in its wake, pulling her head under water. By the time she managed to dislodge it, choking against the pressure in her lungs, they were in the middle of the stream at its deepest point, and heading quickly away from the temple. As if that wasn't enough, she'd lost her cane.

'Kick harder,' she sputtered as she sculled frantically with her free hand to bring them into the correct line. She felt like her lungs were going to burst. They pressed painfully against her broken ribs. The minutes passed like hours until they were out of the current and back into calmer water. Soon, Leon's feet hit the ground and they could stop, waist-high in the river. Kala could have collapsed there and then.

'We can't stop,' Leon said, looking back across the valley to the wall.

Kala knew the rest of it could give way at any moment, but she was so exhausted that she was struggling to care. The current pulled at her dress, as though the river wanted her back.

Leon had waded a few paces towards the bank before he realised she wasn't following.

'Kala?'

'I lost my cane,' she said.

He splashed back in her direction.

'Hop on,' he said, crouching down in front of her.

'Leon…'

'No arguing. You carried me across the water. Now it's my turn to carry you.'

'Just until we reach the bank,' she said, climbing gratefully onto his back. When they got out of the water, it was enough to have his arm to lean on.

They had been washed a mile or so off track. The river had carried them south, away from the temple and the line of swimmers running towards it. The rising tide chased Kala and Leon as they struggled away from it, so that no matter how close they got to the temple, they never seemed to shake the water from their heels.

They were the last ones to reach the path up to the temple. No one else would make it out alive.

The lower levels of the wall held until they were halfway up to the temple. When it finally fell, the crash echoed around the whole valley. A wave higher than the city rolled towards them, flattening everything it touched.

'Go!' Leon shouted, helping Kala along with an arm around her waist until he was practically carrying her.

The water crested the citadel as they ran, engulfing even the tower as it barrelled down the valley towards them.

'Leon!' came a shout from above their heads. It was Eulalia, peering down over the edge of the temple plateau. 'Hurry!'

'We're trying!' he shouted back, but they were too far away. The water was moving too quickly, and they weren't climbing fast enough.

'Go,' Kala wheezed. Her chest felt like it was collapsing and she knew she couldn't push any harder. If he went on alone, he might just make it in time.

'No,' he said, and then there was no more need to argue. A rope appeared in their path, tossed down from above.

'Grab on,' Eulalia yelled.

Leon twisted the rope around one arm and one leg, then crushed Kala close to his side. She wrapped herself around him as the water hit.

Their feet were swept out from under them. Water filled Kala's mouth and nose, forcing its way down her throat as they were jerked along with the tide. There was a jolt as the rope pulled taut, so sharp that her fingers slipped from Leon's neck.

But he didn't let go. His arm pressed hard around her broken ribs, pulling her back to him.

Slowly, so slowly that it took Kala a moment to understand what was happening, they were drawn upwards.

By the time they broke the surface, Kala had given up on ever breathing again. They were both coughing when they were finally dragged onto the temple plateau, and their arms and legs were bleeding from the rocks, but they were alive.

Kala rolled onto her stomach and looked back towards the city, but there was nothing to see. The water filled every space that she had once known as her home, churning around the cliffs as it forced its way into the valley. In the opposite direction, the great wave was still pushing towards what they had once known as the eastern sea. Now everything was the sea, everything between the cliffs to the north and south. The temple itself was only twenty feet or so above the water level, low enough that spray fell like rain on its arid ground.

Eulalia and Ariston pulled them close. Kala saw Zotikos over their shoulders, and some of Ariston's cousins, a little way off. How many of his household he had lost today? How many households had been lost entirely? The plateau wasn't crowded. Hooded acolytes flocked everywhere, but there were few city faces amongst them. The Archon and the Hierophants were conspicuous by their absence.

'You're both all right?' Eulalia asked.

'Where's Lissa?' Kala said, wheezing against the stabbing ache in her ribs.

Eulalia frowned and looked away. 'She's not here.'

'What?' Kala stood shakily, despite the pain, and looked around, as though she could find her where Eulalia had failed.

'She's not here,' Eulalia repeated. 'Agathe said she took one of the horses and went to fetch Eirene. She never arrived. I'm sorry.'

'No.'

Kala couldn't breathe. Her knees buckled beneath her and then she was sobbing into her hands, each gulp pricking more tears into her eyes as they stretched her ribs and sent pain ricocheting around her chest.

Why had Lissa done it? It would have taken hours to make the trip, even on horseback, more hours than the wall had given them.

She had been down there when the wave hit.

She was gone.

Kala had lost her father. Her mother. And now her Lissa.

Lissa was gone.

Zotikos and Leon were the only Dekocrats who survived the flood. The others had been too stubborn, too disbelieving or too slow to gather their possessions. The succession wars were already being played out on this tiny plateau, as though they still mattered, but no one was fighting for Nikos's title. They were all just glad he was dead.

None of the acolytes mentioned the possibility of a life on the cliffs above, so the survivors were settling in, hoping they could eke out an existence here with only fish and wine to nourish them.

But Kala wasn't giving up on the Plain. Losing Melissa had only strengthened her determination. She was leaving, broken ribs and all.

'But does it have to be tonight?' Ariston asked.

They had been arguing for an hour already in the small house the acolytes had given them, and he couldn't seem to accept it.

'Yes, it does,' Kala said, still holding back tears. 'Lissa is gone. Kepos is gone. Someone, I'm betting the Archon, killed Theodora. Someone killed Neophytos, and someone's tried to kill me three times now. I've had enough.'

'To be fair,' Leon said, 'the first two times might have been my father. He went a little nuts about you.'

'Either way, we're going. We'll tell Zotikos about the Plain, then we're going scouting.'

No one wanted to argue with her. Her eyes were red-rimmed and her body was shaking with a mixture of anger and grief. She was holding it together, just barely, and the others were anxious not to break her composure.

'Maybe we should tell everyone, though?' Ariston suggested, his voice soft.

'We don't know that it's safe up there,' Leon said, taking his cue from Kala. 'Even if we can convince the others that it's real.'

'Grandpa would believe us,' Ariston said.

'Which is why we're telling him,' said Leon, 'but he still won't stake the lives of his people on trust. He'll want proof.'

He was right.

Ariston brought Zotikos to them just before sundown, and they told him everything. He knew a little already from Kala's father, but not enough to trust it blindly. The people were desperate, but at least they could survive here. They needed something tangible if Zotikos was going to encourage them to leave, and the Plain sounded like a drug-addled vision. If it did exist, they needed to know whether the Kepians would be welcomed, enslaved or slaughtered on sight.

There were many things worse than a lifetime spent on this plateau.

Zotikos agreed that they should scout, but disagreed on the members of the party. He wanted Kala and Eulalia to stay behind, especially since Kala was so obviously fighting against her grief, but neither of them would be dissuaded. In the end, he simply wished them luck and assured them he would keep his wits about him until they returned.

Leon had made Kala a new cane from a bit of driftwood he'd snatched from the floodwater. It wasn't a beautiful thing, and it wouldn't last forever, but it fit her hand well enough. It was the best gift he could have given her. She was able to make decent time under her own power again. She caressed the pommel with her hand, and couldn't help but recall what had happened to her favourite one.

Her owl, lost to the waves along with Lissa.

The image threatened to break her all over again.

But there was no time to dwell on it, by Kala's own design.

They left as soon as night fell. They took water, wine, and a few cakes, but they were meagre supplies. There wasn't much to spare. Kala just hoped that Theodora's story had been accurate and that the Empire's Heart was really just a day's walk away.

The houses by the cliff were dark and silent, but when they reached the one next to the pulley lift, light was spilling from its windows. There were figures moving around inside. They paused by the open door: a woman and a man, one past sixty and one barely forty, one a slave and the other a Hierophant.

They were locked in each other's arms. Hagne and Straton.

Kala's mouth dropped open as she watched them kiss. She was so shocked that she stopped dead in the alleyway, and Ariston walked into her back. The collision wasn't loud, but the unexpected lovers heard it and turned to look.

They had no time to hide.

'You,' Hagne said.

'And you,' Kala replied, 'with him.'

They would have known each other, of course. Straton was Charis's brother, Kala's uncle. He would have been raised in Glauks, probably by Hagne.

Kala had made the mistake of forgetting that he was not just the Hierophant. Once, he had been a child of Glauks, just like her. Apparently he had formed a relationship with a slave, just like her. But unlike her, he was homicidal.

'It was you,' she said.

'Kala, you have to understand. I love her,' Straton said, 'but they couldn't accept it. They sent me to the priests. But now, with everything changed, maybe we won't have to hide it anymore.'

She couldn't believe he was appealing to her for sympathy.

'You expect me to care? It was you, wasn't it?'

Guilt suffused his expression, and she knew she was right. 'I had no choice.'

'No choice? You tried to burn me alive.'

'What? No.' To Kala's surprise, his confusion seemed genuine. 'I was talking about the acolytes, Theodora and Neophytos. They were going to leave, and then the soldiers of the Plain would have overwhelmed us, the Archon said, because of her. He said Theodora's captivity was the only thing keeping them away. Don't you see? I had to kill her. I was just trying to protect the city, to keep the peace.'

'Then why did Hagne drug me,' Kala said, 'and set the library on fire, with me in it?'

Straton turned to Hagne. Either he was an excellent actor, several orders of magnitude better than Ariston, or he hadn't known.

'What did you do?' he said.

Hagne glared at Kala, but the look she turned to Straton was tender.

'I just wanted you to have what you'd always wanted: a way to unite the priesthood and the Dekocracy. If you'd been the Glauks as well as the Glauks Hierophant, then you could have done it. You could have changed things. You could have ruled this city, and then there would have been a way for us to be together.'

She stroked her fingers down the side of his face as she spoke. Perhaps they truly loved one another, but Hagne was delusional. Straton was too weak for that much power.

'You wanted me out of the way,' Kala said.

'Of course I did,' Hagne said. The words were bitten out, sharp and loud. 'How could they let you live anyway, when you were so cursed? They exiled him here just because we fell in love, but ignored your twisted blasphemy. I was doing the city a favour to rid it of you, and your barbarian father.'

Leon stepped forwards, his expression filled with intent, but Kala held him back.

'My father?' she said. 'My mother killed my father.'

'Your mother was so blind she didn't even know he was planning to leave. Someone had to warn her, advise her.'

'Manipulate her, you mean. You're the one who broke her mind.'

'No,' Hagne sneered. 'What broke your mother, girl, was your little brother's death. He was the only pure thing she had. I just levered her open. Then I dosed your father so he'd be asleep when she suffocated him.'

'Hagne...' Straton was visibly reeling.

'You knew that this would come at a cost,' she said. 'You killed for this too. Nothing that's worth having comes without a price, so I took it for you, so you could have what you wanted.'

'By killing my family?'

'What family were they to you? They disowned you. Do you think you owed them anything, your whore of a sister and that savage she let into Glauks? They took your rightful place from you and gave it to this burden to the earth.' She spat at Kala. 'A cripple marked with the gods' disfavour, and now she's given your title to a drunkard boy. If she'd died like she was supposed to, then you'd have everything.'

'Have you even seen the valley?' Leon said to her. His rage was barely contained, simmering in the cracked edges of this voice. 'I might be a drunkard, but even I can see there's nothing to be had here. You tried to kill the woman I love, for this?'

Hagne turned on him, her eyes flaring with wildness.

'She's a curse on us all,' she said. 'They should have killed her when she was blighted, and maybe then the gods would have saved us from this. This is their judgement on us.'

'This isn't what I wanted,' Straton stuttered.

'But you still killed your acolytes to keep the Archon's secret,' Leon said. 'And now he's dead, along with most of Kepos. You were just his puppet, and a shit-eating coward.'

Straton was diminishing in front of their eyes, shrinking back into the room as his paramour grew in her outrage. Hagne screamed and then she was lunging at Leon, tearing at his face with her fingernails. She was uncontrollable, flailing with her arms so none of them could get close.

'It's too late!' Kala yelled. 'Kepos is gone. Give up.'

But Hagne wouldn't be restrained. Eulalia managed to sweep her legs out from under her, but in seconds she was clawing her way back up Leon's body, reaching for his eyes. Straton was close behind her, gripping her shoulders as he called her name and tried to pull her away. There was a mess of elbows and fingernails until all six of them tumbled over.

Hagne fell backwards.

Straton had pulled too hard.

There was a sickening crack as her skull hit stone, and everything went quiet.

The combatants drew away. Leon was missing some hair and had some new scratches on his face and neck, but given the number of cuts he'd sustained being dragged up to the temple, Hagne hadn't made much of a dent. Eulalia and Kala were unharmed, but Ariston had taken an elbow in the face.

Straton was uninjured, physically at least. He was bent over the body of his lover, whose lifeless eyes stared at nothing as her head drooped to one side.

'No,' he was whispering, over and over. 'No, Hagne, no. I'm so sorry.'

He didn't respond to their voices, drowning in his own loss, so they left him there to mourn. Without Hagne, they had nothing to fear from him.

Nothing he cared about mattered anymore. It had all been for nothing. He had murdered the acolytes for nothing.

Kala's parents had died for nothing.

The escape itself was easy. After spending so many days worrying about climbing that last stretch to the top of the cliff, it turned out to be a breeze compared with what they had suffered already.

Leon and Ariston went first to test the strength of the lift, but managed to pull themselves to the top of its reach without any problems. Its apex was so high that Eulalia and Kala watched the bottom planks disappear out of sight before it stopped moving. Leon came back for them one by one, Eulalia first and then Kala, to carry them up to a small outcropping next to the lift's highest point.

The wide sill was cluttered with birds' nests and greenery, and now with the four of them too. Ariston didn't wait for volunteers before he started climbing the last fifty feet, a rope slung around his shoulders.

'You see the handholds?' Leon pointed as Ariston climbed.

The cliff wasn't vertical here, but it slanted backwards as though a corner had fallen or been cut out of it. At regular intervals along its height, there were chunks excised to allow for climbing.

'Someone's been this way before,' Kala said.

'More than once,' said Leon.

'Do you think they were spying on the Plain? Or were they trading?'

'Straton said Theodora was the only thing keeping the people of the Plain away,' Eulalia said. 'She was the ransom that kept Kepos secret.'

'Well,' said Leon as he started climbing, 'we're about to find out if that's true. You two stay here. We'll throw the rope down.'

When it appeared, Kala tied the rope around Eulalia's waist and helped her up the first few steps. After that, the boys kept it tight to take her weight as she climbed, then dropped the end back to Kala. She had delayed her own climb as long as possible.

'Can you manage?' Leon called down to her.

'Yes,' she said impatiently, tying the rope in loops around her legs and hips to serve as a sling. It wasn't very dignified, but she couldn't face the pressure around her ribs, so it was the only option. She stuck her cane down the back of her dress and then she was off, hauling herself up the final stretch that would take her away from the temple, away from the valley, and away from the sea. Every inch felt like liberation.

When she reached the top and fell into Leon's arms, she could almost believe the pain in her chest was from joy rather than broken bones.

'We made it,' she whispered against his lips as she kissed him.

'Not yet,' he said. 'We still have to find the city.'

'But we're free, Leon.' She kissed him again, overcome with competing emotions. 'I just wish Lissa were here to see it.'

'I'm so sorry, my love.' He pushed the loose hair away from her face and rested his forehead against hers. 'We'll remember her every day. I could never have repaid her for everything she did for us, and for you.'

'She liked you a lot,' Kala remembered, 'right from the start. She always said you'd make a good husband.'

'I liked her too. She loved you.'

'I loved her,' Kala said, wiping a tear from her cheek. 'I love you too, Leon.'

He smiled at her gently for a long moment then kissed her again, picking her up in his arms as he did so.

'Come on, you two,' Eulalia shouted back at them. She and Ariston were already some way across the dark grassland.

'All right then, my Kallista,' Leon said. The endearment was a painful echo of Lissa. 'Let's find this homeland of yours.'

They walked all night, keeping the ocean to their left, and as the dawn broke they got their first glimpse of the Empire's Heart. It was the biggest space Kala had ever seen. The horizon went on forever.

The stone of the palace gleamed in the sunlight with pale iridescence. This wasn't like the stone of Kepos, which was painted in every colour of the rainbow. Here, the colour of the rock was unadulterated. Marble shone white, brick red, sandstone yellow and mud orange in a warm splash of architecture across the immense plain, dotted green here and there with lush trees and gardens. This land of rich hues was where her father had come from and, indescribably, it felt like home.

They took the path her father must have followed down the coast, and a dozen soldiers met them on the beach. They were wearing trousers, an artifice Kala had never seen before, and split tunics. Their weapons were curved and vicious.

They stopped about fifty feet away.

'State your purpose here,' one of them shouted across the distance, his words accented but in their common tongue.

Kala stepped forwards, trying not to wobble on her cane. But gods, she was tired.

'Kepos, the city in the valley,' she pointed, 'has been taken by the sea. We're here to ask for refuge for our people.'

A soldier from the back of the cluster, clearly the man in charge, pushed through his fellows to face her. He squinted.

'Princess Soraya?' he called.

A murmur went up from the soldiers behind him. Kala fingered the stone that still hung from her neck as Leon wove his fingers through hers.

'You could be, you know,' he whispered.

'Answer me,' she called. 'Will you take us in?'

'The King may be minded to shelter your people,' the soldier said, 'but your Archon and his priests, the ones who kept you from us, they will find no protection here.'

'Good enough,' Leon said. Ariston and Eulalia concurred.

'Very well,' Kala called.

The soldiers approached and fell to their knees in the sand at Kala's feet, pressing their heads to the ground.

'I am Tigran,' their leader said. 'We are honoured to welcome you back to your home.'

'Er, thank you. This is my… husband, Leon.'

He squeezed her hand, his grin wider than ever. Well, if she was to be a princess, then why shouldn't he be a prince?

'And these are his siblings,' she went on, introducing Eulalia and Ariston.

The soldiers rose from the ground, wiping the sand from their foreheads. Tigran bowed from the waist, then gestured along the coast towards the city.

'Please allow me to escort you home,' he said. 'Your family will be overjoyed to see you, Princess Soraya.'

She smiled. 'In Kepos,' she said, 'they called me Kala.'

Epilogue

They found her by the water. It kissed her toes, icing the skin with foam.

'How long has she been here, do you think?' The man's tone was hushed, muffled further by the damp in the morning air.

'Must have come in with the flood,' his companion replied. He leaned down by her side and gently rolled her onto her back.

There was rich mud clinging to her clothes, the meagre remainder of what had once been fertile flood plains. There was nothing left now but sea and salt marsh.

'Is she dead?' the first man asked.

There was a moan from the woman, and she mumbled words in a language they didn't recognise. She was clutching something in her hand. It looked like a wooden carving, some kind of bird.

'Not dead, no,' he said. He tried to pry the object from her hand to see it more clearly, but she only gripped it tighter.

'So, what do we do now?'

His companion thought for a moment before replying.

'We clean her up, and we take her to the Pharaoh. Let him decide her fate.'

Author's Note

This book is inspired by Plato's account of the island of Atlantis, a once utopian society destroyed by the gods for its sinfulness. I've adulterated Plato with some creative licence, and a heavy dose of pure fabrication.

Plato's account is just one of many deluge myths that might have formed the basis of my story. A similar tale appears somewhere in the annals of most Mediterranean cultures and religions (Noah's flood being one of the better known examples). Ignatius Donnelley's book Atlantis: The Antediluvian World is a fascinating starting place for those interested in reading more, although it is based on the premise is that Atlantis was real.

Which, of course, it wasn't. At least, not in the way that Plato describes it.

However, there is evidence of extensive, and possibly sudden, flooding in the Black Sea that might have inspired the stories we have today. It was the Black Sea deluge hypothesis that gave me the idea for a great flood resulting from a sill breach, and so eventually led to my creation of Kepos.

Since Plato was my inspiration, the civilisation of Kepos is loosely based on that of Ancient Greece (and the Plain on that of Ancient Persia), but I've contorted it for the purposes of my story. In particular, I have made Kepos's women a little less invisible and its slaves (mostly) less mistreated.

The fixation on cake is mine, although the Ancient Greeks did seem to eat a lot of it.

Thank you so much for reading this book. I really hope you enjoyed it, and I appreciate you taking a chance on an indie author. If you'd like to read more from me, then I have suggestions!

***

Join my Readers' Club and receive a FREE short story!

www.josiejaffrey.com/subscribe

You'll also receive my monthly newsletter, including exclusive news, giveaways and offers.

***

If you enjoyed *The Wolf and The Water*, why not read *The Gilded King*? It's the first book in the *Sovereign* trilogy, a young adult fantasy series featuring vampires and zombies.

***

Support me on Patreon!

My patrons receive draft chapters and a new short story every month, together with other exciting perks for higher-level patrons.

www.patreon.com/josiejaffrey

***

Please leave a review!

If you enjoyed *The Wolf and The Water*, I'd be so grateful if you would please review it. Book reviews can make a huge difference to the success of a novel, particularly those of self-published authors like me. If you have time to leave a review, even if it's just a sentence or two, then I'd really appreciate it.

***

Get in touch!

I love hearing from readers! If you'd like to contact me, you can do that through my website, Twitter, Facebook or Instagram.

Acknowledgements

Huge thanks to Vicky and Asha for proof-reading and beta reading, and for everything they do behind the scenes as my publicist and author assistant, respectively. Without you, I would have been too overwhelmed to get this book out on time.

Thanks to Ali Jinks for reading an early draft, and for suggesting some major changes that I think hugely improved the story.

Thank you to Susan Davis for her manuscript feedback through Jericho Writers, which helped to polish an early draft.

Thanks to Rosie Fickling for reading a late draft and providing her editorial feedback. It was so helpful. This book is better as a result of her input.

And finally, a huge thank you to Max, who makes sure that I never fall so far into a manuscript that I forget to eat cake and drink tea. I would be a wreck without you.

CONTENT WARNINGS

Violence: murder and attempted murder; violent amputation; poisoning; arson, including characters trapped inside buildings on fire; injuries described.

Death: Parental death and aftermath, including discovering the body (on page and remembered); sibling death (remembered); death in childbirth (briefly described on page); death of a spouse (remembered); children left exposed to die (remembered); detailed description of funeral pyre/body burning (on page and remembered); grief explored for multiple characters.

Racism: from side characters, including the use of the words 'savage' and 'barbarian'.

Ableism: heroine has a bone abnormality in her foot (caused by polio) and walks with a cane; she suffers ableist bullying from other characters, including the use of the word 'cripple', and has internalised a lot of ableism to the point she feels worthless.

Slavery: the book is set in an Ancient Greece-inspired setting and slaves are present throughout. They are mostly treated kindly. The main character's family owns slaves; a prominent secondary character is a slave of the household.

Misogyny: women are seen as possessions of their male head of household.

Parental abuse: both emotional and physical.

Miscarriage (remembered).

Attempted sexual assault of heroine.

Romantic/sexual relationship between slave and owner (presented as consensual).

Romantic tension between step-siblings (not raised together).

Implied romantic relationship between unknowing siblings.